13 AND ¾

ALSO BY LISA GREENWALD

A FRIENDSHIP LIST NOVEL

13 and 3/4

LISA GREENWALD

 KATHERINE TEGEN BOOKS

An Imprint of HarperCollins Publishers

Katherine Tegen Books is an imprint of HarperCollins Publishers.

13 and ¾

Library of Congress Control Number: 2020935399
ISBN 978-0-06-287527-3
20 21 22 23 24 PC/LSCH 10 9 8 7 6 5 4 3 2 1
❖
First Edition

In loving memory of Margaux "Gaux" Untracht—
a firecracker of a person and a bright light to anyone
lucky enough to cross her path.

And for my camp girls, the ponies on my carousel, you
know who you are—thank you for showing me the beauty
of friendship, for loving me at my best and at my worst, for
sharing your lives with me. I am forever grateful to Eisner
Camp for bringing us together.

1

KAYLAN

IT'S KIND OF AMAZING HOW the human brain works. I am here, in this moment, at the pool, having fun with Ari and the lunch table girls, but inside I'm completely and totally freaking out about leaving home for a full month. Freaking out in a way I've never freaked out before. And I'm pretty used to freaking out. It's basically my middle name(s).

"We were thinking something interactive," M.W. tells all of us. "Go up on the diving board and yell out your list ideas and then jump in and swim over to the group. K? But quick, one after the other."

Ari and I are about to start our fourth list to help us stay close while we're apart this summer. Of course, she's sooooo happy to be going back to her favorite place on earth, Camp Silver, while I'm a looming skyscraper of agita. I mean, I know it was my choice to go to Laurel Lake Camp for the Arts and focus on comedy. I applied and everything. And I was beyond excited when I got in.

But right now? I'm scared out of my mind. I'm regretting all of that.

Ari and I made our first list of Eleven Fabulous Things to Make Us Even More AMAZING Before We Turn Twelve before sixth grade because we were so nervous about starting middle school and we thought it would calm us down to have a project. Then we just couldn't stop making them. The thing is, we hadn't really planned on doing another list so soon since we just finished the last one, but, well, we couldn't resist. And of course, the lunch table girls want to share some of their brilliant ideas with us.

"I'll go get my phone in the waterproof case so I can record everyone jumping," June suggests. "And then I'll text you guys the video so you'll remember all of our amazing ideas."

"Everyone at the pool will hear," I say, biting my pinkie nail. "But I guess who really cares? We're leaving!"

I laugh my nervous laugh and look over at Ari, praying we can unpack some of this leaving-home agita tonight at our sleepover.

I lean closer to her and rest my head on her shoulder.

She whispers, "Kay! So amazing you're not stressing about people hearing this. You've come soooo far since freeze dancing at the pool two summers ago."

"I have, right?" I raise my eyebrows and pull her into a sideways hug. "OMG, Ari, I'm out of control nervous about leaving home and going to camp for a whole month. A month is a realllly long time. Completely freaking out right now."

"Shhh." She tries to soothe me. "We'll talk tonight. I kind of can't believe they came here with all these list ideas, totally surprising us. Can you?"

"Guys! Stop whispering to each other," Amirah scolds. "For real. Join the group. We planned this day! We even got you a balloon arch!"

It's true that they really did go all out with the decorations. They wrapped the lounge chairs in streamers too and got a gold foil A balloon and a gold foil K balloon and an arch of gold and silver balloons that they tied to the trees. It's all pretty remarkable. I guess they're really gonna miss us.

"And we love it!" I yell. "Really and truly love it!"

Cami stands up and walks behind me and wraps her arms around my neck. "Kay! I can't believe you're leaving. What am I gonna do without you?"

I turn around to face her and whisper, "Don't say that; it makes me feel bad."

"Why? You don't want me to miss you?" Cami asks.

I clench my teeth; I need her to stop. "I don't know. I'm

a jumble glob of emotions right now and truthfully anything can send me over the edge."

"Hey, guys!" Cami turns and shouts like she wants everyone at the pool to hear her. "Can we discuss that we're going into our senior year of middle school in the fall? I mean . . . this is big-time stuff, people."

"We know," June groans. "But school just ended and it's summer. Let's not talk about the fall. K?"

"K." Cami rolls her eyes. "I'm going first!"

She runs over to the diving board and stands there for a few seconds like she's about to make some kind of acceptance speech. Then she says, "Ready? Here are my three brilliant ideas. Actually, wait, I have four. I forgot. Okay, ready?" She pauses for a second before she jumps. "Sneak a gigantic pool float into your bag and use it in the camp pool, dye your hair blue, teach the entire camp a dance you've made up, and . . ." She jumps in and screams, "Make a difference!"

We all clap for Cami. She gets out of the pool and grabs her towel off a lounge and comes back to sit with us.

June finishes recording Cami and then hands her phone to M.W. to record. She calls out her list items as she jumps. "Keep a gratitude journal, have a conversation in another language, and this is a no-brainer: get a younger kid at camp to start their own list!"

I look at Ari and she looks at me. Brilliant. All three of June's ideas are keepers. I know they'll make it on the

4

list. Cami's? Not so much. But maybe we'll keep *make a difference*. That feels like us.

M.W. hands the phone back to June and goes up on the diving board, looking sheepish and embarrassed. I'm not sure if it's because her bathing suit is too tight or because she doesn't like talking in front of groups. "I only have one," she says. "But it's a good one. Get two counselors to fall in love." She jumps in and stays underwater for a few seconds and then pops up.

"Ooh!" Cami yells. "I love that one. Wowie!"

I love how Ari and I are on the side of the pool, watching and listening to all of this like it's a show they've prepared for us. I guess it kind of is. I'm still shocked they organized it and got it together. I mean, we didn't ask them to come up with ideas for our fourth list, but we also didn't expect to be working on another list so soon and, well, we are. It's happening. We might as well go with the flow.

"My turn!" Marie says, hopping up from the side of the pool.

"Take it away, Marie Mundlay Burns." I laugh. For some reason, I'm obsessed with saying her full name.

"Write to each other once a week," she says as she jumps. And when she pops up from the water she adds, "And draw a portrait of each other from memory!" She swims over to us. "The second one can be done while you're apart or when you're back home, either way." She widens her eyes. "Amazing, right?"

"Amazing!" I stand up and shimmy from side to side. "Ah-may-zing!"

Amirah is the last to go. Before she walks over to the diving board, she says, "I'll admit, I had trouble with this. I feel like I had good ideas for the last list, but this one was tough because I don't know anything about what it's like to go to camp or even what happens there or whatever, so I only had two but anyway." She climbs up the ladder, all chic in her hijab swim cap, and yells, "Do something daring. Master the art of tie-dye." She jumps and swims over to us. "Also, can this please be the last list? I know I'm not really part of it, but it kind of stresses me out. I'm always a little worried you won't be able to complete all the stuff."

"For real?" I ask her, giggling a little. "But it's not even your thing to worry about."

"I know." She bobs under the water and hoists herself up to the side of the pool. "But still. How do you always manage to get it done?"

Ari and I look at each other. "We just do," we say at the same time. "Jinx." Everyone cracks up.

"I like your ideas, though, Amirah," I say. "Don't you, Ar?"

"Yes!" Ari picks at a cuticle. She seems like she's ready to be done with this.

A minute later, she gets up to do some jumping jacks off to the side, away from the pool. "Guys, I have so much nervous, happy, excited energy! Can we pause the list stuff and just have fun? All of your ideas are amazing, but I need your help . . ."

"You do?" Cami tightens up her face. "You never need help with anything."

I don't know how it's possible, but even Cami's compliments sound mean sometimes.

"Yes, I do," Ari says, all matter-of-fact. "And I need help now."

She stops the jumping jacks and sits down on the edge of the pool with everyone else, dangling her feet into the water again.

"Fine. What do you need help with?" Cami asks, leaning back on her elbows.

"Okay, so, don't hate me because of my feelings that change from minute to minute, but here's the thing." She pauses and pushes her sunglasses to the top of her head. "I'm in love with Golfy. I never really stopped being in love with him even though, ya know, my brief love of Jason thing. And I'm so nervous and so excited to be back at camp with Golfy, but what if he doesn't like me anymore?"

We all stare at her because obviously we don't have an answer. We don't even really know Golfy. How can we know if he loves her now or if he ever loved her or anything at all really?

June tilts her head to the side like she's waiting for

someone else to respond, but then when no one else does, she says, "Ari, hate to break this to you, but I'm pretty sure everyone would like you—boys and girls. You're gorgeous. You know this, right?"

Ari's cheeks turn red. "Um, thank you, but I don't think that's true."

"It is." June smiles. "Also, hello, remember the giant bear thing? That Golfy sent to school on Valentine's Day? He's obviously still going to like you when you're back at camp together. I mean, he just came to see you run the 5K for your last list only a little over a week ago! I feel like you don't have to worry *at all* about that boy. He is one hundred percent pro Ari Nodberg."

"Maybe. I don't know. I just feel like I messed things up," Ari says. "We didn't really talk that much when he came for the 5K. And now I'm going to camp with all these expectations and then what if he likes someone else this summer? What if he just wants to be friends now?"

"That would be terrible, I guess," Marie says, "but how can we possibly know the answer? And what's the point in worrying about this ahead of time?"

"Yeah, you're right," she says, not looking entirely pleased with this help.

I raise my eyebrows, telling her in eye-speak that we'll hash all of this out at the sleepover later.

She scrunches her eyes back with a half smile.

The lunch table girls are awesome, and so kind to plan this pool day for us, but we need a one-to-one sleepover to prepare for this monumental summer. That probably should have been on the last list, but I guess it didn't need to be.

It's one of those things that goes without saying, without listing.

2

ARI

WE DON'T TALK ABOUT THE list for the rest of the day and it's kind of a relief. Since we just finished a list and we're starting a new one right away, it almost feels like too much to have all the lunch table girls weigh in. I'm glad we got their ideas, but I just couldn't debate and analyze it all with them. I didn't have the energy.

After snack bar lunch (Kaylan and I shared our favorite: a combo platter of mozzarella sticks and chicken fingers), some swim races, soft serve from the ice cream truck, a zillion hugs and sniffles and goodbyes, Kaylan and I walk back to my house just the two of us.

When we get there, Lion follows us up the stairs, licking our ankles on the way. He rests on my bed as Kaylan and I take turns showering. We change into comfy clothes and hang out in my room, surrounded by my camp stuff. It's all pretty much packed up in my giant duffels and my chest of plastic drawers, and I like seeing it in the corner of my room, ready to go. It's like even my stuff is excited to be back at Camp Silver.

"I don't get why you have to bring your own drawers," Kaylan says. "Should I be bringing plastic drawers to Laurel Lake?"

"It's just a thing we all do," I tell her. "We only get one cubby that has three shelves. So I like to put my undies and bathing suits and pj's in these drawers. Keeps them neat and protected a little." I lean back on my bed. "You may not need to."

"And what's with all the nail polish?" Kaylan asks, swiveling around on my desk chair. "You never do your nails."

"It's a camp thing." I put my arms behind my head and stretch my legs out as far as they can go.

I need Kaylan to stop asking questions. I love her, and I'm happy she's here, and I'm happy we're having a sleepover, but I can't handle the questions right now.

We're quiet for a minute as I read over the packing list for the millionth time to make sure I didn't forget anything. Kaylan's staring out my window. I know she spies on Jason whenever she's here, even though I never admit that I realize she's doing it. It's just one of those things, a secret kind of BFF code where we both know what's happening but we don't discuss it.

I'm not even sure she likes Jason; I think she just likes to spy on people, him especially, and know what he's up to. He was her first kiss, and even if feelings change, the fact of the matter never will. He's a big deal in her life for that reason.

"Is someone crying?" Kaylan asks.

I crinkle my eyebrows because I hear it, too. We move closer to my door. My heart pounds because every time anyone cries, or the phone rings at an odd hour, or I hear my parents whispering, I always assume the worst.

Bubbie.

"If I don't like it, can I come home?" I hear my little sister say between sobs.

Okay, phew. Nothing happened to my grandmother. It's just Gemma being scared about camp. Again. Not that I want her to be scared and crying, but I'll take that over a tragedy two days before I leave for the summer, or anytime, really.

"What's not to like, Gem?" my dad says softly. "Sports and arts and crafts and carnivals and swimming and singing . . ." His voice trails off and then he adds, "I loved camp as a kid!"

"I don't know," Gemma says. "I don't think I'm ready."

"She sounds like me," Kaylan whispers, coming over

to sit next to me on my bed and resting her head on my shoulder.

"Maybe you should've had a sleepover with her!" I crack up and she smacks me with a pillow. "Okay, enough of this eavesdropping, enough of the agita—for you, for Gemma, for me about Golfy—we need to just get to camp already. Too much anticipation."

"You're right." Kaylan sniffles and curls her body up tight. "List time. Let's finish this thing so we can play Best Case Scenario in your backyard!"

"Yes!"

"Ya know how the last list was all organic and stuff and everything just kind of came to us over time?" Kaylan asks, adjusting herself on my bed. "We have so little time with this one, it's kind of like an extra list since we didn't plan to do it. For this one, we need to go with gut instinct."

"Totally! A gut instinct list," I agree. "And also that makes total sense because this is our fourth list! We have this down to a science."

"Right."

We grab snacks from the kitchen, then cuddle together back in my room and watch the video of the girls jumping. We crack up over and over again, so loud that we can't even hear their ideas and then we need to watch it again and again to jot everything down.

Lunch Table Girls' Ideas for our Fourth and Fabulous List

Cami:
Sneak a gigantic pool float into your bag and use it in the camp pool.
Dye your hair blue.
Teach the entire camp a dance you've made up.
Make a difference.

June:
Keep a gratitude journal.
Have a conversation in another language.
Get a younger kid at camp to start their own list!

M.W.:
Get two counselors to fall in love.

Marie:
Write to each other once a week.
Draw a portrait of each other from memory.

Amirah:
Master the art of tie-dye.
Do something daring.

"Okay, let's do a yea or nay," Kaylan says. "I'll say yea to both of Marie's ideas—write to each other once a week and the portrait thing. You?"

"Yes." I crack my knuckles. "Yea to both."

She nods, and writes a check mark next to both.

"No to most of Cami's." Kaylan rolls her eyes. "Except maybe the *make a difference*. I like that one."

"Totally. I don't even really know what that means, but I like the soul-searchy element of it."

Kaylan nods. "Yeah, same. I think some of my favorite list items are the ones that start out vague, when we don't even really know what they mean and then we figure them out as we go."

I rest my head on her shoulder and breathe in her coconut papaya shampoo. "You smell so good," I say. "Do you have an extra bottle of that new shampoo you got that I can take to camp so I can use it on my hair and smell good but also feel like you're with me? Smells are the most important triggers of memories, did you know that?"

"I'll see if I have an extra bottle," Kaylan says with her eyes bulged like I'm going a little loony tunes, but also kind of into it.

I look over our notes. "Okay, and yea to both of Amirah's, right? I feel like she nailed it—*master the art of tie-dye* and *do something daring*? It's like she has a soul-searchy one and a totally camp one."

"Yeah, she seriously nailed it the most of anyone, and she was the one who said she didn't know anything about camp," Kaylan reminds me. "Kind of amazing, right?"

"Totally."

"M.W.'s seems kind of tricky though, no?" I ask.

"Kinda. No clue how to do that one, but I feel like we need to include it. She only had one idea." Kaylan crinkles her eyes, unsure.

We watch the video three more times, and review the notes, and then we come up with a somewhat formed list.

"Definitely yea to all of June's," I say. "She pretty much crushed it, too. The language one will be tricky, though. We'll need to agree on a language."

"Yeah," Kaylan says. "We'll figure out a language when we write back and forth at camp. Or maybe we'll even save that one until we get home. Too much to do now, and we need some quality hang time."

"Duh." Right now, I feel like I'm in two places. Or maybe even more than two places. Part of me is here, with Kaylan, in my room. Part of me is already at camp. And part of me is just lost in my thoughts. It feels like a literal jungle that I'm climbing through. Voices are muffled and I can't really hear what's going on. My thoughts are taking over.

I think back to all I learned about mindfulness and letting thoughts pass and being in the moment. I try as hard as I can.

Kaylan flips the notebook to a fresh page and starts writing.

Kaylan and Ari's Fourth and Fabulous List to Stay Together While We're Apart for the Most Epic Summer Ever

1. Write a letter to each other at least once a week.
2. Draw a portrait of each other from memory.
3. Make a difference.
4. Master the art of tie-dye.
5. Do something daring.
6. Get two counselors to fall in love.
7. Keep a gratitude journal.
8. Inspire a younger camper to start their own list.
9. Be able to have a conversation in another language.

"It's looking gooooood," I sing. "And the thing about inspiring a younger camper." I pause and clear my throat. "It's basically like a continuation from *make our mark*, ya know? Our legacy . . ."

"OMG." Kaylan's eyes widen. "You are totally right. Mind is medium blown right now. You?"

I nod, feeling pretty impressed with ourselves. "Yeah. Same. Wait. So how many more do we need?"

Kaylan counts on her fingers. "Um, five, or basically four and three-quarters, I guess, right? I mean, we're finishing this list at the end of summer, before our birthdays, right, so we can't have fourteen things, but we already did a thirteen list, so that doesn't work either."

"Yeah." I get up and walk around my room. "I sort of think of our three-quarters thing as an infinite one, ya know, like not necessarily that we need to do three-quarters of something, but more it's something that goes on forever and ever . . ."

"Agree," Kaylan says. "The three-quarter should keep our friendship strong since we'll never actually complete it but we're always kind of doing it."

"Right, it'll be something we're working on and making a priority forever and ever and ever and ever." I do a few jumping jacks, all pumped up and excited. "Or . . . if we can't finish one, this is kind of an out?" I smile.

"That's some negative thinking, Ar. I think Amirah got inside your head a little." Kaylan shakes her head and giggles. "Put that aside for now, K?"

"K. Come, let's go hang in the backyard. I'll grab some snacks on the way out. Meet me there!"

I run down the stairs, not paying attention to Gemma crying to my parents in the den. I grab some mini bags of pretzels and a bag of those organic gummy worms my mom loves, and we go outside.

I sit down on the red Adirondack chair and stretch my legs out on the ottoman, close my eyes, and breathe in the smells of summer: fresh-cut grass, a citronella candle. I hear the crickets off in the distance. I exhale. Even though it doesn't usually occur to me that I'm using my meditation skills, I kind of always am, focusing on my breathing, letting my thoughts come and go.

Summer is here. It's all out in front of me, and it feels as big and expansive as the ocean.

I want to live in this moment for as long as I can.

3

KAYLAN

"DID I TELL YOU THERE are rumblings of my dad and his person—or I mean wife, I guess, eww—moving back to Brookside?" I twist a gummy worm around my finger and then eat it like I'm a third grader. It's still just as fun as it was then.

"Seriously?" Ari gasps and sits up straight. "No, you didn't tell me."

I kick off my flip-flops. "I mean, Ryan just said it in passing, so who knows if it's really true. It's not like my dad and I really communicate that well."

Ari's quiet for a minute. "Actually, I don't think my dad and I do either, really. It's like everything is filtered through my mom. My dad and I never even talk one on one."

I raise my eyebrows. "List item! For sure."

"In what way?" Ari looks confused.

"Have a mature discussion with our dads about their flaws, the way we did with our moms on our first list," I explain. "Or maybe tell them one thing we'd like to improve about our relationship."

"Wow, that's hard." Ari laughs. "I'm not sure I can do that. My dad is just so dad-ish, ya know?"

"Aren't all dads dad-ish?" I ask, laughing too. "But honestly, my dad is way more dad-ish than yours."

Ari gets up and pours herself a glass of lemonade. "Okay, I can't hear the word *dad-ish* again."

"Same. Adding it to the list, though."

Ari leans over my Adirondack chair and says, "Listen, I think the rest of the list should be figured out when we're apart. Stuff might come to us at camp, and we can write each other to discuss it." She pauses. "This just feels like too much pressure to finish tonight, and I really want to play Best Case Scenario." She takes a big gulp of lemonade and then *aaaahs* about the refreshment. "I'm going over to the hammock."

Ari walks away, but I feel frozen in place, unable to move, even though a gentle hammock swing sounds lovely.

"Fine," I reply, feeling tiny droplets of agita creep all over my skin because we'll be apart without a complete list. But maybe it's a good thing; maybe the list will be something to focus on if I get scared or homesick or even more agity. "Let me just read it over, aloud, so we know where we stand."

"Cool," Ari says, swaying on the hammock. "Go!"

I stand up straight on her patio and grab a stick off the ground to use as a microphone.

Kaylan and Ari's Fourth and Fabulous List to Stay Together While We're Apart for the Most Epic Summer Ever

1. Write a letter to each other at least once a week.
2. Draw a portrait of each other from memory.
3. Make a difference.
4. Master the art of tie-dye.
5. Do something daring.
6. Get two counselors to fall in love.
7. Keep a gratitude journal.
8. Inspire a younger kid to start their own list.
9. Be able to have a conversation in another language.
10. Tell our dads one thing we want to improve about our relationship with them.
11. To come.
12. To come.
13. To come.
13 ¾. Keep our friendship strong.

"Amazing, Kay," Ari says. "So we need three more things. That's totally doable for when we're apart. They'll probably be really important camp-inspired things that aren't even coming to us now while we're at home."

I put the stick and the list down on the table and come to sit next to her on the hammock. I nudge her to scooch over so I can lie down. "So basically this is half gut instinct list and half organic."

Ari puts an arm around me and readjusts the hammock pillow. "Right, and that feels like the ideal list, in my humble opinion."

"I guess." I pull a strand of hair out of my mouth and turn over onto my hip. "I kinda wish we were going away with a full list, but I'm going to muster any inner chillness that I have and go with it." I think back to how far I've come since the first list, when I was a gigantic ball of agita all the time about starting middle school, and how one of the main goals of the list in the first place was to keep me calm. I can do this.

"That's what I like to hear, Kay-kay." Ari kisses me on the cheek. "This is gonna be good. I promise."

Deep down I know she's right, but on the surface, and probably a little below the surface, too, I really don't agree with her, not at all. It goes against everything I am and everything I believe in. But there are times in friendships and in general life when you have to trust your best friend and follow her lead because maybe she knows more about camp than you do, and maybe she's chiller than you are, and maybe she's just better at dealing with new things than you are.

I look at Ari and push down the tears that are creeping into my eyeballs. I wish I was better at this stuff. I wish I wasn't so scared of going away from home. I wish I could go with the flow.

"Best Case Scenario?" Ari asks.

"Yes. And I really want the best best *best* case scenario, so give me a good one," I instruct. "I want my scenario first, by the way."

"I figured." Ari squints and makes a silly face. "Give me a minute to brainstorm."

We lie back on the hammock and listen to the birds chirping, the gentle breeze of an early summer evening, and deep down, I wish it was the summer after fourth grade, the year when Ari and I met. I wish we were little and we were staying home together and we could go to the pool every day and do crafts in her backyard and run through the sprinkler in our one-piece bathing suits.

I don't want to be thirteen and three-quarters. It's too hard.

I want to be little, still. Little, forever.

Of all of my friends, I feel like I was the one who wanted to grow up the least. I didn't want boobs or my period. Even kissing a boy was something I pretty much only wanted to complete for the first list, or in a way, it was just something I wanted to get over with so I'd know what it was like, so I didn't have to worry about it.

"Ready?" Ari asks, pulling me out of my wistful thoughts.

"Yup."

"Here is the Kaylan Terrel Best Case Scenario Laurel Lake Camp for the Arts experience . . ." Ari pauses and taps her fingertips together like she's about to deliver something great. "You're going to meet a Summer BFF (because duh, I'm the only one in the universe who gets actual BFF status) on the bus and you'll hit it off right away. I feel like her name will be Poppie or something eccentric. She'll be chill—maybe she's wearing a vintage dress, her hair is in braids, she's one of those people who's smiling even when they're not, ya know?"

I nod, relief washing over me. "Go on, I love it already. Tell me more."

"Anyway, you'll be summer besties and you'll become like a thing, like Kaylan and Poppie. People will know you guys together as a team, but they'll also know you apart. She won't be there for the comedy part, though. I see her in fine arts. Maybe painting? But you'll still do everything together, except for the stuff for your actual program."

"Got it." I smile, propping myself up a little bit.

"You'll totally crush it on your comedy stuff. Everyone

will think you're hilarious, because duh you are. You'll make friends in the comedy part, too, and then Poppie will hang with them sometimes, but basically you'll be one of those girls who are friends with everyone and can sit at any table, and you won't feel like you'll need a buddy for the summer, even though you'll have one."

"Yeah." My voice catches my throat. I'm suddenly choked up, really hoping that this will happen, but then worrying it won't. "Will I be homesick?" I ask.

"Maybe for like the first day or something," Ari explains. "Not even. Maybe when you're unpacking, but that's it. Then you'll be totally fine and relaxed and it'll feel like you've known these people your whole life pretty instantly."

"I love it, Ar." I lie on my back and stare at the sky, relief and gratitude taking over all of my thoughts.

"I love you, Kay." Ari shifts in the hammock. "And I swear to you I have zero doubts that this experience is going to be amazing for you. You're gonna come back and say you wish you had listened to me, and you're gonna be so mad at yourself that you wasted so much time worrying. Honestly."

I sniffle. "I'm always mad at myself that I've wasted so much time worrying."

"I know." Ari laughs. "So can you stop?"

"I'll try."

"Ooh, you have an eyelash on the apple of your cheek,"

Ari says. She pulls it off gently with her fingertip and shows it to me. "Make a wish."

I blow it away. *Please let my summer be good, great even, as wonderful as Ari's Best Case Scenario for me.*

"K. My turn, please." Ari claps.

I take a few minutes to map it out in my head, and I wonder why it took me so long to come up with this game. It's so calming to hear someone predict how a new experience is gonna go.

I pull out a wedgie and adjust myself on the hammock. "Okay. I'm ready."

Ari flops over onto her side so she's facing me.

"So you and your friends are gonna be tight as ever, of course, but for whatever reason you and Hana are gonna become close. You'll still be Camp/Summer BFFs with Alice, but you and Hana will really bond. Golfy will love you, but there will also be this new boy, and let's face it—we know how you are with changing your mind and stuff—so you go through a little bit of a debating period but then you officially decide on Golfy and you're together all summer and it's super romantic. You're the kind of couple that everyone wishes they were part of." I smile.

Ari says, "I like it. I feel good about it."

She seems pleased, but not like she's on the edge of her seat (or in this case hammock) worrying and depending on my vision.

Best Case Scenario is more fun when you're going to

an unknown, new place. But it's fun this way, too. I think that I just need it more than Ari does, because I'm always shaky and uncertain.

"You haven't talked to Golfy at all since the race?" I ask her.

"We texted a little that night but that was it. I mean, it was only, like, a week ago, but whatever. I think things are still awkward between us." Ari scrunches her face tight. "I hope it all just feels normal when we're back at camp."

"I think it will," I reply. "I'll add that to your best case scenario."

"Thanks, dahling." Ari puts her arm over my shoulder, and we sway back and forth on the hammock, staring at the sky.

Ari's mom brings us grilled cheese sandwiches for dinner and tall glasses of mango iced tea. We stay out in her backyard so late that we get goose bumps all over our skin, and by the time we go inside and crawl into Ari's bed, it's after midnight.

There's something about sharing your best friend's double bed on a summer night that makes the whole world seem perfect. It's the comfiest, coziest, safest feeling in the world. And you feel that if you can just stay like this forever, in this space, nothing can ever go wrong. Her windows are open and I can hear the comforting, consistent cricket sound. The whir of the ceiling fan lulls us to sleep, pure peace surrounding me.

I wake up and look at the clock and notice that it's almost three in the morning. *Please let this night take a long time. I don't want to say goodbye. I don't want it to be morning. I don't want it to be the day before I'm leaving.*

I look over at Ari as she sleeps and I wonder if some of her confidence will rub off on me, some of the Arianna Simone Nodberg chillness.

I hope so. I'll need it.

4

ARI

MY MOM MAKES US HOMEMADE muffins in the morning and she puts out a fruit bowl and she even fresh squeezes some orange juice. Gemma is moping in the den but we're all ignoring her because there's really not much we can do right now.

"My mom just texted me again," Kaylan says between bites. "I have to go home after this muffin."

My mom smiles and puts her hands on my shoulders and it makes me wriggle a little away from her. "That's probably a good idea, Kaylan. She needs to soak you in before you leave."

"Ew, Mom," I scoff. "That sounds gross and weird."

My mom shakes her head. "Okay, I can never seem to say anything right these days." She heads over to the counter. "More muffins?"

"Yes, please," Kaylan replies.

Kaylan and I stare at each other from across the table, doing our eye talk, and I can tell that she's about to cry. I shake my head gently, reassuring her that she shouldn't cry, that it's all okay, and it's gonna be better than okay, actually.

After we finish breakfast and she grabs her bag from my room, I walk her outside.

"We're not really saying goodbye," she tells me. "I refuse."

"Agree. No goodbyes. Ever."

"Ever ever ever."

I pull her in for a hug and squeeze her tight, and I whisper, "You're gonna crush it, Kay," right in her ear. "For real, you're gonna be the coolest, chillest girl at comedy camp and everyone will love you. Best Case Scenario. Just remember that."

She pulls away from the hug, sniffling, tears rolling down her cheeks. "I hope so."

"Stop," I say. "I know so. We'll write all the time, I promise, maybe even more than once a week. And it'll feel like we're together, and then before you know it, you'll be home and then I'll be home."

She's crying so hard she can't talk. "But I don't want to rush summer away."

"So don't. Be in the moment." I pause. "Oh! That should be on our list. Focus on the present, the moment you're in, what's right in front of you. Remember meditation? Mindfulness? We have the skills!"

"I like it, but it's a hard thing to really complete, kind of ongoing, ya know?" She stops crying as soon as she starts talking about the list. It's like magic. "So we can do it, but let's not list it."

"Whatever you say, Kay-kay." I hug her one more time and then say, "Okay, you really should go now."

"Talk as soon as I get to my house?"

"You can text me as you're walking if you really want to." I shrug. "Nah, don't do that. Not safe. You'll trip over a dog or something."

She picks her bag up off the ground. "Love you, Ar. Don't forget about the bus note I wrote you."

"Love you, Kay." I smile. "Don't forget about the bus note I wrote you!"

I watch her walk away for as long as I can see her, and I'm smiling and crying at the same time. Little Kaylan going away for the summer, on her own. She'll be okay. I know she will.

I walk back inside and right away my mom says, "Ari, I need to ask you for a favor."

I roll my eyes at the ceiling, a sense of dread creeping all over me. I sit down at the table and take another muffin out of the basket and mentally prepare for some kind of last-minute thing I need to do, like clean out the entire playroom. When my mom gets stressed, she comes up with a thousand things that need to be done immediately and if they're not completed she acts like the world will explode. I'm not sure if this is a *my mom* thing or a mom thing in general, but it's annoying and so predictable.

She sits down next to me and sips her coffee. "You'll look out for Gemma, right? She insisted on going to camp this summer, and Dad and I weren't sure she was ready, and now she's falling to pieces," she whispers, and my throat goes clumpy. I don't want her to be sad; I don't want my mom to worry. "I think it'll really help if you reassure her that you'll be there for her."

I stay quiet and wait for her to continue.

She says, "I'm counting on you to help her, okay? I remember when I went to camp and all the siblings loved each other in this totally different way than they ever loved each other at home. A new closeness came about."

"Huh?" What is my mom even saying right now? My throat clumpiness fades away because it seems like she's just speaking nonsense.

"Just look out for her, Ari, okay? Check in during free time, make sure she's adjusting to everything . . ."

"Mom, in all fairness, you know that this is my summer, too? I'm not just Gemma's chaperone?" I say, trying to stay respectful, but now I feel like she's taking advantage of me and not thinking about me at all, only about Gemma. "I will of course look out for her, but I can't have her homesickness or whatever ruin my time. I've waited

33

all year to get back to camp!"

"Lower your voice." My mom's eyebrows turn inward. "She's not going to interfere with your time. Just keep an eye out. That's it."

"Fine." When my mom's paging through a magazine on the table, I sneak another muffin and wrap it in a napkin. "May I be excused to go pack now, Mother?" I laugh.

"Yes, but please don't make crumbs in your room. I saw you take that muffin." She looks up at me. "Oh, Ari, you make me positively nuts, but I adore you, you know that, yes? And I'm going to miss you."

"Oh, Mom." I shake my head. "I'll be back so soon you won't even realize I've been gone."

"I'm not so sure about that."

I traipse up the stairs, taking small bites of my muffin so I don't make any crumbs, and try to ignore Gemma huddled in a ball on the couch. Lion follows me up to my room and we cuddle on my bed together for a minute.

"Oh, little Lion baby, I'm gonna miss you the most." I smoosh my face into his head. I wish I could sneak him to camp.

After a few minutes of listening to a thud-thud-thud sound coming from outside, I go over to the window to check it out. Jason playing basketball. I knew it. I watch him for a moment or two, wondering if he'll look up, but he doesn't.

Oh, Jason. I laugh a little to myself about him and how my feelings change from one second to the next. I wonder if I'll always be like this, or if one day I'll settle down a little and feel confident and pleased with my decisions about boys and all things, really.

I look at the calendar above my desk and all the Xs marking the days of my countdown that have passed, every one leading up to tomorrow!

Tomorrow at this time I'll be at Camp Silver. Unpacking my stuff, saying goodbye to my parents, hanging my pictures on the wall, sitting on the bunk porch with Alice, Hana, and Zoe, overflowing with gratitude that we're all together again.

When the moment you're waiting for finally arrives, you need to appreciate it, breathe it in, take pictures of it with your mind. That's exactly what I'll do.

Later that day, I take Lion with me and we walk over to Bubbie and Zeyda's. I know we're all getting together for a "final dinner" tonight, but I want my own time with them.

"Hi, doll," Bubbie says when I get to the den. I have a key to their apartment now and I let myself in. I'm always a little nervous that I'll walk in and find Bubbie weaker or sicker than the last time I saw her, but that hasn't happened recently. "Camp tomorrow! How wonderful!"

I sit down on Zeyda's recliner, wondering if he's at the

clubhouse playing cards or if he's in the bathroom. Lion hops up onto Bubbie's lap and she strokes the fur on his back.

I snap a picture of the two of them on my phone. "I know! I am so excited."

"I loved camp. You know that. Partly because it was the best place in the world. Partly because I got away from my sister." She laughs her throaty laugh. "Either way, you need to make sure you enjoy every second."

I lean back against the chair. "I will. I'm worried about Gemma, though. What if she doesn't like it? What if it ruins my time?"

Bubbie shakes her head. "She'll like it. It may take a bit of time for her to adjust." She pauses. "But she'll like it. All will be marvelous. And she's only staying for four weeks; she's not married to the place!"

I smile at Bubbie because it really doesn't matter what she says; I always believe her. In a way, she's my own private fortune-teller.

"What else, doll? Seems like there's a lot on your mind." Bubbie looks at me wide-eyed.

I exhale. "Well, here's the thing." I pause. "And I haven't told Kaylan yet, so shh if you see her." I put a finger to my lips and pause again. "I kind of want to go to boarding school for high school. I don't know how to approach it with my parents. I've sort of talked to them about it but only in passing. I don't think they believe me. The only reasons to stay home are because you're here now and I love seeing you so much. And Kaylan, of course." I sniffle a little. "But we have so many breaks. I think it could be an amazing experience."

"When would you have to apply?" Bubbie asks. "By the way, Zeyda's out for coffee with Charlie. He'll be at dinner tonight."

I nod. "I think I'd have to apply in the fall. I requested some information online. And all the schools are on the East Coast."

Bubbie's quiet. "I see," she says.

"What do you think?" I ask her, tentative.

"I think we can table this until the fall," she tells me. "Right now, all you need to focus on is having fun at camp. Pure, consistent, wonderful fun. That's it."

"That's it?" I giggle. Bubbie says it like it's an instruction, a command. I guess it is in a way.

"That's it." She laughs. "Now go home, get ready. We have a celebration dinner tonight!"

"Will you talk some sense into Gemma?" I ask her, scooping Lion up off her lap.

"I'll do my best." Bubbie leans out a little so I can give her a kiss. "See you later, darling."

Lion and I walk home together, and I focus on what Bubbie said.

I already know the first thing I'll write in my gratitude journal tonight.

Having a fortune-teller for a bubbie.

In a way, she's the inventor of Best Case Scenario. I can't believe I never realized that until now.

5

KAYLAN

MY THIGHS ARE SWEATING ONTO this cloth coach bus seat and three things are running through my head: I wish I'd worn longer shorts, I hope the seat won't be visibly wet when I get up, and I wonder how long I should wait to read this bus note from Ari.

Actually, other things are running through my head, too, but I'm trying as hard as I can to push them away, down deep into a corner. So it's basically just the three.

On the one hand, the bus just pulled away from the parking lot and it's a two-hour drive, so I should probably save Ari's bus note since I have a good chunk of time. On the other hand, I already miss her something fierce, like someone pulled my arm off, and I want to read it right now so I can hear her voice in my head.

I didn't have to take the bus, my mom could have

driven me, but I felt bad about her driving two hours just to drop me off and then turn around and drive home all alone, without me.

Right now I'm really regretting all of my decisions. First of all, the bus is only half-full, and I'm still not talking to anyone. I'm sweating and I'm already homesick.

Also, my mom is probably with Robert Irwin Krieger right now. Out to lunch in the city. I feel a little guilty that I interrupted her every time she tried to talk to me about him, or said la-la-la-la in my head over and over again when she was talking so I wouldn't have to hear any of it.

I'm happy for her, I really am. I just don't want to know the logistics, or anything about their future plans, or how serious it really is.

It felt like too much. Especially right before I was leaving home.

So far no sign of the Poppie that Ari came up with in Best Case Scenario.

Okay, that's it. I have to read Ari's note. She'll have some words of wisdom for me, I'm sure.

My dearest Kaylan,
Right now you're on the bus to comedy camp. You're probably freaking out. Actually, I know you're freaking out. So here's the first thing to do: think about all of our meditation skills

and remember to breathe. Breathe in. Breathe out. Breathe in. Breathe out. Feel better? No? Okay, try again. Now? Any better? I hope so. Just remember how awesome you are, and how much you wanted to go to Laurel Lake. Look around the bus, at all the strange faces. It's weird, right? I know it is. But by the end of the session, you'll probably know everyone. And some of these kids may even be your new best friends. How crazy is that? That's the magic of camp. You don't even know what lies ahead in the coming weeks, but I promise you, it will be unforgettable.

Are you still freaking out? No? You feel calm now. Good. Put your head back against the seat. Close your eyes. (I hope you've opened them now so you can finish reading.) Just relax, take it all in, know that you're in my heart and I'm cheering you on every step of the way. I miss you, and I love you, and you're the best friend any girl could ever hope for. If you're still feeling anxious and agita-ridden, you can write to me.

Don't forget about our one letter a week thing. Who am I kidding? Of course you won't forget. It's on the list and you have three copies with you. There's no way you could forget.

Okay, I'll stop now. Go talk to the person in the seat in front of you, or maybe the seat behind you. Either way.

I love you, Kaylan.

Xoxoxoxox Ari

PS If you're feeling sad, remember Best Case Scenario! And even if you're not, remember it! ☺

41

I choke back the tears, and I do a casual head-to-the-side move so I can get a glimpse of who is behind me. Nope. That won't work. Two boys who look more scared than I do. I see long hair in front of me but I can't tell if it's a girl or a boy—not that it really matters. So I take a deep breath, push away the agita, and do a shoulder tap and wait for the person to turn around.

I smile. "Hey, I'm Kaylan," I say.

"Cleo." She smiles a big toothy smile and her teeth are the whitest and straightest teeth I've ever seen in my life. Seems like a natural, no-braces-ever kind of smile. The person next to her is asleep. A boy. I wonder if they're a couple, or friends, or if they even know each other. "Is this your first summer?"

I nod. "Yeah. Yours?"

"No." She giggles. "I've been coming since I was a baby actually; my mom used to be on faculty here for theater." She pauses. "She died, though, three summers ago, but I still come. I love it. All of my friends get rides, but I like the bus. Feels like the whole experience starts sooner." She looks over to her sleeping seatmate and whispers, "I don't even know this kid."

Wow, that is a lot to take in. I wonder if I should say something about her mom or just let it go since she mentioned it so casually.

"So sorry about your mom," I say, without really planning to.

"Yeah, thanks. It's been rough, but you get through it."

She seems super confident and low-key. Is Cleo my Poppie?

"I'm getting carsick sitting like this," she tells me. "Let's talk when we get there. I'll show you around and everything. I promise."

I lean back in my seat, pleased with my first camper-to-camper encounter. It's true that I don't know Cleo's age. I wonder if she's in high school. She's definitely at least thirteen, but she could also be fifteen or sixteen. It's hard to tell. She's nice, though, and friendly, and not even the least bit awkward. I hope we can be friends. And I mean friends-friends, not just first-day friends. She doesn't really need a first-day friend, but I do.

I take out my copy of the list, wishing we'd had time to send it to work with Ari's dad so he could laminate it for us. But it's not even complete, so that would've been a waste.

A last-minute list is a last-minute last. We haven't really done one before.

Kaylan and Ari's Fourth and Fabulous List to Stay Together While We're Apart for the Most Epic Summer Ever

1. Write a letter to each other at least once a week.
2. Draw a portrait of each other from memory.
3. Make a difference.

4. Master the art of tie-dye.

5. Do something daring.

6. Get two counselors to fall in love.

7. Keep a gratitude journal.

8. Inspire a younger camper to start their own list.

9. Have a conversation in another language.

10. Have an honest conversation with our dads about one thing we want to improve about our relationship with them.

11. To come.

12. To come.

13. To come.

13 ¾. Keep our friendship strong.

I kind of wish there was one thing on the list I could do right now, to keep myself occupied on this bus ride and to keep my mind from going into the dark places: the thought of grabbing my bag and running off the bus and pretending none of this happened, the agita that I'll be so homesick when I get there that I won't even be able to think about comedy, the fear that I won't have any friends or that no one will even think I'm funny. All of that.

I could write Ari a letter now but I don't really have anything new to tell her yet, and all the other list stuff is too big to do on a bus. So instead I brainstorm some new list items.

Ideas for the list
Nominate each other for some kind of award.
Make and bury a time capsule when we get home.
Quit social media.

   I decide I'll write Ari a letter tonight, right before bed, to tell her all about the first day at Laurel Lake, and about my ideas. The only one I'm really feeling is the time capsule one, and we won't be able to do that until we get home, and I think that's why I like it. The pressure is off. Sometimes you need to push things away for a bit, let them wait. So much of life is an immediate, right now, hurried, rushed kind of thing. I want to get away from that. I'm hoping camp helps.

   I'm putting my journal in the front pocket of my backpack when Cleo turns around again. Then she gets up and comes to sit next to me.

"Your name is Kaylan, you said?"

"Yeah."

"Cool. Just wanted to make sure. I'm not so good with names. Ya know how people say them and then you immediately forget?"

I giggle. "Totally."

"So I feel like I need to say them a few times to really remember, and spelling—forget it. I'm a terrible speller." She clears her throat. "Luckily we don't need to spell too much at camp."

"Imagine if there was a spelling camp, though?" I muse. "Like a focus at Laurel Lake for spelling or even just a camp all about spelling?" I crack myself up and Cleo starts laughing, too.

"Oh goodness, I bet it exists," she says. "Everyone is obsessed with school stuff and being the smartest and getting ahead! I bet there is a spelling camp somewhere."

"I'd google it if I had my phone."

"Same." She giggles again. "It's good they don't allow phones, though. So good to have a break from all that." She nods like it'll help make her point. "I'm really excited for you to meet my friends. What grade are you going into?"

I hesitate a second, scared that if I tell her my real age, she'll think I'm babyish or something, but there's really no reason to lie about it. "Eighth."

"Me too! This is gonna be so fab, Kay-lan." She says my name slow like she's trying to commit it to memory.

"I agree. Cle-o."

Cleo cracks up. "Wait, I didn't even ask what focus you're in," she says, stretching out her neck. "I'm doing two: jazz and painting."

"Oh, um. I'm doing comedy."

"I mean, of course!" She laughs. "I could tell you were really funny right away."

I scrunch my nose. "You could?" To be honest, I don't even feel funny right now. The fear is covering up the funny, I think. But maybe since I'm on the bus—on my way to comedy camp—the funny is coming out. It's possible.

"Yup!" She leans her knees on the back of the seat in front of her. "Where are you from?"

"Oh, um, Brookside, Connecticut." I laugh. "I almost forgot for a second. What about you?"

"So convenient since that was one of the bus stops!" She raises her eyebrows. "I'm from Pleasantville. Isn't that so funny that there's a real town with that name? Like the movie."

I giggle. "Yeah. Is it oh so pleasant?"

"Sort of, yeah. Kind of a basic suburban town." She shrugs. "What about Brookside?"

"The same, I guess. But I love it. I've lived there my whole life and it's basically like the comfiest pair of jeans for me at this point. Even going away for four weeks feels kind of painful, to be honest."

"You've never been away from home before?" Her voice squeaks at the end.

"Not really. Not for this long, anyway," I explain.

Her eyes bulge. "OMG, Kay-lan! This is HUGE. You are going to return a changed person in every sense of the word."

"That sounds kind of scary, no offense." I turn my body so I can make better eye contact. "In what way?"

"In every way!" She drums her fingers against the side of her face. "Stick with me, girl. It's gonna be literally epic."

Cleo sits with me for the rest of the ride and she tells me all sorts of stories about simple things like her neighbor and how he lives alone but he fosters dogs and she helps with them sometimes and this restaurant in her town that serves all the food in Chinese food containers but it's not a Chinese restaurant.

There's something about Cleo and the way she talks that's just so fascinating. Like she makes even the simple things seem exceptional and beautiful and interesting. I can't totally put my finger on it but I kind of just want her to talk and talk and talk and tell me stories the whole time we're at camp.

She speaks and my insides relax, my agita fades.

This is gonna be good.

Great, possibly.

Maybe even epic, as Cleo says.

6

ARI

I'LL ADMIT—THE MAGIC OF DRIVING through the Camp Silver gates is heavily diminished when you have a crying little sister in the car seat next to you.

"But can I please, please, please go home if I don't like it?" she asks for the zillionth time. "Promise me? Please? Can I get it in writing?"

We all crack up.

"It's not funny!" She stomps her feet on the floor of the car. "This is serious."

"Gem." I put my hand on her arm. "Camp Silver is literally the happiest place in the universe, happier than Disney World, I swear to you. It's bliss. It's perfection. People wait all year to come back here and we only have seven weeks, so can we please just try to enjoy it?"

"Seven weeks!" she gasps. "I'm only staying first

session, Ari! Four weeks is wayyyyyy more than enough for me. Don't scare me like that."

"First of all, Gem, remember how you begged to come this summer? Second of all, you're gonna love it so much you'll want to extend," I whisper. "Mark my words."

She sniffles again. "I don't even know what that expression means."

Outside the car, all the counselors are holding home-made posters and screaming, "Welcome home!" "We're so glad you're here!" "Get ready for the most incredible summer ever!" and on and on and on.

"Roll down the windows, Dad!" I instruct, and he does, and then Gemma hides her face in her sweatshirt sleeve.

I never should've agreed to this. I wish I'd said Gemma wasn't ready, or maybe I should've suggested another camp. Little sis does not have the right to ruin my happy place or spoil my good time. I just won't have it. My goal for this summer is to achieve perfection, to feel the magic at all times, and not let anything get in the way of that.

As we drive slowly into camp, following the line of cars, I soak it in: all the cheering and wooing and excitement. All the happy energy. I breathe in the most beautiful-smelling Berkshire air as deep as I possibly can.

The day we've waited for all year is finally here.

We pull over and park on the quad and we get our lice checks (Gemma cries the entire time) and then we get our bunk assignments. So far I haven't seen any of my friends. I wonder if they're here already.

"OMG, are we allowed to use those?" Gemma asks the people handing out the camp T-shirts on the quad (after she takes a sobbing break).

"Use what?" one of the counselors asks, flipping through the pile of T-shirts to find an extra small for Gemma.

"Those floats!" Gemma points to the pool, and I can't believe I hadn't noticed that there are two giant unicorn floats in the water. They're rafts so a few people can sit on them at the same time.

I think back to the whole *find a unicorn* thing from the last list. A little twinge comes over me, a missing-Kaylan kind of twinge where all I want to do is call her and tell her about these floats and reminisce about our last list. I know I can't, though. I'll write her later.

"Yup! During free swim." The counselor smiles. "So, okay, you guys know where to go? Up the hill and to your right. You're both on the same side of camp."

I knew this was going to be the case, but I hope our bunks are far enough apart that Gemma doesn't feel like it's okay to come and visit every other minute.

Gemma hugs me again, her tears landing on the middle of my T-shirt. I wish I could zap this sadness and fear out of her brain or at the very least just say *enough already*. I let her stay in the hug for a little bit, and then I pull away.

The counselor says, "Don't cry, you're really gonna love it here. I promise!"

Gemma nods, wiping tears away with the back of her hand.

"That's what I keep telling her." I shrug.

"She'll get there," the counselor says, and then gets interrupted to go help another family.

"Okay, parents." I turn around to face them. "You guys can just drop me off at my bunk with my bags and I'll unpack myself." I smile, hands on my hips. "Go help Gemma settle in and then come say goodbye on your way out."

"You sure, Ari?" My mom pushes her sunglasses down from the top of her head. This usually means she's about to cry. "I wanted to help make your bed."

"I got this, Mom." I reach over and hug her and then whisper in my sweetest tone, "Gemma needs you more than I do right now."

"She's got this," my dad repeats. There's a certain calmness to him when he's at Camp Silver. I'm not sure if it's the nostalgia element since he went to camp for so many summers and loved it, or if it's the feeling that he's going to be rid of his children for a few weeks. Or maybe it's that he's wearing shorts. He never wears shorts at home.

Shorts kind of have transformative powers. They're like literal fun in clothing form.

No clue what it is, but it's working for him. My dad is kind of a different person as soon as he drives through the gates. The Camp Silver euphoria rubs off on everyone—even dads. Let's just hope it works on Gemma, too.

Oh! I should have the conversation with my dad on visiting day because the Camp Silver magic can work wonders for our relationship! Mental note to write to Kaylan about that at some point.

Maybe bonding over camp is just the thing my dad and I need to be close again.

We get back in the car and drive up the hill, and pretty soon we're all standing outside of bunk twenty-seven—my new home for the summer. On the door is a bright pink piece of poster board that says Bunk Twenty-Seven Flamingos! in chunky black bubble letters, and a few miniature blow-up flamingos are glued to it. All of our names are written on the poster in matching bubble letters. Alice. Zoe. Hana. Ari. Sadie. Claire. Ava. Josie. Rebekah. Mira. Phoebe. Karina. The counselors' names are in curlicue script in the corner. Noa. Charlie. Annie.

This is it. The moment I've been waiting for. My insides are like one of those squishy stress balls, all soft and gooey.

I'm home. Really and truly home.

My dad gets my duffel bags and plastic drawers out of the trunk and he helps me carry them inside while my mom and Gemma wait in the car.

"You sure you can handle unpacking on your own?" he asks.

"Oh, I'm sure."

My dad nods like he believes me but also isn't sure what else to say. I want him to say something sentimental for some reason, some little bit to acknowledge that this is a big moment, and we've reached it. But he just stands there awkwardly.

"So, I'm gonna go unpack, I guess . . ."

"Uh, yeah." He looks around. "We'll be back. And, Ari, just remember to—"

"Ari!" We hear someone yelp and the loudest thud of feet on the floor, and before we even realize what's happening, Alice is hugging me and lifting me up in the air and squeeing over and over again and it feels like magic, like pure happiness in a sound, the sensation of love and appreciation and connectedness. "Eeeeeeee, Arrriiiiiiiiiii," she sings. "You're here, you're here, you're here!!"

"Okay, well, I guess I should be getting back to the car," my dad says while slowly backing away. I wonder if he's relieved that Alice just interrupted this on-the-verge-of-emotional moment. He just can't handle it. Mental note for list item: discuss lack of emotion with him. "I'll, um, be back to say goodbye."

"Bye, Mr. Nodberg!" Alice yells. "Arrriiiiiii!!"

"AlKal, my sweet!" I say, grabbing one of her braids

and brushing it against the side of my cheek. Some people might think this is odd, but it's just something we do. "AlKal!! We are back togetherrrrrrrr. For seven whole weeks!"

"I knowwwwww!" she squeals again. "We're the first ones here. Come, let me help you unpack. I need to show you my Shabbat dresses, OMG, and you're gonna be obsessed with these overall shorts I brought. I look SO cute in them. Like beyond cute."

"You look beyond cute in everything," I remind her.

She helps me drag my duffel bags to the corner where my bed is.

"How adorable is this?" she whispers. "The counselors taped a little pink flamingo thing to each of our beds! They're like mini pool floats!"

"The cutest ever," I reply. "Speaking of counselors, though. Where are they?"

"No idea!" She laughs. "Anyway, come on."

"You've just been chillin' in the bunk alone this whole time?" I ask, laughing.

"No, they're around. You know how it is. One of them is already crying about the guy she was with last summer, and she's still in love with him but she's not sure he likes her or something . . ." She rolls her eyes. "Typical camp drama."

"Yeah." I smile, and a light bulb goes off in my brain. The list! Help two counselors fall in love. Mission one!

Right at my feet. I contemplate mentioning it to Alice, but I decide to save it for later. Sometimes Alice wants to feel like she has all of me, and if I'm drifting off to do list stuff, she'll get upset. Especially since I just got here.

"You make your bed, and I'll unpack your cubbies," Alice says. "You know mine are always the neatest in the bunk."

"That's true," I reply, starting to feel kind of confused about where everyone else is. I'm quiet for a bit and then Alice bursts out with, "I know what you're thinking but not saying," while neatly folding a stack of my T-shirts on the first cubby shelf.

"What?" I look down from the top bunk bed after smoothing my fitted sheet in the corners.

"Golfy. Duh. And yes, I've seen him, and no, he hasn't asked about you." She pauses. "But I could tell he wanted to, so there's that."

"Okay, um, cool, I guess." I nervous laugh.

She eye-bulges at me. "You'll be back together by tonight at evening program. I predict this with almost one hundred percent certainty."

"Are you sure?" I ask. "Like how come you're not at one hundred percent, you're only at *almost* one hundred percent?" I prop up my pillows and lean back and take in the view from my bed.

"I mean, I can't say anything with one hundred per-cent certainty," Alice says defensively. "You know how—"

"Where my girls at?" Hana runs into the cabin and jumps up and down three times when she reaches the middle. "AlKal! Ari! I know you're here. I heard the rumors."

She heard the rumors?

"Up here!" I yell. "Al is unpacking for me." I jump down off my bed and survey all that she's accomplished. It's true that her folding skills are unmatched. There's still a lot for me to do, though.

Alice and I run to the middle of the bunk to meet Hana. We're in the middle of a deep, intense, passionate hug when we feel more arms on our backs.

"Zo-zo?" I ask. "Is that you?"

"Yup!! Guysssssssss." She starts crying while hugging us. "It's here. It's really, really here. We're back! I know we just saw each other at Ari's race last week but somehow it feels like forever ago."

We stay in this weird mishmash hug for a few more moments and then our counselors finally make an appearance.

"Hi, girls!" one of them yells. "Sorry, we were tending to some important business." They giggle for a second and that's when I realize that the counselors aren't really so much older and wiser than we are. I guess that's the fun part.

They introduce themselves: Annie, Charlotte (but everyone calls her Charlie), and Noa. I can already tell that Charlie's gonna be my favorite. I don't know why; I just know. Come to think of it, I haven't seen any of my counselors from last summer yet. Hope we get to chat at dinner!

Hana and Zoe go unpack, and Alice helps me finish folding my clothes and putting them in my cubbies, and right when I'm back up on my bed hanging my pictures, my parents and Gemma traipse in.

They say hi to my counselors and Gemma pulls her sweatshirt hood down over her eyes, and I wonder if I acted this immaturely when I was her age. Maybe I did. Hard to say for sure.

"Let's make this quick, guys," I say, reaching out to pull them both in for a hug. "And please take Gemma back to her bunk before you go."

"Ari," my mom warns, pulling away from the hug. "Please. We talked about this."

"We did," I agree. Gemma grabs my hand and rests her head on my upper arm, almost like she wants to crawl inside my T-shirt and stay there. "But you should take her back and then leave her there with her bunkmates and that'll help her settle in. Trust me. I know how this works."

"Okay," my dad replies. "We love you. Have fun. Don't forget to write."

My mom sniffles, and I pretend not to notice her crying under her sunglasses. "Ditto. Love you, Ari."

"Promise to keep me updated on Bubbie," I whisper.

"We promise, Ar." My dad pulls back from the hug. "But just have fun, okay? You know Bubbie loved camp more than anyone, so she really wants you to have fun."

"I'll have fun. Of course. My number one mission," I reassure them. "But I still need to know what's going on. And please don't lie to me."

My mom replies, sort of worn out, "Okay. We hear you."

Gemma hugs me again, and I whisper in her ear. "It's gonna be great. I promise you. Go back to your bunk and make some friends and I'll see you at dinner."

She nods because she has to, not because she agrees. But finally they leave my bunk and I exhale.

I say a little silent prayer that Gemma will love it here as much as I do, maybe even more, if that's even possible. Doubtful, though.

"Ari, I need to show you something," Hana says, giggling behind her hand. "Come see."

She leads me to a corner of the cabin and points to the wall. *Shira Malkin was here.*

I love that Golfy's older sister was in this bunk. I love that Hana thought to show it to me. I love everything right now.

It's all magic perfection.

Summer is now officially really and truly here. At last.

I'm going to enjoy every single second. I won't have it any other way.

7

KAYLAN

I'M NOT SURE HOW THIS happened since it's pretty much the opposite of anything I'd ever do, but when I applied to Laurel Lake I didn't really look into the accommodations. I figured it's camp and there would be cabins like at Camp Silver and maybe it would be a little rustic but it would be fine. Since the only camp I ever visited was Camp Silver, last summer on visiting day, that's all I really had in my head.

Turns out I was totally wrong.

We're not in bunks at all. We're in tall dorm-style buildings, and we only have one roommate, and the whole thing kind of feels like a college campus with a gigantic lake in the middle of it.

I'm in my dorm now and my roommate isn't here yet,

so here I am just casually unpacking, making my bed, putting my stuff in the drawers. They don't have cubbies here like they have at Camp Silver. Good thing I didn't bother to buy plastic drawers like Ari's.

I choose the bed near the window because it looks cozier over there and I always feel better when I have natural light. I spread my fitted sheet over my mattress and the saddest feeling of aloneness washes over me. It's not loneliness really; it's aloneness. I am all alone. I don't even know what building Cleo is in because we got separated as soon as we got off the bus. She sort of got swallowed up by a big group of kids and counselors and I lost her. It's not like she tried to get away from me. At least I don't think so. But that's what happened.

I rush through unpacking so I can crawl under my covers and close my eyes for a moment and hopefully zap myself out of this gloom.

As I'm lining up my shoes under my bed, I hear a knock on the door. I whip around, expecting it to be my roommate. I smooth out the sides of my hair and put on a smile, ready to muster a sense of happy, chill excitedness.

"Uh, hey," the deep voice says.

"Hi," I stammer.

"I think I'm in the wrong building," he says. This kid is tall and lanky with a backward cap on. He's wearing mesh shorts and a jersey like a soccer game is about to break out at any moment. "They're not coed here, are they?"

I laugh even though I'm not totally sure if he's joking. "Uh. I don't know. I'm new and I just got here, and basically I have no idea what's going on."

"Yeah, we're in the same boat." He shrugs. "I better go find my building." He leans against the doorframe for a second and then walks over to me.

"I'm Chad," he says, reaching out to shake my hand like we're adults about to agree on a business venture.

"Kaylan." I look at him sideways.

"I'm here for the jam band focus." He steps back a bit, all sure of himself like he's the first person in the history of the world who was into jam bands. My mind flashes back to Ryan and the time we sabotaged his jam band audition and a feeling of slithery, slimy guilt creeps over my brain. I push it away because there's no room for another bad feeling at the moment. I already feel alone and slightly weirded out by Chad and concerned my roommate might never show. "What about you?"

"Oh, comedy." I shrug for no apparent reason. I should be proud of my comedy, wear it as a badge of honor.

"Trying to prove girls can be funny, eh?" He cracks himself up.

"Not at all. I know girls can be funny, eh," I mimic him, and then clear my throat.

He stands there silent and awkward, and I add, "Um, you should probably go, though. Don't you want to unpack?"

"I do." He hesitates a little before leaving, like maybe there's more to say, but the bottom line is I have nothing more to say to this arrogant doofus. "Later, Kaylan."

"Later." I wish he'd forgotten my name. That would have helped prove his doofiness even more, not that I really needed to. But the fact that he remembered my name from the beginning of the conversation to the end means he does have at least one redeeming quality.

Ew to this Chad kid and his sexist comment. Ew to the fact that my roommate isn't here.

When I was on the bus, it all felt great. I'd found Cleo and things were smooth sailing and it seemed like Ari's Best Case Scenario was totally manifesting itself. Now I'm not feeling so great about stuff. Not a bit.

There's a sexist doofus on the loose. One who likes jam bands. Ew to the extreme.

I crawl onto my bed and pull myself into a fetal position, writing a letter to Ari in my mind but not feeling the energy to grab my stationery and actually write it for real. And then I try to pull myself together. I talk to myself a little. *Kaylan, you're here. You wanted this. You wanted to be here. Just chill. Relax. Hang in your room for a bit. Your roommate will get here. It'll all be okay. Best case scenario. Positive thinking. Mindfulness. Breathe in. Breathe out.*

A few minutes later my door opens again and to be honest, I'm feeling like this next visitor has to be better than the first. I sit up and smile.

"Am I in the right place?" the voice asks.

Seriously, why is everyone so lost here? They have counselors all around guiding people and all the buildings are labeled. I don't get it. I look up and see a petite girl standing in the doorway with her parents.

I smile. "Um, this is the Chelsea Building, room forty-six. I'm Kaylan Terrel. Is that what it says on your sheet?"

The girl looks down at her paper, and her parents peer over her shoulder to read it.

"Yup!" she says, and does a little shimmy. "I'm Indigo. Here for modern dance." She pauses. "You?"

I'm starting to realize this is how every conversation is going to go for the foreseeable future. I'm kind of bored by it already and I wonder if that's a bad thing.

"Comedy." I pull my knees up to my chin and debate if I should get up to help them bring stuff in.

"Wow, that is so cool," Indigo says, bouncing on her toes a little bit, like she has so much excited energy and she doesn't know what to do with it.

"Thanks."

So far we're already off to a better start than with Chad.

Indigo and her parents come in, and they help her unpack. She has one of those giant tapestries for her wall and it seems the only clothes she brought are long, flowy flowery skirts and ribbed tank tops.

Maybe *she's* the Poppie from Ari's Best Case Scenario.

Her parents are in and out pretty quick and they're not super chatty. They look older than my parents and not that interested in the whole first-day-at-camp process.

"Bye, Indi," her mom says, wrapping her in the tightest hug I've ever seen. Her dad doesn't hug her at all but instead he tousles her hair and then fist-bumps her and tells her to *keep it real*. They're sort of half hippie, half fancy people. It's hard to really figure it out.

"Bye, parentals," she says. "I'll write but not that often, so don't expect much." She giggles.

"We know how it is," her dad says. "No worries. Bye, Kaylan. Nice to meet you."

"Bye!" I yell out cheerfully when they're mostly in the hallway. Indigo follows behind them and shuts the door, and then she leans against it and exhales an extremely deep sigh of relief.

"Yesssssss," she says. "This is the moment I wait for all year."

"It is?" I giggle. "Why? Your parents seem super chill."

"They are, but it's a second marriage for them and they both have two older kids and I think they're just, like, sort of over the parenting thing but they won't admit it." She pauses. "I mean, I'm named after the Indigo Girls. Like, that's the best they could come up with for my name?"

I nod, realizing that Indigo has a lot to say, but not really minding it. It's filling the air with stuff, and also keeping my mind off the glooms. I have no idea who the Indigo Girls are, but I feel like it's embarrassing to admit that.

"Do you know the Indigo Girls?" she asks.

I hesitate, unsure if I should be honest. "Um, no." I laugh, relieved that she asked me.

"They're actually okay, and I do like them, but it's just weird for a name. Anyway, I'll play some of their stuff for you later."

I wonder how long she can go on about this. Also, if she's come here before, I wonder why she didn't request someone to room with and how she ended up with a newbie like me.

"Anyway," she continues. "Wanna go hang by the lake? Did you see the new hammocks they put in?"

"No! And I love hammocks." Seriously, this is the most peppy I've felt since the bus ride, which was oddly enough only an hour or so ago, but already feels like at least a decade.

"Me too!" Indigo bounces on her toes again, and I wonder if it's going to end up being appealing or annoying. Hard to say. "Come. Let's go. It's awesome over there."

As we walk down the dorm steps and then outside and over to the lake, Indigo talks nonstop. I like not having to worry about what to say, but it's also kind of hard to get a word in.

"I mean, we're living in a crazy time," she says, referring to our politics and stuff but not mentioning names. "Women are on the cusp of something extraordinary and we've always been but now it's all out there, and we are seizing the moment. Do you know what I mean?"

"I do." I wonder if I should bring up the Chad comment but it feels a little wrong to gossip about another camper on the first day. Maybe I should wait for the second day for that.

"I mean, I'm really glad that places like Laurel Lake exist," she goes on. "Because we can be totally ourselves here. And it's not just about our focuses. We have really meaningful discussions. That never happens at school."

As she talks, I realize who she reminds me of: Ari! Not in her intensity but in her deep, passionate love of camp.

I've always rolled my eyes about it, and deep down (or maybe not so deep down) kind of hated Ari's camp obsession, but now I wonder if I'm going to end up like that.

Part of me hopes I will and part of me hopes I won't. It feels like a lot of pressure to have a place that means so much to you, that you love and care about so deeply. Because what if it lets you down? What if something goes wrong?

Indigo is still talking but my mind has trailed off, and something dawns on me.

My dad! The discussion! The issues I have with him and with stuff in general. It hits me like I just walked into a brick wall because I wasn't paying attention and my head hurts.

He's let me down so much and that's why it's hard for me to have expectations, hard for me to really care about stuff, because I'm afraid other stuff is going to let me down, too.

I'm not sure why it took me so long to realize this, but there it is.

This is one of the things I'll discuss with him for the list. It's here, in front of my eyes. Out in the open now. It has to be talked about.

I'll write a letter to Ari tonight before bed—about this and the bus ride and Cleo and Indigo and Chad and everything.

It's a little shocking to realize how much has happened in such a short time.

It's just as Ari says: the days at camp feel like weeks and the weeks feel like years.

Completely true.

8

ARI

WE WALK DOWN THE HILL to dinner and it feels weird that we've been here half a day pretty much and I still haven't seen Golfy. I'm trying to be chill and not bring it up but I think my friends can sense that it's on my mind.

"You look cute, Ar. I'm obsessed with those cutoffs." Alice links arms with me. "What do you think evening program is going to be?"

"Thanks." I smile. "Some kind of get-to-know-you thing. Right?"

"Yeah. For sure. Can I borrow those shorts? And the tank top, too? And the Birkenstocks?" Alice laughs. "Can I borrow your whole outfit?"

I laugh a little and nod. She doesn't need to ask; she knows she can borrow any of my stuff.

"You seem kind of out of it," Alice blurts like it's been

on her mind for a bit. "Is it Golfy? What?"

"Kinda, yeah," I reply. "It's weird we haven't seen each other yet and it feels like the longer we go without seeing each other, the more awkward it'll be. Plus I'm worried about Gemma, and there's always the lingering, back of my mind Bubbie worry."

Alice puts her head close to mine. "Ari! Come on! It's the first day! You're at camp. This level of stress is not allowed here."

"I know." I laugh. I don't know why I'm letting it get to me.

Truthfully, I think I'll feel better when I see Golfy. It's just so up in the air, and it may be for a while, but I won't know for sure until we have our first interaction. I need that to happen soon.

Alice nods and we're quiet for a moment. We make it to the dining hall and Alice says, "Oh no. Don't look."

"What?" My heart pounds.

But there's no way *not* to look.

Gemma's on the bench by the front door, sobbing into a counselor's shoulder.

"I'll meet you inside," I say under my breath, icky gloom creeping all over me. I want to pretend I don't see this, pretend it's not happening. I don't want any icky gloom to affect me at camp, but it's unavoidable. "Save me a good seat."

I walk over to them, hopeful that her counselor is

already cheering her up and pulling her out of this moment of sadness.

"What's going on?" I ask, arms folded across my chest.

"I want to go home, Ari." Gemma bursts into tears. "I don't want to stay. This was a mistake. I don't feel comfortable here. I don't have any friends. I already miss my bed. I miss Lion. I don't want to be here. I feel like I'll be all alone at night. I don't even know my way around this place. Four weeks feels like forever."

"Gem." I sit down on the edge of the bench, with half a butt cheek dangling off the side. "First of all, you're not alone at night. There's a whole cabin of girls, and all the counselors sleep in the bunk, and one counselor stays there after lights-out, even. You're never alone. Second of all, you need to give it some time. You don't know anyone yet. Come on, okay? It takes time to settle in. People don't always love things right away. It's a basic fact of life."

Her counselor nods. I don't really recognize her; I wonder if she's new this summer. "I was telling her how much fun we're going to have and how it's okay to miss our parents and our home and everything. But we'll see them soon. There's a time for home and there's a time for camp, and now we're in the camp time."

I smile, relieved that Gemma's counselor seems really great. "It's so true. I wait all year for this."

"Maybe I'm not meant to be at camp! Not everyone likes the same stuff, Ari." Gemma wipes her runny nose with the sleeve of her shirt, and her counselor hands her a tissue.

I lean in close to her and whisper, "That's true, but you begged to come this year. Please promise me you'll give it a chance? A real chance?"

She doesn't respond.

"You can go inside," her counselor tells me with a smile. "I got this."

"Sure?" I mouth.

"Yes."

I tousle Gemma's hair before I go and then I walk inside the dining hall. They're already starting the *motzi*, the blessing we say in Hebrew before meals. I do a quick scan of the dining hall, looking at each table for a second, to see where Golfy's bunk's table is, so I have a sense of where to locate him.

There it is. The boys our age. In the corner on the left side. Our table is directly across the dining hall from them. Two salad bars and the stage separate us. That's it. So close but also so far. As soon as I spot the back of his head, I turn away and walk quickly to my table. I don't want him to notice me looking at him.

Thankfully Alice saved me a seat next to her, and I sit down without causing too much of a distraction.

"Is she okay?" Alice whispers.

I shrug. "Eh. We'll see."

First night dinner is spaghetti and vegetarian

meatballs, but I never eat the meatballs. Instead I pile up the Parmesan cheese on the noodles and mix in some butter and voilà—my favorite meal in the world.

I'm mid-bite with spaghetti hanging out of my mouth when I feel someone's hands on my shoulders. They stay there for a second before I turn around.

"Where have you been all my life?" he asks.

My heart pounds. I'm unable to speak.

Golfy.

His hair is a mess and one strand of his eyebrow is sticking straight up, but his freckles are already at summer level and he's wearing his Barney Greengrass T-shirt and when I see him my heart flops over like a pancake on a griddle.

"I've, um, been here," I stammer. "Where have you been?"

"Here." He shrugs.

"Okay, so we've established that we've both been here," I muse, smiling.

"Come find me after dinner," he says.

"I will."

I watch him walk away, this confident, goofy swagger that is unmistakably Golfy Malkin. And when I turn back around to my table, all the girls are pretty much heart-eye emojis.

"Give it up for the couple of the decade," Hana says way too loud, quoting the movie *Bridesmaids*. "For real, though, they are," she explains to everyone and no one at the same time.

"My parents met at camp," our counselor Noa says. "Not this camp, but another one that went out of business. They're so into it. People think it's literally the cutest thing in the world."

"It is the cutest thing in the world!" Alice squeals. "Hello, life goals!"

"Okay, calm down, AlKal. For real." My heart is still flipping and flopping all over the place, so much so that I'm not sure I can finish this delicious plate of spaghetti.

"He loves you still," Zoe reassures me. "I mean, obviously, but I know you were worried and he definitely loves you. I think he'll love you for the rest of his life."

"Zoe!" I yell. "Intense much?"

She raises her eyebrows. "Yeah. But so what?"

The conversation turns to other things and we stack our plates and wipe down the table with a soggy sponge and we sing the prayer after the meal. It's called the *Birkat Hamazon* and it's really long and all in Hebrew but no one really minds it. There are all kinds of silly hand motions and dances that go along with it, too.

After that, all the unit heads announce where everyone's going for evening program. Our unit head says, "Chaverim to the quad," into the microphone.

Chaverim is the name of our unit, for kids going into eighth grade; it literally means "friends" in Hebrew. I was

kind of hoping we were meeting somewhere a little far-
ther away so I'd have a longer time to walk with Golfy
before we got there.

I wait for him outside the dining hall and all of my
friends go on ahead of me, oohing and aahing and making fun of me about the Golfy thing.

"So. Arianna. Hello." He puts an arm around me. He
smells like tomato sauce and iced tea.

"So. Golfy. Hello."

I'm trying not to focus on the complete awkwardness
of this conversation because I wonder if it's even that
awkward. Maybe it's not. It's lighthearted and funny and
silly and who even knows what it is. Plus he came up to
me first, so that's something.

"Um, I just wanted to say sorry about the whole thing
over the school year," I blurt out without planning to. "It
was just a stressful time."

"I get it," he says, and we walk quietly for another few
seconds. He takes his arm off me in a slow-motion kind
of way and I wish that it was still there.

"So, um, ya know. I didn't know what would happen
between us this summer, so, like, anyway, I, um, just
wanted to say I was sorry." I wonder why he's not saying
more or jumping in.

"It's okay, for real. We'll see what happens."

We'll see what happens?

I'm so stunned by this comment that I don't say

anything else. In a way, this kind of feels like he's getting back at me for deciding I needed a break during the school year, wanting to just be friends.

We get to the quad and we have to sit with our bunks, so he goes to sit with his and I go to sit with mine.

"So?" Alice presses, sitting as close to me as humanly possible. She's practically on my lap.

"I don't know," I mumble. "It's kind of hard to explain. I'll tell you later."

"Um, okay." She looks concerned.

It takes all of my effort not to be slumpy and distracted for the rest of evening program. I'm so happy to be here, back with my friends, but there's that lingering Golfy confusion.

I see him across the quad and he takes his hat off and puts it back on and takes it off again. It seems like he's nervous, like he has to do something with his hands to keep occupied. I wonder if he can feel me staring at him. He doesn't look in my direction.

"Ar, you can't let this take over the whole summer," Alice whispers after a rousing round of Would You Rather with all of our bunkmates.

"It won't. I know that," I say more rudely than I'd intended.

"Okay, cool, just making sure. You were kind of zoning out just now, not even very into one of your favorite games." We're sitting so close together that the edges of our knees are touching and even though I've waited months for this, all I want right now is some space. I need to figure things out. I need to understand why this Golfy thing is bugging me so much, when a few months ago I didn't even like him.

After evening program, we walk up the hill. The stars are shining so bright in the sky that it seems lit up. The air has a cool crispness to it. I pull up the hood of my sweatshirt and link arms with Alice.

There's a feeling that washes over me; a sense that I'm exactly where I'm meant to be. That if I could stay here forever, I would.

We make it back to the bunk and change into pajamas. Soon we're all on our beds reading and writing letters with flashlights. All of the counselors are still here; they haven't gone out for the night yet and I'm eavesdropping on their conversation.

"I can't take a whole summer of this," Charlie says. "It's majorly stressing me out."

"We know," Noa says. "The whole camp probably knows."

They start laughing after that, but I know how Charlie feels. I don't know who the guy is or anything about their story—but the feelings are real.

I look over the list again before I start to write a letter to Kaylan. And if I have the energy, I'll write one to Bubbie, too.

Dear Kaylan,

How are things at Laurel Lake? Tell me everything. First things first, there's something we need to add to the list ASAP. It occurred to me tonight when the counselors were talking about upcoming events and they brought up the talent show. At Silver, they always have it near the beginning of the summer because it's kind of a get-to-know-you, highlight-our-strengths thing and obviously this is never something I'd want to do, but I will! For the list! And I bet Laurel Lake has one, too, and you'll do it, too! How listy is that? Right? Especially since you crushed the school talent show in sixth grade. Okay, write back soon and tell me if you agree. It's next week, so let's hope the mail travels quickly.

The Golfy thing is still up in the air, and Gemma is mega homesick, but other than that, all is amazing. And my counselor has a broken heart, so I think she's the one I'll try to get to fall in love. She's in a terrible "but last summer he loved me" zone. So sad, right? UGH.

Also, I decided I'm gonna have the conversation with my dad on visiting day. Hopefully the Camp Silver magic will help it along. Guess what? They have giant unicorn floats in the pool this summer. Hello—list appreciation! Find a unicorn! Woo!

My gratitude journal is in high gear. I love it so much. Also it's such an awesome way to record what happened in a day.

Here are a few snippets:

Being at camp.

Alice making me laugh so hard bug juice flew all the way across the table.

Ice pops for dessert.

Golfy coming to say hi to me in the dining hall.

Okay, write back. I miss you SO SO SO much.

Always and forever your BFFFFFFFFFFF,

Arianna Simone Nodberg

Dear Bub,

How are things? It's the first day of camp and I am sooooooo happy to be here. I'd live here if I could. I remember you telling me you always wished you could live at camp. I'd miss you, though, if I lived here. But you could visit? Anyway, hope you're feeling good. I've been thinking about how I'm not so close to my dad these days, not the way we used to be when I was little, and it's bugging me. Since he's your son I wondered if you had any pointers. ☺ I'm gonna try and talk to him about it on visiting day.

Love you so much! You're my hero. Never forget it.

xoxoxox Arianna Simone Nodberg, your amazing granddaughter

9

KAYLAN

TIME AT LAUREL LAKE PICKS up speed really quickly. It's kind of hard to believe I've been here for three days already. We only have forty-five minutes a day to lounge on the hammocks, which is kind of a bummer. I love to lounge!

But I came here for comedy, and comedy is what I'll do!

"This is the smallest concentration at Laurel Lake," Dan reminds us from the stage. I only remember his name because he wears a name tag all the time; all the counselors do. I'm grateful for that. I even wrote it in my gratitude journal the past few nights. I'm not totally sure if we're allowed to write the same thing more than once; I should probably check in with Ari on that.

Dan continues almost like we're medium in trouble,

like something has happened that I didn't notice. "It's the smallest because it's the only one that requires an audition. We take this seriously. We've had years where we didn't require auditions and the whole thing just got too silly. Zany is good. Funny is great. Silly can sometimes be okay, but also sometimes not." He pauses. "We need to take our art seriously. Even if that means being wacky." He pauses again. "Does this make sense? Nod your head if this makes sense."

We all nod.

I guess something *did* happen. Who knows. I don't really have anyone to ask.

So far I haven't made any friends in comedy, but I smile at people and they smile at me and it's fine. At meals I sit with Indigo sometimes and Cleo and her friends sometimes, and there was even one BBQ where we all sat on the grass together.

It's hard to say who Indigo's friends are. She seems to be friends with everyone and no one at the same time. But there's one issue: it doesn't seem like she's friends with Cleo. To be honest, it doesn't seem like Cleo likes her at all.

"So after a few days of our group exercises, today is when the real work, cough-cough, fun begins! You're all getting paired up with a writing partner. We'll spend the morning writing, and then you'll do some peer review." He looks down at his clipboard. "And then maybe we'll have some brave souls who want to share their work. Actually, you should all be brave souls and want to share your work because that's why you're here!" He cackles. "Okay, let's get started."

He reads off a long list of names, and I pray silently that I'm paired up with a girl. Unlikely, though, since there's only one other girl in this concentration and she's fifteen.

The thing is, I don't want to have to prove to some dumb boy that girls can be funny. I know we're funny but I don't want to focus on it. I just want to work on my writing and my stand-up and my improv and whatever else we're doing here. Wasting time proving yourself again and again is just that—a total waste of time.

"Kaylan Terrel and Otis Alstadt."

Okay. Not a girl. I'll make this work. I don't have a choice.

Dan finishes reading over the list and we all go to meet our partners. "Take some time to get to know each other," he tells us all from the front of the room. "Be friendly. Kind. All that jazz. You know the drill."

Otis walks over to me. Yeah, um, definitely not a girl. A medium-tall boy in jeans on a kind of hot day and a faded navy T-shirt that says *Fun* across the front. I don't know what to think of him, except to worry that he'll overheat in those pants.

"Hey, I'm Otis. I mean, you probably already guessed

that." He sits down and then leans back on his elbows. "I'm from New Jersey, so please refrain from the Jersey jokes."

I don't totally know what he means but I smile anyway, just to start things off on the right foot. "Cool. Uh, Kaylan, from Connecticut. Are there any Connecticut jokes?" I laugh.

"Good question. Maybe something about why it's spelled Connect-I-Cut," he muses. "Say that five times fast."

"Connect-I-Cut. Connect-I-Cut," I start. "Twice is probably good enough."

"Yeah, makes sense." He nods, and we're giggling together, and maybe being paired up with a boy isn't so terrible. Maybe they're not all like Chad. "Are you most into stand-up? Or improv or sketch or . . ."

"I think stand-up," I tell him. "But sketch is cool. Improv, nah. I'm way too anxious for improv. I need to have stuff Planned. Out."

"I hear that," he says.

"What about you?"

He ponders. "I like it all. I kind of want to try everything and see what I'm best at, because let's face it, I really hate to fail and I'm a typical first child overachiever and I'm way too arrogant to not be good at something, so . . ." He stops. "Just putting it all out there."

"Obviously. Isn't that why we're here? Pretty much

free therapy." I pause. "Well, not really free because we're paying to be here, so I guess scratch that whole thing."

"Well, now you need to tell me why you need therapy," he says. "Because you seem like a very well-adjusted person to me."

I hesitate a minute, wondering why I even made that comment. But now it's out there, swirling around in the air, and I can't take it back. "The usual: divorced parents, remarried dad, general anxiety."

"I get that." He scratches an itch on the top of his head.

He doesn't elaborate more, or share anything about his own life, so we're left sitting there in an awkward lump of silence for a moment.

Thankfully, Dan makes another announcement and calls out an improv exercise to get us started. Something about a glass of lemonade, and we need to team up with the pair next to us.

"Ahhhh, this lemonade," I start, trying to sound like an old woman. "It takes me back to my childhood days on the porch in Alabama. And I'm sittin' there sippin' and relaxin' and feelin' the wind in my bones."

Otis taps my shoulder, jumping into the exercise. "Remember me, Gloria? Do I look familiar to you?"

"Yes, uh, you do, but I'm ninety-six, so please refresh my memory, dearie." It's all I can do not to laugh because Otis is making this confused and frightened face and it's so over the top.

"Gloria!" he yells. "I'm your son!"

One of the other kids—his name is Teddy and he's a few years younger than I am—tries to tag in. "Did anyone order a pizza?" he asks.

For some reason the way he says it is so funny we all burst into laughter and the improv exercise is over for the moment.

I lie down flat on the floor and catch my breath.

Maybe Teddy is the younger kid I convince to start his own list. When we first made the new list, I figured it would be a younger girl, but there's something about Teddy that's just so cute and funny.

It might work.

That night, Indigo and I are chatting before we go to sleep. "Pillow talk is essential in any relationship—couple, friend sleepover, roommate sitch," Indigo says, and I agree with her completely.

"Did I tell you about the girl who snuck out last summer?" she asks.

"No." I shift onto my side. "You mean snuck out of camp?"

Indigo giggles. "No! I mean, like, snuck out of the building. She went down to the lake and sat there for a while and then dipped her feet in. She didn't get caught until she walked back to her room. And she didn't really get in that much trouble. Her parents were called, though, and the directors said that if she ever did that again, she'd be kicked out of camp." She pauses. "I'm really not a rule breaker, but I just have this itchy feeling that I want to break some rules this summer."

"I know what you mean," I reply. "Summer is the time to do that; camp too. We're so good all year. I think it's good to break rules sometimes."

Indigo goes on about this for a few minutes and I zone out, and then the list pops into my head! *Sneak out of your room/bunk without getting caught.* It's so listy that I can't believe it took me this long to figure it out.

We have a few more minutes of pillow talk and then I say, "Okay, I'm tired, gonna head to sleep. Nighty-night."

But I can't fall asleep, of course, because I need to tell Ari about our new list item. I wait a few minutes and then I get out my gel pens and my lap desk, and I write.

Dear Ari,

Things at Laurel Lake are going well. I feel like I'm getting close to people (no one who compares to you, don't worry) and my comedy partner is awesome. This kid Chad is kind of a doofus and now he thinks we have this running joke about girls not being funny but we don't. He's just sexist. Need to figure out what to do about it.

I may have found a younger kid for the list, but I haven't told him that yet. I will soon. He's so cute and smooshy—he's like ten, I think—and I feel like he'll be really into it. Have you found anyone yet?

I loved your first letter and I love your idea about the talent show. And I have another idea! I think we should both try to sneak out of our bunk/room at night without getting caught. It's such a camp-y thing to do, and it's a little more dangerous than we usually do, but I'm up for it. Are you? It came to me when I heard this story about a girl who snuck out last summer to swim in the lake at night. Spoiler alert, she did get caught when she wasn't even really swimming. But anyway, we're not going to swim in the lake, we're just going to sneak out. We'll figure that part out later. Anyway, let me know what you think.

I miss you so much but I'm surviving. I LOVE YOU FOREVER & EVER & EVER & EVER.

Xoxoxooooxox Kaylan

PS Did I already mention my time capsule idea? I can't remember. Anyway, we are making one when we get home!!! And burying it!!! List complete!

10

ARI

ZOE AND I ARE LYING side by side on towels during free swim while all of our other friends are in the pool. Zoe had period cramps so she wanted to avoid the pool, and I, being the good friend that I am, decided to sit out with her.

Alice and Hana are on the unicorn float, and they're having a really hard time both staying on. They keep cracking up and falling into the water, and it's making Zoe and me laugh, too.

Zoe flips her hair upside down and pulls it into a bun. She says, "Did you hear my dad and Kaylan's mom talked about getting married?"

It almost feels like my heart stops for a second. "Wait. What? Like they're engaged?"

"No, I mean, I don't think so. It's not, like, an official thing." She clears her throat. "He mentioned it in passing.

I don't know if Kaylan knows, so maybe don't say anything to her? It wasn't like an official declaration and they don't have, like, set plans."

My voice catches in my throat a little bit. "Does that mean you'd move to Brookside?"

"No way. My dad loves the city."

My heart stops again. *Would Kaylan move to New York City?*

This feels like way too intense of a conversation to have by the pool during free swim when everyone is screaming and splashing. I wonder why Zoe mentioned it now. I wonder how long she's known.

"How do you feel about this?" I ask her softly, sort of scared to know the answer, but sensing it's the right question to ask.

"Um, not sure." She flips over onto her stomach and faces away from me so we're not making eye contact. She fiddles with the unraveling threads on her towel. "I'm kind of hoping it takes a while. Not that I don't like Kaylan's mom, or Kaylan. I mean, actually, I don't know them *that* well. But a stepmother? A stepsister? It's just, I don't know. Weird, I guess."

"Totally. It is weird." My mind is blank right now, literally a white sheet. I can't think of anything to say or anything to offer.

"So anyway," Zoe says. "Has Kaylan mentioned anything?"

"Nope. Not a word." I flip onto my back and stare at the fluffy white clouds floating by. All of a sudden I feel older and heavier, like life is harder than it used to be. I wonder if Kaylan knows about it and felt too awkward to discuss it with me. I wonder if she keeps more secrets than I realize. I start to feel guilty about my boarding school secret, even though it's not really a thing. It's just something I want to do. I wonder if all friendships have secrets. "Should I write to her about it?"

Zoe jerks upward. "No, definitely not. Maybe she doesn't know yet, and I don't want her stressing. Or saying something to her mom. Maybe her mom isn't even aware of it, but I doubt that. Right? Maybe it's just something my dad hopes will happen. I dunno. Grown-ups are weird."

"Okay. Yeah. They are soooo weird." I move my fingers across my lips—the universal sign for "lips are zipped," and I think about the conversation I need to have with my dad and all the secrets that seem to be popping up between Kaylan and me.

We were TH, Total Honesty friends, I thought? Oh wait, no. I was. She was PF—Protecting Feelings. I think? I sigh and push all of this away and ignore it for now. I don't want anything to get in the way of Camp Silver euphoria. That's my mission for this summer. And every summer. "I won't say anything; I promise."

After swim, we're traipsing up the hill with our towels

around our necks and everywhere I go, I'm thinking about Golfy: where he is, what he's doing, what he's thinking, if there's ever going to be an Ari and Golfy again.

I feel pathetic about it. I don't know why it's consuming me. I can tell my friends are getting annoyed when I bring it up, and yet I can't seem to help it. We've been at camp for five days already and the situation is still so unclear. We say hi and talk sometimes and we all hang out together at night before bed, but it's like we're just friends in a big clumpy group, and that's it.

When I get to the bunk, Gemma's already there, head slumped toward her knees, sitting on the porch steps.

"Hi, Gem."

Every day she waits for me here during *breira*—the free time in the afternoon for the whole camp. We're allowed to be anywhere and do anything (except stay in the bunk) and somehow this has turned into my babysitting-Gemma-and-listening-to-her-cry time.

"Hi." She's barely able to get the words out through her sobs.

"Gemma!" Zoe scoops her up like a baby. "Come on, girl! You gotta have fun. Enough of this sad business!"

I sort of want to remind Gemma that Zoe knows about true sadness—her mom is literally dead—but I don't. It's inappropriate and it also won't really help her.

"Okay, enough is enough." Alice bursts out of the bunk. "I am not watching this sad breira scene for another day!

Gemma, you're coming with us."

I glare at Alice through my sunglasses, but obviously she can't see me. I don't want to have to share my friends with Gemma. Maybe that's mean, but it's how I feel. I don't want to waste my precious Camp Silver days dealing with my little sister's whining.

"But after this, we're done trying, Gem!" I blurt out.

"Ari!" Alice yelps, shocked.

"No, seriously, time for tough love," I continue. "She needs to make her own space here, and find her own fun and make an effort. She's lumped herself into this pattern of sadness and now she's comfy this way and it's not right."

"But I don't have any friends here," Gemma mumbles. "And I'm miserable!"

"You're miserable because you think you have to be. Bottom line: you don't have to be."

We take Gemma to the art shack and we all make lanyard bracelets. She finds a few of her bunkmates there, and they're all friendly to her. They smoosh together on the bench to make space for her to sit with them. For a few minutes she's happy and she seems to be enjoying herself. What happens later is anybody's guess.

Near the end of breira, we leave Gemma in the art shack and go hang out at the top of the hill. We lie down, fold our arms behind our heads, and stare up at the sky.

When we're back at the bunk showering and getting

ready for dinner, Noa yells out, "Girls! Reminder that tonight Chaverim/K'tanim buddies meet, so please bring your best selves. Remember, these kids are gonna look up to you! You seem like real adults in their eyes."

"We do?" Hana scoffs. "That's kind of scary."

Everyone starts laughing after that, and Noa mumbles, "Well, I tried," under her breath.

The K'tanim kids are the littlest ones at camp. They're going into second and third grade and they only stay for two weeks. They get matched up with us, the kids going into eighth grade. Gemma's ten and going into fifth grade; it's kind of amazing that in the camp world she's not the littlest even though she still seems little to me.

"I hope I get a good buddy," Alice says. "I want someone who loves camp, who I can see summer after summer and we can hug and I can kind of follow her progress and then when she's a counselor I can be so proud and everything."

"Um, I kind of just want someone who doesn't run away from me," Zoe muses. "These kids are so little."

I'm excited to get my buddy and hope some of the little kid energy will quell my lingering agita. What started out as Kaylan's word has kind of become my word, and sometimes it's really the only way to explain how my insides are doing.

It's not major agita but it's there, and if Kaylan were with me, I'd put it all out for her to analyze and pick apart.

I don't want this feeling at camp; it shouldn't be here.

I'm not sure why I feel guilty knowing the thing about Zoe's dad and not sharing it with Kaylan. Maybe because I wonder if she actually knows but was too nervous to tell me, like the thing with the Cami trip over spring break and the application for Laurel Lake. What if this is another one of those secrets? I need to talk to her and go back to the conversation we had about Total Honesty friends or Protecting Feelings friends. I need a refresher on what she said.

We finish dinner and say the Birkat Hamazon, and then we walk over to Universal Lawn for our buddy program. Golfy runs up behind me, the way he always does right after dinner. His mood seems to change at that time of day and some kind of signal goes off in his brain and he remembers that he loves me, but then after evening program, when we're all up on the hill and the stars are twinkling and it's dark out and everything's relaxed, he kind of disappears. It's like he's scared to make it official, somehow.

"Hey," he says. "Excited to get your buddy?"

"I think so." I laugh a little. "You?"

"Yes! I've been waiting for this moment since I was in K'tanim! I remember my buddy—Joel Slossberg—he was the man!"

I'm sure Golfy is the only boy in the unit who remembers his buddy's full name.

"I'm still confused why Olim isn't paired up with K'tanim. Wouldn't it make sense to have the oldest and the youngest?" It feels like a relief to be having an actual conversation with Golfy about a real thing. So far it's just been nonsense, really, and the whole time we're talking all I can think about is if he'll ever kiss me again.

"It used to be Olim/K'tanim buddies but then they changed it to Chaverim/Tzofim and Olim/Bonim since K'tanim is like soooo young and sort of like a trial unit," he explains. "Bonim is like the real start of camp, ya know!"

"Um, okay. So you're saying we'll get another buddy next summer and another buddy in two years when we're in Olim?"

"Kinda, yeah, but buddies are FOR LIFE!" he yells, all over the top, and drapes an arm over my shoulder as we walk. "Oh, Nodz, you're such quality."

My skin prickles. "I am?"

"Oh yeah, the qualitiest of the qualities!"

"Golfy, I don't even know what to do with you," I say, because it just seems to fall out of my mouth.

"Be my girlfriend," he says. "But for real this time."

My throat clenches up and I feel like I'm about to fall over. This is happening. Really happening. It took almost a week, which is three decades in camp time, but it's happening. It's happening now.

"So?" he asks. "What say you, Arianna Simone Nodberg?"

"Um, yes. Hello! I've been waiting for this." I regret saying the last part because I think it's coming on too strong, like I've spent this whole time pining away for a boy, which is truthfully something I'd never do even though I was kind of doing it in my head, and I really didn't like it.

"You have?" he asks.

"Um, well, sort of. You know what I mean."

He side-eyes me. "Maybe. But this time you can't just ditch me out of the blue. Okay? My heart is a fragile flower and it can't be bashed around."

I burst out laughing. *His heart is a fragile flower.*

"It's true!" he yelps. "Here I am baring my soul to you, and you laugh! Why do I subject myself to this? Why?"

I shrug.

"Because you're the awesomest, that's why." He pauses, and pulls me in close for a second. "I guess you're worth the risk."

Our conversation ends there because we need to sit with our bunks on Universal Lawn and then the unit heads are going to call out the buddies.

"Eeeeeeep," I loud-whisper into Alice's ear.

"What?" She bulges her eyes.

"Golfy. Me. Good news. We talked." I pull her in for the tightest sideways hug. "I'll fill you in tonight. My bed after lights-out. K?"

"K!"

Our unit heads—Rachel and Andy—call out all the names of the buddies, and then we're broken up into little teams to do things like three-legged races and egg toss and get the Oreo into your mouth from your forehead.

I meet my buddy, Margaux, by the big tree at the far end of Universal Lawn. She has bright blond hair and she's missing a few teeth. She seems to bounce when she walks.

"I'm Margaux," she says, sitting down. "But everyone calls me Gaux. Like the end of my name, but said like you're spelling it out—*gawks*, not the French way, like *go*. Get it?"

I smile and sit across from her. "I get it. Very cool. I'm Arianna but everyone calls me Ari." I play with the grass in front of me. "I love nicknames."

"I just moved here from California. I haven't even seen my new house yet. I came to camp first. Can you believe that?"

I shake my head, trying not to laugh and to take this little girl seriously, but she's so cute that I kind of want to eat her up. "I can't believe that. Is this your first summer?"

"Yeah," she says. "But I love it already."

"It's only my second summer," I tell her. "I wish I'd come earlier, when I was younger, but oh well."

"Yeah. Oh well. You're here now," she says.

Margaux tells me everything: about her house on the beach in California and how she's moving to Long Island and her parents are there right now setting up the house and about her bunkmate who was able to eat five hamburgers at dinner last night and not even throw up and about the shower wheel in her bunk.

"They make us shower every day," she says. "I kind of expected that, though."

"It's important to be clean," I say, stating one of the more obvious things about life. "Were you nervous to come to camp for the first time?" I ask her.

"Not really." She braids together three strands of grass. "You?"

"I was, yeah," I admit. I almost tell her about Gemma but then decide it's a bad idea to bring up a sad, homesick camper. Gaux might seem fine now but who knows what's lurking under the surface. I don't want her to get upset.

"I went to camp in California last summer for a few weeks, so I'm used to it," she declares proudly. "My mom says I was made for camp. She's right."

It takes a good deal of effort not to crack up at everything Gaux says.

Rachel speaks loudly into the megaphone. "Okay, time for relay races! We're dividing up by buddy teams. Soooo . . . if you're in Chaverim and your bunk ends in an odd number, come over here." She moves her hands to the left like she's guiding people into parking at a gigantic sports stadium. "And if you're in Chaverim and your bunk ends in an even number, go over there." She does the same gesture with her arms, just in the other direction.

"Ready for this?"

"Oh. I was born ready."

Gaux links arms with me and we head to our section of Universal Lawn.

Younger kid to start his or her own list? No doubt about it.

I can't wait to see what kind of stuff Gaux comes up with.

11

KAYLAN

"STILL TRYING TO PROVE GIRLS can be funny?" Chad seems to appear out of nowhere, plopping himself down on the hammock next to mine by the lake.

I roll my eyes. "Um? What?"

"It's just a joke, Terrel." He talks but doesn't look at me; he's staring straight up at the sky. "Aren't you supposed to get jokes? Since you're in comedy . . ."

"How do you even know my last name?"

"I know things," he says. "Haven't you ever heard the expression 'Alvig knows all'?"

"Definitely not." I laugh. "I'm guessing you're Alvig?"

"Yup. People say it around here."

Seriously, who is this kid? He was confused on the first day like he'd never been here before, but now I'm beginning to see that was just a charade. And he seems to find me at the randomest times. It's not like I'm scared, although maybe I am a little bit, but more just confused.

When I don't respond to that, he says, "So when did you first get into comedy?"

I hesitate to answer because I have so little interest in talking to Chad. I came here for some quiet R&R by the lake, Cleo and her friends stopped by for a bit, which was okay, and now I'm forced to make conversation with someone I don't even want to talk to. Is this what adulthood is? I mean, I know I'm not an adult yet, but I kind of feel like doing things out of obligation is one of the big things about it.

"Um, I'm not sure. I guess last year I got really into it, but I've always loved making people laugh. It's the best feeling in the world."

"It totally is. I considered doing comedy, too, but the whole jam band thing is just incredible to me. These bands just jam and play for soooooo long at concerts, like forever basically. It's amazing. I mean, the band Phish is totally my inspiration and I need to be like them one day. It's my only goal."

I wonder if I should admit that I've never heard of the band Phish and also that I don't care at all. My main goal right now is to end this conversation and go back to my relaxing before the time is up and I have to go to afternoon session.

"Very admirable," I say. "Listen, Chad, I kinda just want

to relax a bit now. No offense or anything. But I'm gonna close my eyes and maybe doze for a little."

"No offense taken," he replies.

I expect him to get up and walk away but he doesn't. He stays on that hammock, and he's one of those heavy breathers even when he's not sleeping.

Chad Alvig is the personification of that time that Ari and I went to Ultimate Pizza Kitchen and they put salt in the whipped cream on my sundae instead of sugar.

Such a small thing has the power to really ruin something great.

When Indigo and I get back to the room later that night, there's a pile of mail on our little entryway table. We don't get mail every day; it's more like every few days.

The first letter that catches my eye is one from my dad.

Oh Lord.

I scan through the rest of the pile, hoping for something from Ari, but nothing. It's just this one letter from my dad; the rest are for Indigo.

I hand Indigo her envelopes and brace myself before I open mine, wishing Ari was here to help me through this. Anything from my dad is always nerve-racking. It's this constant feeling that a bucket of ice is about to pour from the heavens all over my head at the moment I'm least expecting it.

"Are you okay?" Indigo asks me, ripping open a letter.

"Oh yeah, I'm fine." I laugh.

She looks at me through one eye, not convinced that I'm telling her the truth.

I slowly open my dad's letter and read:

Dear Kaylan,

Hope comedy camp is going great! I can't wait to hear all about it. Just wanted to let you know that we're coming for visiting day. I cleared it with your mom already. I have some exciting news to tell you, but it's better to wait for in person.

Write back and tell us all about camp.

Love, Dad (and Amy)

Barf bag in a pile of poop: that was gross to the extreme. I hate that he included Amy—not that I hate her, but it's not like she had much to do with the writing of that letter, so why does she need to be included? And visiting day! Both of them! And my mom. Obviously Robert Irwin Krieger won't be coming since my visiting day is randomly the same as Camp Silver's. I push away the thought of that, too, though.

Every time I wonder about what my mom's doing at home without me, I think about her with Robert Irwin Krieger and I feel happy that she's not alone, but then also kind of icky and grossed out.

I'm about to launch into the horrors of second marriages when I remember that Indigo is a product of a second marriage and I stop myself.

"You know what's weird?" Indigo asks.

"Um, a zillion things, but what are you referring to?" I laugh.

"How little kids always say *stop following me* but then as we get older we all want to be the one being followed, like with trends and social groups and stuff?" She stops talking for a minute and stacks her letters in a neat pile. "It just came to my mind because I had this friend growing up who always said *stop following me* in this obnoxious tone and it really hurt my feelings."

I'll admit that I have no idea where this is coming from, but that's just how Indigo is. At this point I'm used to it. I'm interested in the inner workings of her brain but I'm not sure I'll ever really figure it out.

"I know what you're saying," I reply. "Little girls are kind of mean. I guess so are big girls, though." I think back to Brooke and Lily and that friendship breakup debacle and how they just moved on without me. It all happened before Ari moved here. It feels like another lifetime. We seemed like big girls then, but we really weren't.

"Yeah, totally." She dangles her legs off the side of the bed and scratches a mosquito bite. "It's cool how you're friends with Cleo and them. You just met her on the bus and now you're besties?"

"I wouldn't say besties!" I get up to get some stationery out of my cubby. "I mean, she's nice to me and everything, but I don't think I'm part of the crew."

"You're more part of the crew than I am."

I'm quiet for a second because I realize that I've been here a week and a half already and I haven't spent much time worrying about having a crew. I've been so focused on the comedy. I have people to sit with at meals and I enjoy my quiet time by the lake and that's pretty much it.

I wish Laurel Lake didn't have a visiting day. I don't need my dad (and Amy) here and I don't need to experience the my-dad-and-my-mom interaction, and the my-mom-and-Amy interaction, for that matter.

I wish I could call my mom and discuss this with her but we can't make phone calls. And a letter will take a few days to get to Ari.

For the first time since I got here, I feel slumpy and alone. And it's all my dad's fault.

At least I figured out what I want to discuss with him to complete the list item. Why everything he does makes me nervous and shaky and uncertain and how we can change that, drop the cryptic stuff, and who knows what else.

A girl can't live like this forever.

Dear Ari,

How's camp? My dad and his person are coming on visiting day. How crazy is that? I'm freaking out. I think we both need to have the dad discussions on visiting day, though, for the list, because I don't know if I'll see my dad when I get home and I kind of want to get it out of the way. When's your talent show? I think mine is at the end of the session. This kid Chad is still driving me crazy. Ugh. Other than that, things are really good.

I miss you so much! xoxo Kay

"Oh! Kay! You missed a letter," Indigo says, hopping up from her bed and dropping it on my lap. "And it's a postcard from Ari!"

"Really?" My voice rises at the end. "How did I miss that?"

Dear Kay,

The mail is so slow from here, I'm not even sure they pick it up every day. Anyway, I've been thinking so much about our list and I love it. Also I know we haven't fully completed one thing yet but we can JHH the letters thing and the gratitude journal since we're doing it and obv crushing it!

We always feel better when we're checking stuff off and celebrating with a Jump in the air, High Five, Hug. I couldn't

106

sleep last night and I got worried you were stressing about list item completion. Don't fret, my pet! I LOVE YOU!!!!

XOXOXO Ari

PS Have you given any thought to what language our conversation should be in?

12

ARI

"I STILL CAN'T BELIEVE YOU'RE doing the talent show," Alice says, when we're standing side by side in front of the full-length bathroom mirror, getting ready for dinner and evening program. We've been at camp for almost two weeks and it feels like time is literally flying by. "You hate being the center of attention."

"Loyal to the List, baby." Truth is, I can't believe it either, and I'm kind of regretting suggesting it. "Want to do it with me?"

"Would that count?" she asks.

"Yeah, totally. We can do it together." I turn to face her. "Hand-clapping games? That would be so funny if we just went up there, did three hand-clapping games without talking, and then sat back down."

"Um, this is literally tonight," Alice says. "It's such a Camp Silver thing to have people sign up and then not ask them in advance what they're doing. I mean, any other camp would have this planned out. No?"

"I have no idea! This is the only camp I've ever been to."

"Same, actually." Alice cracks up, and then I do, too, and before we realize, we've collapsed on the disgusting bathroom floor in hysterics.

"Okay, ew, can we get up off the floor?" I stand up and brush off the butt of my jeans. "Seriously, you'll do this with me? Honestly? Because my only other idea was begging Golfy to sing a duet of 'Summer Nights' with me but I keep chickening out of asking him."

"Ari, this is tonight. You know this, right?" Alice looks deep into my eyes. "So what was your plan if I didn't say yes to the hand clapping?"

I shrug. "Um, I was also going to ask everyone in the bunk to a borrow a letter from a parent and then read them all aloud; it sounded funny in my head."

"I like that you didn't say letter from a mom," Alice whispers as she finds her hairbrush in the bathroom cubby. "Because, Zoe, obviously."

"Well, obvs. Yeah."

"Ari!" Charlie yells from her bed. "You have a visitor!"

I walk to the front door of the bunk and find Gemma there. She's wearing a hot pink tank top and black bike shorts. Her cheeks are red and her eyes are swollen; she looks like she's been crying for hours.

"Hey, Charlie," I say. "Is it okay if I walk with Gemma for a bit? I'll meet you guys at dinner."

"Yes, but stay on the hill for the walk. Don't go far."

I nod.

As annoyed as I am about this, I try to hide it. Gemma needs me. She shouldn't but she does. I want to help her.

"Gem." I put an arm around her as we walk. "Talk to me. What is it?"

She's quiet for a bit. Then she says, "Sometimes I feel okay here. And then it hits me that I still have a lot of time left and I get scared I'll get sad again. So then I'm sad."

I think about it for a minute and only sort of get what she's saying.

Then something comes to me. Mindfulness!

"Gem, the only way to do this, to really experience camp to the fullest, to really have fun—the kind of fun Bubbie tells us about—is to be in the moment. Don't think too far ahead. Don't think about the past. Just be." I pause and watch her wiping the tears with the bottom of her tank top. Her belly button is showing and she doesn't even care. "Only focus on what's right in front of you. Take in all the sights and sounds and smells and touches of camp. Think of it this way: try to find five things you can see around you, four things you can touch, three things you can hear, two things you can smell, and one thing you can taste."

"You think that can work?" Gemma sniffles again.

We've walked all the way across the hill to the boys' side and we're about to head back. "I know it can. Mindfulness keeps us centered. You're getting too wrapped up in your fearful thoughts. Feel them, and then let them pass. And be in the moment."

I can't totally tell if this is sinking in, but I'm trying.

I think there's a way for Gemma to love camp. She just has to allow herself to not let the sad, anxious, impatient feelings take over.

After dinner (taco night) we're all in the Chaverim Beit Am (our unit's meeting space, which translates to Friends House of the People) sitting on the floor, and Alice and I are practicing our hand-clapping games. I hope people won't catch on that it's our (my) talent show act but even if they do, it'll still be funny.

I realize that I kind of know a lot of Hebrew and I wonder if I could ask Kaylan to pick Hebrew as the language of our conversation. I wonder if that's selfish of me to even bring it up. But she did say at my bat mitzvah that she kind of wanted to become an honorary Jew so she could have the experience.

"I hear you're doing the talent show." Golfy sits down next to me and leans his head on my shoulder. My whole body turns tingly and all of a sudden I don't know where to put my hands or how to hold my arms or anything. I'm just frozen, sort of suspended in time with him there, and it feels like the world stops.

"I am."

"Me too."

"What's your act?" I ask.

"You'll have to be surprised," he says.

"Oh, Golfy, I hate surprises, you know this about me." I clench my teeth in his direction. "Please. Tell me."

"This isn't a big surprise." He looks at me sideways. "You can handle it."

He gets up and goes back to his friends. "Good luck," he says as he walks away.

"I wonder what he's doing," Zoe whispers to the group.

Hana adds, "Well, with Golfy it's gotta be something totally random. Like he stole one of those little ride-on things from the day camp and he's going to pedal across the stage."

I laugh. "Yeah, exactly. Or he somehow swiped the dining hall menu for the whole summer and he's going to read it aloud."

I kind of regret not asking him to do the duet with me, even just now when he came over, but Alice and I have a good plan. I don't think Kaylan will be annoyed with me about Alice joining. But maybe she will. I did tell her not to let Cami do list things with her when they were on vacation together.

Ugh. I'm hit hard in the stomach with a boulder-sized wad of guilt.

Also I hope Kaylan realizes this is a talent show just for our unit and not the whole camp. Whatever. I can't second-guess all of this now. It's just one list item, not the whole thing, and I'm doing the best I can. Plus this was my idea!

Suddenly my head is spinning and I feel like I'm about to faint.

"I need to go outside for a minute," I whisper to my friends. I get up and walk carefully so I don't step on anyone and then when I get to the little porch area, I lean back on one of the railings and breathe in the beautiful Berkshire mountain air. In and out. In and out, remembering all of my skills, especially the five-four-three-two-one I just talked to Gemma about. I need to make sure I remember it myself!

Okay, Ari. Get ahold of yourself (whatever that means). This is a unit talent show, one thing on the list, not the end of the world. I just don't know if it's cheating to do it with Alice but I've already decided and I can't bail on her now.

Then something hits me. An idea! A solution!

I could do two acts. One with Alice and one on my

own. I wonder if our unit heads would let me.

I meditate for a minute and then go back inside; I tap Rachel on the shoulder.

"Hey," I say, trying not to sound out of breath even though it's kind of hard to hide it.

"Hey, Ari. Can I help you? We're gonna start in a minute. I have you down on the list." She looks at me, all confused.

"I kinda want to do two things." I scrunch up my face and pray she says yes. "One with Alice and one on my own. Kinda last minute, I know, but if there's time . . . pretty please?"

"Um." She looks down at the list again and brushes some hair away from her eyes. "I guess? Sure. Let's see how it goes. You know we'll have another one at the beginning of second session. You're staying all summer, right?"

"Yeah." I think about it for a second and realize this can be a test run, and then I can do something on my own for the second session one if I need to. This way Kaylan can't be mad, and if she's okay with me sharing it with Alice, then we're all good, and if not, I can do second session. Perfect! "Okay, so then I'll do my other act for second session. Thanks, Rachel!"

I skip back over to my friends, flooded with relief that this entire list item doesn't rest on this day, this talent show, this experience.

I think about it for a little bit and realize that so much

of life is wrapped up in that fear; the sense that we won't have another chance, the feeling that time is limited and we want to make the most of it, and we want everything to go exactly the way we want it to go.

This is it. I've nailed down the root of all agita. I feel like I've just unlocked some major epiphany, all because of this list item and the list in general.

It reminds me of the song we sing at camp that translates into: "The whole world is a narrow bridge, but the most important thing is not to be afraid." I never realized it before, and I'm not sure why since it's kind of obvious, but that whole song is pretty much talking about agita. I should tell Kaylan about it at some point.

"Welcome to the Chaverim Talent Show!" Andy yells out, and tries to do a little tap dance as he talks. "The moment you've all been waiting for! The chance to see your friends as the stars that they are! Can I get a woo from the crowd?"

We all yell out a lazy *woo!*

"C'mon, guys, you can definitely do better than that!" Rachel yells. "Can we get a WOO from the crowd?"

We try harder this time. WOO!

"Okay! Let's get started! The first person who signed up for the talent show," Andy says, looking down at his clipboard (the number one unofficial Camp Silver accessory), "this will probably not come as a surprise to anyone . . . Golfy Malkin!"

It cracks me up inside that he has to say his full name because it's not like there's another Golfy. And if anyone ever called him Jonah, it would sound so completely ridiculous.

Golfy runs up to the stage and stands there with his hands in his pockets. The whole unit is silent, waiting to see what he'll do, and I guess we're extra patient since the talent show just started. My nervousness has faded away a little bit. Now all I feel are little excitement bubbles. This kid. This place. It's pure happiness.

"Picture it. The year is 2005. Little Jonah Abraham Malkin—yes, my initials spell out *jam*—is five years old. Shira Malkin is nine. Yael Malkin is twelve."

He pauses and the whole unit is staring at him. My heart pounds, waiting to see what he's going to do. I'm a mixture of scared and embarrassed and one thousand percent in love.

"Have you pictured this? A household in suburban Boston." He pauses again. "Nod your head if you've all pictured it."

We do and then he says, "Great. I'm going to read you a few pages from the Malkin family calendar. Yes, I snatched this from the family archives before the summer just for this very purpose. What could be more fun than listening to an average American Jewish family's day-to-day schedule?"

The whole unit cracks up as he says, "Shira dance

rehearsal, three p.m. New prayer book committee meeting, seven p.m. Fill out permission slip for Fenway Park field trip. Pick up Mom at Sadelle's."

And on and on and on. The whole unit is literally freaking out with laughter even though he's just reading an old calendar.

One billion percent in love. That's me right now.

After Golfy goes, all the girls from bunk seventeen sing a medley of Disney songs and then the boys from bunk forty-two do an interpretive dance that they made up to go with a counselor's white noise machine playing sounds of a rainstorm.

"And now we have Ari Nodberg and Alice Kalman!" Rachel leads the cheering and the clapping from the stage.

Alice and I run up there and we jog in place for a few seconds to get fired up. I don't make eye contact with anyone in the audience; I focus on Alice, and smile, and try not to laugh. We do a superfast *double-double this-this, double-double that-that* and then *Avocado, avocado, name of the game. If you mess up you have to change your name.*

After that Zoe throws two jump ropes on the stage, careful not to hit anyone, and we jump in complete unison for four whole minutes. We bow and curtsy and hug and then run off the stage.

Everyone claps and cheers for us and Golfy yells out, "Yeah, Ari! Yeah, Alice! Yeah, Zoe!"

"That was amazing." Alice pulls me into a side hug. "Really truly."

"Really truly. I agree."

I'm out of breath and randomly kind of sweaty but I feel euphoric. There was something about being on that stage with Alice that just felt so awesome and exciting and almost powerful. We weren't doing anything all that important but it still felt like an accomplishment.

Back at the bunk that night, I write in my gratitude journal, like I do every night.

Rocking the talent show with Alice.

Golfy cheering for us.

Having a heart-to-heart with Gemma and then seeing her smiling and singing with her bunk during dinner.

Getting an awesome letter from Bubbie and Zeyda.

Moving up a swim group.

I write a quick postcard to Bubbie about the talent show and then I write to Kaylan.

Dear Kay,
We had the talent show! Now, please brace yourself, because you may see this as cheating, and if so, don't worry, because there's another talent show second session! But I did

hand-clapping games with Alice and it was SO awesome. I am super proud of myself since you know I'm not a talent show kind of gal. But here's how I see it: I couldn't do hand-clapping games on my own! They require another person. So it's really not cheating. I hope you agree.

What's the latest with Chad the doofus? I hope he's not still bothering you.

I agree with you about the conversation with our dads on visiting day. I'm gonna do it then, too. To get it over with. Have you heard from Cami or any of the other girls? Marie wrote me a note on a diner napkin but that's it. I haven't written anyone. Oops! How's your gratitude journal going? Mine is great.

Miss you beyond beyond beyond.

Xoxoxoxoxxoxoxoxooxoxox Ari

13

KAYLAN

"I STILL CAN'T BELIEVE YOU got paired up with Indigo," Cleo says.

We're on the hammocks by the lake, soaking in the sun before it's time to go to afternoon session. I've been trying to learn Hebrew during hammock time using some sheets I printed out from the computer lab a few days ago. I'm getting pretty good at it. I just need to figure out if I should surprise Ari with it being our conversation language or if I should tell her in a letter.

I think Cleo can tell I'm not paying complete attention to her because she does this slow crinkly-eye look at me before she talks.

She continues, "I mean, almost half the session has passed and we haven't discussed it really, but she's just so over the top. Isn't she?"

"Yeah, she's kind of funny, though," I reply. I don't know why I suddenly feel the need to prove how great Indigo is to Cleo and her friends. It almost seems like just because Indigo is my roommate she's a reflection of me or something. I know she's not. I know that sounds ridiculous. But I'm pretty sure that's how I feel. "She's been to, like, thirty concerts."

"Oh, well, that's cool, I guess," Cleo mumbles like she's already bored with this conversation and falling asleep.

I decide to close my eyes, too, and not worry about this. I haven't really focused on it much at all since there's actually so little time to even spend with people outside of your focus. I spend most of my time with Otis and he's a delight. Plus we're crushing it at comedy. Not like I timed it or anything, but people laugh the longest at our routines, longer than for anyone else's.

We hear the wind chimes, signaling that it's time to go to the afternoon session, and Cleo and I wake up slowly from our little nap, widening our eyes to help us to energize.

"See ya, Kaylan," Cleo says. "Find me at dinner, K?"

"Yup," I reply. "Will do."

I walk over to the comedy building at the far end of camp and I'm kind of glad my location is the farthest away. I like having the time to myself to think and regroup and work on some routines in my head.

For some reason I'm the first one there, so I take out my wrinkled-up copy of the list and look it over, trying to make a game plan for what I have to do next. Probably tie-dye, but we've barely even had time for activities like that and who knows if we will. Actually, maybe I'll wait until I get home for that and beg my mom to let me tie-dye in the backyard. It'll give me something to do when I'm home all alone for three weeks without Ari.

Ari and Kaylan's 13¾ Things to Build and Improve on Our Complete and Total Amazingness

1. Perform in a camp talent show.
2. Write at least one letter to each other a week.
3. Sneak out of the bunk/room at night without getting caught.
4. Keep a gratitude journal.
5. Get two counselors to fall in love.
6. Be able to have a full conversation in another language.
7. Draw a portrait of each other from memory.
8. Do something daring.
9. Get a younger kid at camp and/or at home to start their own list.
10. Master the art of tie-dye.
11. Make a difference.
12. Tell our dads one thing we'd like to improve about our relationship with them.
13. Make a time capsule to capture our lives at exactly 13 ¾

years old and bury it somewhere in Brookside.

13 ¾. Keep our friendship strong.

Just having this list in my hands feels calming. Not that I was all that stressed but the Cleo/Indigo thing tugs at me a little. I just wish it wasn't a thing at all. So when I look at this list, I feel peace. I feel as if Ari's beside me and we're together and when that happens, everything feels right in the world even if it's not.

I'm overcome with gratitude and I wish I had my journal to write this down, but I promise myself I'll remember to write it down tonight. Everyone needs to have at least one person in his or her life who makes them feel like everything is right in the world even if it's not. Just one person. Could be a romantic person or a sibling or a grandparent or a neighbor or anyone, really.

Just one. That's all it takes.

"Do they ever have tie-dye here?" I ask Otis as soon as he arrives.

"Is this a bit?" He laughs.

I crack up. "No, one hundred percent serious question."

He hesitates. "Um, I don't think they do. I hope this isn't a deal breaker for you, though. Don't go and write home and say you need to leave right away because of a lack of tie-dye, okay, Terrel?"

"Okay, when you put it that way . . ." I smile. "I'll rip up the letter."

"If you have any overwhelming need to tie-dye something, though . . ." His voice trails off. "I know a secret way."

"Is *this* a bit?" I ask him, laughing.

"No, for real. My mom's really crafty. She gets into this stuff and once we tie-dyed all our old white T-shirts with Sharpies and rubbing alcohol. We used droppers from eye drops."

"You're saying you have all of that here?" I back up a little, slightly spooked.

"The infirmary has rubbing alcohol and they probably have some kind of eye drop, too." He pauses. "I have Sharpies. We can make this happen, Kaylan. I'm not sure why you have this burning desire to tie-dye, but I'm here for you. I'll help make it happen." He puts a hand on my shoulder.

Oh my goodness. Otis. He likes me. There's no doubt in my mind. I never even thought about him that way. But he just put his hand on my shoulder. This is real. This is happening. All because of a discussion about tie-dye. I mean, that's not why it's happening, but that's what made me realize it.

"When will we do it, though?" I cough. "Tie-dye, I mean. We have no free time, and the little bit we have I reserve for my hammock session. I'm trying to learn Hebrew then, too."

"Hammock session? Hebrew?"

"It's very real and very important to me. I'm always on the hammocks during our rest time or free time or whatever you want to call it. And the Hebrew thing is a long story. I'll explain later."

"Um, okay. Welllll, good to know. I can't help with the Hebrew thing." He smiles. "As for tie-dye . . . we'll find a time."

After that discussion we get to work on sketch comedy. So far I've come up with a woman who wears so much jewelry that she physically can't walk and is weighed down but she can't see that the jewelry is the problem. I think it'll work well once we actually start doing the sketch but in the writing it's coming off as kind of weak.

"Anything so far?" I inch closer and read over Otis's shoulder. He smells like bug spray.

He's only written three things down: *cartwheel*, *race car*, *bouquet of roses*.

"Well, not sure. I'm trying to write down words that come to me and go from there." He looks down at his paper again. "But I also have this idea about a couple who is stranded in NYC after they have to leave a terrible Airbnb and then they end up sleeping on someone's fire escape and every few minutes they pop their heads up to look in the window and make this face."

He makes this eye-bulged, scared yet goofy face at me, and I fall on the floor laughing. The face sells the whole thing. Makes it all come together.

"So you think it can work?" he asks.

I can't stop laughing long enough to answer him, so I nod and offer two thumbs up and keep laughing.

As I walk back to my room to shower and get ready for dinner, I think about Otis and his tie-dye offer and then I realize I can combine that with *sneak out of the bunk without getting caught* and check two things off the list at once. Maybe I'll invite Indigo, too, since she brought it up in the first place, and Otis can help with the tie-dye. And then maybe Indigo will go back to the room and maybe, just maybe, I'll kiss Otis.

I haven't kissed anyone since Jason and it was awkward even after the redo. Maybe I need to reset my kissing experience, start fresh.

And after Ari talked to me about the magic of a camp romance and everything with Golfy—I kind of feel like I need to have one, too. But it has to happen fast if it's gonna happen at all.

When I first left for Laurel Lake, four weeks away from home seemed like forever, but now I only have a little less than two weeks left here and it doesn't seem like enough time at all.

Dear Ari,

I just got a letter from the lunch table girls. They were all going to the pie place again and they said they'd send us a crumb of the raspberry cream in the mail. Kind of gross,

126

but cute? I think something is happening between Otis and me. I know he likes me (I can just tell). I'm not sure how I feel about him but I kind of want to explore it. Also, I think I found a way to do tie-dye without actually having a tie-dye session. Indigo is still a little awk about the Cleo crew but I kind of just ignore it.

All good about you doing the talent show with Alice. Totally counts! I mean, you're right. No way to do hand-clapping games on your own, and you don't really have a specific talent. No offense!

Visiting day is this weekend! Craziness. Time is flying here!

I still have so much agita about my dad. We'll have to discuss when we're home.

Also I'm still thinking about the language, considering a few. Stay tuned. Is it okay if we wait to agree on a language until we get home? We'll still have time to learn enough for a conversation.

Write back soon. I miss you so much!

Oh! And here's a snippet of yesterday's gratitude journal:

Pink lemonade at dinner.

Otis making me laugh (duh).

Indigo teaching me the words to "Closer to Fine" (that's an Indigo Girls song) and playing it for me on the guitar.

Cleo wanting to borrow my jeans.

Not getting any mosquito bites during hammock time.

♡ ♡ ♡

xoxooxoxoxoo FOREVER Kaylan

14

ARI

Dear Kay,

We need to discuss this whole make a difference thing. It's so big. It's like our make our mark and start a movement things. Why do we do this to ourselves? Anyway, I feel like I have made a difference, in getting Gemma to like camp. I kind of did half tough love and half encouraging her to use mindfulness techniques and she seems mostly happy. Does that count as making a difference? What's your plan for that?

Camp is amazing but I miss you so much.

Xoxoxo Ari

"Let's amp this up," Golfy says, an arm draped over my shoulder. Our legs are stretched out in front of us on the hill and the air smells crisp and clean because it just rained. The sky is a perfect blue, only a few clouds, and if I had to guess what heaven was like, I'd guess this. This place, with this boy, in this weather. "Let's see how many things on the list you can do in one day."

"Why, though?" I ask. He's holding the list on his lap like it's an ancient text and he's scared to get fingerprints on it.

"Just for fun. I dunno." He leans over and kisses me on the cheek. "I'm excited to be part of this. It's an honor just to be nominated." He cracks up.

"I saw Gemma in the art shack literally having the best time ever," Alice says, out of breath from sprinting up the hill. "That girl is in it!"

"In what?" Golfy asks, concerned.

Alice plops down next to me and takes a sip of my water bottle. "In camp. She's gotten into it. I don't know how and I don't know when but she's all happy and great. She's tie-dyeing a tank top right now!"

I pat myself on the shoulder. "Thanks for the report, Al. I think it was my tough love/mindfulness combo approach. That really seemed to make the difference."

"Oooh!" Golfy yells, looking at the list. "Make a difference! Check!"

I think he just read my mind or my hand, I guess, since I wrote that exact thing in a letter to Kaylan. I'm too shocked to speak.

Alice lies back on the grass. "Hope I'm not interrupting something but I can't get up again, so just pretend I'm not here."

"You're fine," I say. "Golfy was just helping me with some list ideas."

"I thought you had a finalized list with Kaylan. What do you mean?" She mumbles a little and it's hard to hear her.

"I do. He just has an idea." I turn to him. "Golfy, tell her your idea."

"First of all, you should be in the art shack tie-dyeing, too!" Golfy points at the list. "Come on, Ari! You're slacking here. So my idea . . ."

He tells her his do-as-much-as-you-can-in-a-day thing and Alice doesn't sit up but she listens and then she says, "I am in love with this idea, Golfy. For real. Way to really get in it!" She pops up. "Ooh! Things are on fire today. Can you guys feel it?"

Seconds later, Alice is running in place on the hill. "Can I help with the one-day plan too? Please? Pretty please?"

"What is happening right now?" I ask under my breath.

"No idea, but I don't think you can say no to Alice. Not when she gets like this." Golfy lies back on the grass. "But the sneaking out part has to be a you and me thing," he says. "I mean, it's like a fundamental element of camp."

"What is?" I ask, looking over at him.

"That you sneak out to meet the person you're, ya know, going out with . . ."

"Going out," I scoff. "It sounds so ridiculous, since we're not *going out* anywhere."

"I know, but it's just a thing." He stops talking for a moment. "So, leave that to me, but Alice can help with the rest."

"I can help getting Ari safely out of the bunk!" Alice yells, and we shh her. "What she does after that is on her."

My heart starts pounding. This seems scary and dangerous and I'm not sure I even want to do it. I wish I hadn't listened to Kaylan about that one.

"Okay. So getting back to the tie-dye, I'll do that tomorrow during breira. Technically I have to master it, but I have a feeling I'm already pretty good, so . . ." I look at the list mapping out the rest. "Can I do something daring in one day?"

"Um, yes!" Alice finally stops running in place. "Definitely. What's the most daring thing you can do at camp, though?"

"Steal a golf cart and drive down the hill blindfolded," Golfy says like he's thinking out loud.

"Too daring. I don't want to die. Or kill anyone." I clear my throat for emphasis. "Neither of those things are on this list. Or any list."

"Noted," Golfy says. "But I'm definitely getting golf cart vibes here. And it's pretty daring to just drive a golf cart, ya know. First of all, it's not a thing campers are allowed to do; second of all, you don't know how to drive . . ." He raises his eyebrows.

"Hello!" Alice puts her hands on my shoulders. "When else in life will you ever get to do this, except for, like, if you play golf?" She falls back on the grass, cracking herself up. "Golf. Like Golfy. Oh my goodness, I can't even take this. Everything is so funny."

We all crack up. "Okay, getting back to the one-day plan," I say. "I can't start today because I need to mentally prepare for something so big, but tomorrow I'll tie-dye, sneak out of the bunk at night, and drive a golf cart. Even if it's only a few feet, that's still pretty daring. Are we all on board with this?"

I look at Golfy and Alice but I'm not sure why I need their approval. "This is totally doable in one day, isn't it?" I ask when neither of them responds.

"Totally. Ari, you were made for a day like this." Golfy closes his eyes. I'm not sure where all the enthusiasm went. Even Alice seems to have tired herself out.

"Mail!" Zoe screams while walking up the hill. "Bunk nineteen, I have your mail!"

"How'd you get our mail?" I ask when she finally reaches us.

"I ran into Charlie in the main office, and she said I could bring it up and hand it out." Zoe sits down next to me. "Yes, she was crying again. I just need to say this—I don't think he's into her."

"Who's he?" Golfy mumbles, sounding half asleep.

"Pres," Alice replies. "I didn't even know Pres had a girlfriend last summer, but apparently he did and apparently it was our counselor Charlie and apparently they broke up and apparently she's still obsessed."

"Apparently," Zoe mocks her.

"Ouch." Golfy sits up and rubs his eyes. "I did know they were going out actually. I once caught them making out, last summer, on the bunk porch next to mine."

"You did?" I scrunch up my face. "That feels awkward."

"It wasn't. They didn't see me. I didn't stand there and watch or anything."

"Ew. Golfy!" I scream.

"What?" he laughs. "I said I *didn't*!"

"Okay! Enough of this. Anyway, that's another I need to do, and I can start it tomorrow, but definitely won't finish it tomorrow. The getting the two counselors to fall in love thing." I pause while Zoe flips through the letters and hands me one. I recognize Bubbie's handwriting immediately and get a little flutter of relief and happiness. "The question is, do I get Charlie and Pres to rekindle or do I get her to fall in love with someone new?"

Zoe hands me a letter. "She's pretty hung up on him. So I don't think someone new will really work. Rekindling might be best."

I nod, sort of agreeing with her but not totally. What if he's just not into her?

Deep down, I want to bail on this list item. In my heart, it doesn't feel right. We can't control other people. And I sort of think we need to accept that we may fail at something on the list at some point. That time may be now.

I rip open the envelope from Bubbie and push all of those thoughts to the side for the moment. Right now I need to hold this letter in my hands and feel Bubbie close to me.

Darling Ari,

How are you, my girl? All is well here except it's very hot. I don't go outside much. Your parents have been over a few times and it's always lovely to see them, and Lion of course, although it's quieter without you and Gemma. We miss you. I'm feeling much better these days. Everyone takes good care of me. I'm letting you know so you don't worry. Please have fun at camp. Those were such happy summers. Remember to stretch it; make it last.

I love you. Give Gemma a kiss for me.

Hugs and kisses, Bubbie

PS Don't worry too much about talking to your dad. I've known him a long time (ha-ha) and I have a feeling he will be happy to hear whatever you have to say.

I hold the letter in my hands and read it over and again and again, flooded with relief. There's a thing about how on Shabbat, the Jewish Sabbath, we don't ask God for more things; we just show appreciation for what we have. Even though it's just an average weekday right now and not the Sabbath, I am overwhelmed with appreciation that Bubbie is healthy enough to write to me and that she sounds so good.

Gratitude journals, thanking God for stuff—it all works together; the key to happiness, I think.

15

KAYLAN

"WHY DO YOU HAVE TO get two counselors to fall in love?" Indigo asks during our nightly pillow talk session. "Why are you doing this list again? I'm still confused. Explain, please."

I flip my pillow over. "It's just a thing we do. It started when we were nervous for middle school, but we had so much fun doing it, and now we just keep making new ones."

Indigo raises her eyebrows. "That's honestly the craziest thing but also kind of inspirational. I may start one."

I wonder if Indigo can count as the person I get to start the list, even though she's not really younger than I am. Or wait. Maybe she is.

"How old are you again?" I ask her.

"Twelve, almost thirteen because of my September

birthday. I just made the cutoff for my school!"

She is younger than I am. Jackpot! This totally counts. This is even better than my original Teddy idea!

"So the two counselors falling in love is just one of the things on the list?" Indigo asks me.

"Yeah." I sigh. "But I only know the comedy people and not even that well, so I'm not sure who would fall in love with who. I mean, even our dorm counselors are kind of mysterious to me; we don't really ever do anything with them."

"I know exactly," she says. "That assistant director Rob and that drama counselor who's always telling jokes on the microphone at meals."

"Paul?"

"Yeah!"

I consider the fact that I hadn't even thought about setting up a gay couple and then I feel bad about that.

"You think they'd be into each other?" I ask Indigo.

"Definitely." She nods, all forceful.

"Just because they're always hanging out?" I ask her, sort of teasing.

She laughs. "Well, kind of, but I mean, why not? Right? They do seem to have good chemistry. . . ."

"I dunno. I'm starting to feel a little weird about this list item, to be honest. . . ." I yawn and think for a minute.

"Have you ever just skipped a list thing or given up on it or whatever?" Indigo asks, pulling her covers to her chin.

"No." I yawn again. "We never have."

I'm so sleepy and I want to think about this on my own for a few minutes and also think about how I can convince her to start her own list. Plus I still need to map out the sneaking into the infirmary thing with Otis and the tie-dye. It's a triple whammy since it's the daring thing with breaking into the infirmary, the tie-dye thing, and the sneaking out at night thing. "I'm starting to feel really tired, Ind. I'm gonna go to sleep, okay?"

"Yeah, me too. Nighty-night, Kay."

"Nighty-night. Thanks for your help."

Sometimes when my mind is so crowded with thoughts, I can't fall asleep at all, but tonight my camp exhaustion takes over and I seem to fall asleep right away. But then I wake up so early in the morning, and I stare at my clock for a few minutes in disbelief that my eyes are open.

After a bit, though, I start to feel glad that I have all this extra time to map out the next few list items, and also glad that I can see the sun rise through my window.

I come up with a plan in my head. I'll discuss it with Otis during morning session.

After lights-out tonight, he'll meet me on the bench near the infirmary. I'll go in and say I have a sore throat and I need some cough drops. He'll say he has a headache and they'll get him some Tylenol. Since all the medicine is in the back, I'll be able to snatch a bottle of rubbing alcohol and a bottle of eye drops and shove them in my sweatshirt pocket while they're filling out the medicine form and getting him a cup of water and stuff.

Then we'll go to the hammocks and work on my tie-dye under the lights by the lake. The more I think about this, the more I get this tingly, romantic, *what's going to happen* feeling. Otis. I like him. It's a thing.

But as I replay the infirmary plan in my head, I start to wonder if I need a few stops there in advance to really figure out where all the stuff is—the rubbing alcohol and the eye drops. I know they have a supply closet near the door but I probably want to figure out what shelf all the things are on so I can be prepared.

I'll discuss it with him this morning.

And maybe I need to know if I really do like him. There's one way to know. Sort of an experiment.

I look at the last few pages of my gratitude journal to see if I mention him. That could tell me something. Not definitive. But a hint. A hunch.

Tacos for dinner.
Cleo saying she's really glad I came to camp this summer.
Otis going in an amazing direction during improv. ♡
Indigo finding her pink lemonade mix.
Getting a letter from Ari.
**
Having thirty extra minutes of free time.

S'mores after dinner.

Dan saying we're all really funny and meaning it (I think).

My mom writing me about how much fun she had at the beach.

Otis waiting for me outside before afternoon session. ♡

**

It not being as hot today.

Otis laughing at my joke about the pigeon parade in NYC. ♡

Thinking that Teddy could be a good younger kid for the list.

Ignoring Chad when he made another rude comment.

Danny giving out Twizzlers at the end of morning session.

Okay. Yup. He's mentioned three days in a row. This is a thing. For sure.

Now I just need to figure out where to go from here.

I stay up through sunrise, staring out my window and thinking about and missing Ari but also feeling so grateful about so much.

When I'm at the sink brushing my teeth, a slithery, embarrassed feeling comes over me. I can't believe I actually thought I'd be able to accomplish all of these plans—the sneaking out, the Otis meet-up. All of it. I wonder why things often seem so much easier before you've actually started the day. Maybe it's the comfiness of being in bed. Maybe it's the fact that it's not actually happening for a bit. I'm not sure. Whatever it is, right now, everything feels more difficult, more scary. I feel less brave. Once the day has begun, I'm tempted to abandon all ideas and goals and aspirations.

Indigo and I walk to breakfast, and she's still talking about setting Rob up with Paul. I'm not feeling so confident about it.

"You can't just assume that since they both like guys they'll both like each other, though," I remind her. "That doesn't make sense."

"I know that." She rolls her eyes. "Kaylan, my older brother is gay. I get it. Believe me."

An embarrassed ickiness crawls down from my forehead to my face and I feel a need to apologize even though I'm not sure why. There's no way I could have known that.

"So you really think they'll like each other?" I ask again, suddenly feeling very invested in this. Mostly for the list but for the general excitement of setting two people up as well.

"I think they already do," she reassures me. "But since it's on your list or whatever, we can make it happen."

A skip appears in my step and I'm feeling peppy again, closer to the way I felt last night. Maybe we can make this happen. Maybe I can make the other stuff happen, too.

I mean, Loyal to the List. It's always worked in the past.

Plus it's taking my mind off of visiting day, looming

in the distance. That's all of our lists' main mission any-way: to distract from stress and help us prepare for life and all that it will throw at us.

It's magic.

I run into Otis as Indigo and I get to the dining hall.

"Hey," he says, filling up his water bottle at the foun-tain.

"Hey. I need to talk to you." I lean on one leg and then lean on the other, and shove my hands in my pockets, anxious to talk this whole thing through with him.

"I'll save you guys seats," Indigo says, walking into the dining hall.

"What's up?" Otis whispers like we're already on a secret mission even though it hasn't even started yet. I like his dedication. He has an eyelash on his cheek and I'm tempted to grab it and have him make a wish, but I don't think we're there yet. Eyelash touching is more intimate than most people realize.

I take a deep breath. "I think we need to assess the infirmary situation before we go ahead with our plan. I want to make sure I know exactly where the rubbing alcohol is, and the eye drops."

"Right," he says. "That makes sense."

I wait for him to offer up a suggestion but he doesn't. I guess this is my thing and he's basically just my sidekick so I should have the ideas.

"After lunch," I say. "During my usual hammock time,

we'll go and I'll say I need a lotion for my mosquito bites and then I'll quickly scan the supply closet."

"I'll come with you," he says. "Two pairs of eyes are better than one."

"That's a good opening improv scene line!" I yelp.

Otis high-fives me. "K, let's go eat breakfast. I'm starving."

"Another good opening scene line," I say as we walk in.

We find Indigo at the table with Cleo and friends but they're not talking at all. I wonder how this went down but I'm not really concerned about it. Maybe they're actually becoming friends. Who knows.

I plop down next to Indigo, and Otis sits on my other side.

I'm in the middle of eating a plate of pancakes when Otis asks, "How's your friend doing with her list? Do you ever have a contest to see which one of you can finish it first?"

I realize Cleo and the rest don't know anything about the list and I don't feel like getting into it now so I shrug it off. "Not really."

I come off as a little cold and then there's silence at the table but it dissipates after a few seconds when everyone starts talking about the campfire tonight and how the a cappella concentration is going to perform. They call themselves Laurelicious and they're really good.

Otis taps me on the shoulder. "Come with me," he

mouths, and then the table does all this awkward oohing and aahing and I feel my face turn to tomato juice.

We walk a little away from the table, near the breakfast buffet setup in one of the salad bars. "We can go now," he says. "All the kids who take meds go to the infirmary at this time and it gets busy so the nurses won't notice us snooping a little while we wait on line for your bug bite lotion."

"Brilliant. We can just go now?" I ask him. "Even though we don't take meds?"

"Of course. You have a bug bite, don't you?"

"Um, a million." I laugh.

I guess it's because we spend so much time thinking about comedy and working on comedy, but when I'm with Otis, literally everything feels funny and everything feels like a bit and everything feels like it can turn into some kind of routine.

I look behind me at the table, wondering if I should tell everyone where I'm going, but they've already started clearing the table and Rob is already on the microphone explaining the schedule for the day and talking about the campfire tonight and everyone is cheering about the Laurelicious performance.

We walk around the dining hall to the infirmary. The meds table is out front and the nurses are sitting behind it, tending to everyone. There's a neat, orderly line but it still seems like it'll take a while.

"Hi," I say to one of the nurses. "I have a bug bite. Is it okay if I just go in and grab a spray of the lotion?"

"This is a very busy time." She blows some hair out of her face. "I'd rather you come back after med call, but if it's an emergency, sure. Go on in. The lotions are on the first table, on your right."

Otis and I make eyes at each other. Success!

"You need lotion too?" the same nurse asks Otis.

"Yeah." He shakes his head. "The mosquitoes were crazy last night!"

"Oh, I know it," she replies.

Otis and I walk into the infirmary quickly but calmly and I try to soothe the teeny, tiny butterflies floating up from my stomach to my throat.

"Just a quick glance," I whisper. "We can't make it look too obvious because then they'll be onto us later when we come in."

"I know. I got this. We got this."

To the right of the entryway is a giant supply closet, neatly organized, with everything a camper with an ailment could need: Band-Aids, anti-itch lotion, aloe, alcohol pads, tissues, eye drops, and on and on and on. It's all there. Right in front of our eyes.

"Middle shelf. Bottom shelf," I say quietly. "Middle shelf. Bottom shelf."

"This is almost too easy," Otis says as we leave. "Honestly, I'm worried it's not even daring enough."

"Believe me. It is. We're stealing! And the sneaking out part is daring but also that's another thing on the list." I bite my pinkie nail and then stop because it's such a gross habit. "Whatever, it's all daring, but I'm ready. And I'm grateful for your assistance!"

"Here to help!" Otis salutes me. "Pumped to be a part of it."

"Ooh, that's a good sketch," I tell him. "Someone who has a slogan for everything and an over the top salute or curtsy or whatever. It could be really funny. . . ."

"Let's try it."

We walk the rest of the way to the comedy building, riffing ideas and laughing with each other, and it all feels light and airy and fun.

Grateful, grateful, grateful. For all of it.

I just learned that there isn't one word for gratitude in Hebrew; instead it's more of a phrase—*ah-see-rat todah*—which literally means bound by thanks.

It makes sense to me.

We're taught as little kids, over and over again, to say thank you, and then as we grow up, people don't remind us all the time, and sometimes we forget. But we shouldn't. We should all be bound by thanks. As much as possible.

16

ARI

"WANT TO MEET ME AT the art shack during breira?" I ask Gaux after breakfast. I'm all fired up for this intense list completion day and I can't wait to get started. "I want to tie-dye a shirt. Are you good at tie-dye?"

"Um, I'm amazing at tie-dye!" she shouts. "And yes, I would love to. I usually swim but I can change it up for one day."

Gaux seems older than an eight-year-old, but maybe it's the California thing, or maybe because she has an older brother. Or maybe that's just who she is.

"Great! I'll see you there. Have fun cleaning."

"Yeah, right. I don't clean."

"Girl after my own heart."

We always have *nikayon* after breakfast. It means "cleaning" in Hebrew and it's the time of the day when we're supposed to tidy our bunk—make our beds, neaten our cubbies, even sweep and gather stuff from the clothesline outside. I'd say we clean maybe three days out of the week, which isn't great, but isn't the worst. This week my job is garbage so I do have to do it because an overflowing garbage pail is just unacceptable.

"Arianna Nodberg," Alice sings. "She's the awesomest girl. Arianna Nodberg, you're the queen of my world."

Alice has been very into singing lately and it's funny. The tunes are catchy, too, so I find myself singing them to myself.

"I have to tell you something," she whispers, and follows me to the bathroom.

"What?"

"Have you noticed a change in my behavior?"

"Yes. We all have. You're extra zany."

"I'm in love. And I've kept it secret because it's a weird one. Promise you won't freak out."

"Um." I wait for her to tell me that she's in love with one of the song leaders. There's just something so dreamy about an older guy who plays guitar. But they're in college and there's no way she can go out with any of them. "I won't freak out. Of course I won't freak out."

She pulls me outside through the bathroom door, and she starts gathering all the dry towels from the clothesline as she talks to me. She seems a little fired up; more energetic than usual. "You know that new kid. The one from Israel. Oren."

I nod.

"I'm in love with him. He barely speaks English but he's learning and he's literally the cutest and we hung out during tennis yesterday and we communicated a little and I really think he likes me."

"That's amazing, Al. I'm gonna watch your interaction at lunch, okay?"

"Def, but we have to be subtle."

"Obviously. I'm the queen of subtlety."

"You are?" She laughs.

"Yes! Come on. I'm chill. I keep it chill."

Alice keeps gathering the stuff from the clothesline, and I empty the two garbage pails into the big blue garbage bins at the far end of the hill.

"But can it work? If we don't speak the same language?"

"Sure." I shrug. "Plus I bet his English is better than you realize. He's probably just shy."

"True. And I know camp Hebrew and like some lines from Passover, but whatever. I can learn more!"

We traipse back across the hill and Alice helps me carry an empty garbage pail. Only at camp would it be fun to take out the garbage at nine in the morning and walk through morning-mist-soaked wet grass. I keep pulling up my pajama pants so they don't get wet, but I don't think it's really helping.

When we get to the bunk, we attempt a power nap but it actually turns into a real deep sleep. I'm totally caught off guard when Annie yells, "Girls, out of the bunk! Time for swim. Don't forget sunscreen! Bye! Love you! See you later!"

Annie's always the first counselor to tell us to get out of the bunk after nikayon because she has her hour off during swim and she doesn't want to lose a minute of it.

"Want to walk down with us?" I ask Charlie on the way out of the bunk. She's huddled under a blanket on one of the chairs on the front porch. It's not even that cold out. I'm kind of sad she's having such a miserable summer all because of Pres. I wonder what happened between the two of them. Maybe they were together all year and they broke up right before the summer.

"Sure," she says, sort of halfheartedly, but I guess it would be we wrong for her to say no to her camper. She is technically working here even though all she does is cry and sulk and have private chats with other counselors.

I yell back to the bunk to Alice, Zoe, and Hana. "I'm walking to the pool with Charlie. See you guys there!"

I don't wait for them to reply because I really want to take advantage of this walking time. I need to find out the deal once and for all so I can work on the rekindling. I want to make this happen.

"So what's up?" I ask her.

"Ya know, camp," she replies, and I can tell she's trying to hold back tears. "It's camp. It's good. I love it."

"I love it, too." We're quiet then, and I wonder if this walk will be a flop or if we'll be able to get anywhere. "Are you okay, though, Charlie? I know it's weird that I'm asking you since you're a counselor and I'm a camper but we live in close quarters and all of that, so I figured I'd ask."

"I'm really only four years older than you," she says. "Isn't that so weird?"

"Wait. Really?"

"Yeah, you're thirteen, I'm seventeen. I have a fall birthday."

"Same."

We're quiet again then, getting closer to the pool, and I haven't made any progress in delving into her love problems.

"I'm fine," she says finally. "It's just that I went through a really bad breakup this winter and now I'm at camp with the person and it's pretty terrible."

"That sounds really bad. Of course you're struggling."

"Yeah, and the guy, um, I just really love him." She starts crying right there and I don't know if I should reach over and hug or her not.

"Charlie, this is so, so sad." I put an arm around her. "But are you sure it's really over? I mean, maybe it was just a distance thing and you could patch things up now

151

that you're back together at camp."

"I don't know." She sniffles. "We barely even talk now, and what if he ends up with someone else? I just don't even know what to do. And it occupies my thoughts all the time and my friends don't want to hear about it." She starts crying all over again. "I don't even know why I'm telling you this."

"It's okay." We make it all the way down the hill and get to the pool gate. We're about it go in. "I may have an idea, though. Let's talk later. I'll be at the art shack for breira. But maybe after that."

I could probably talk to her during rest hour but everyone will be around then, and Noa and Annie might think it's weird that she's having this in depth of a conversation with a camper. It's okay, though. She's only four years older than I am. It's not even a big deal. Camp ages are weird like that. Gaux is way younger than I am and yet I feel like we talk as real friends.

I spend the rest of the day trying to figure out how I can talk to Pres to get him to realize he's still in love with Charlie. I mean, she's super pretty, with olive skin and dirty-blond curly hair. Sure, she's no fun to be around right now because she's so sad, but I bet she was at some point and I bet she'll be fun again, too.

Gaux is waiting for me on the bench outside the art shack. She has mosquito bites up and down and her leg and she's wearing a plain white T-shirt that says *Gaux*

Rules in her own handwriting (I'm guessing) across the front.

"I'm tie-dyeing this shirt," she declares. "I just didn't want to carry it. I have a tank top on underneath." She lifts up the T-shirt to show me.

"Oh, smart." I give her two thumbs up.

She groans. "I hate carrying things at camp. I don't know why. I just do."

"I get it. Did you ever realize how no one uses umbrellas here? It's all raincoats. I find that interesting."

"Yeah, you're right." She shakes out her hair in front of her up and down three times and then pulls it into a messy ponytail. "What are you gonna tie-dye?"

"I brought a plain white tee. It's kind of a niceish one but I think it'll be okay." I shrug. "Hopefully my mom will forget that it was kind of niceish."

We go inside and Shula the art shack lady is already there, setting everything up: beads and lanyard and string and markers and paper and dye and rubber bands for tie-dye.

"Are there really people who tie-dye every day?" I ask her.

"Some. Not many."

I pull a few stools around the table so everyone will have a seat, and I save the one on my left for Golfy. Gaux sits on my right.

"I want to do a rainbow," I declare, spreading out my

shirt on the table. "I want to really master the art of tie-dye."

Shula laughs. "I'm not sure anyone really masters it. But it's good to have goals."

When Shula goes in the back to grab more supplies, Gaux turns to me with one side of her lip turned up. "Why do you wanna master tie-dye so bad?"

Yes. This is it. My moment.

"It's kind of a long story." I smile. "Wanna hear it?"

"Um, yeah." She laughs.

So I tell her all about the first list and middle school and how the list helped us with our agita and helped us prepare, and then I tell her about the second one because we loved the first one and we don't break traditions and then all about our third one (our winter list) because we knew we were going to be apart for summer and now our fourth one because we are apart and it's keeping us close. How they always keep us connected and keep our friendship strong and how important and awesome they are.

"Did you guys make this up? Are you the only ones who have ever done this?" Gaux looks at me wide-eyed. "I don't really get it, but it's funny and, um, cool."

"We did make it up, but I don't know if we're the only ones. Anyone can do it, really." I shrug, feeling so fired up talking about this.

"OMG, I want to do it!" Gaux yells, and the rest of the

kids in the art shack turn around. "I really wanna do it. Can I do super-zany things? Like zipline between two skyscrapers?"

"Um, not like super crazy like that," I say, trying not to burst her bubble. "But you can make up your own stuff. It's really fun."

"I need to do this! With my friend Astrid from California. My BFFFFFFF who I love with all of my heart and now we're across the country from each other! OMG, I need to do this!"

"Yes! I love it." I clap. "Love the enthusiasm."

"Can you help me do it, though? How should I start?" Gaux leans forward on the table, suddenly deep in thought.

"I'll definitely help!" I nod, completely thrilled about this. "You can write to Astrid and tell her and then I can help you think of ideas, and she'll think of some, too, and it'll be so great." I clap a few times. "But first! Tie-dye!"

Shula gets back and she shows us how to tie a spiral in our shirts because we both want to do the rainbow spiral. She gives us forks to place in the location that we want to be the middle of the spiral and then we twist the forks around the fabric.

"This is gonna look so good!" Gaux yells.

Shula shows us how to maneuver the outer pieces to make folds that will turn into the outer spiral. Then we tie rubber bands all around the shirt to make it into a disc. We soak the shirts in this special solution and then we squirt the dye into all the crevices and areas, to make sure we cover the whole shirt. I try as hard as I can to not let the dye run over one section and into the next.

"These are gonna look so good!" Gaux says again. "What other set of buddies will have matching tie-dye shirts?"

"I know! Right? We're the best set of buddies that ever existed."

"No doubt!"

I'm so into this tie-dye session and thinking about Gaux's list that I don't even realize that Golfy hasn't shown up yet. It starts to nag at my mind and I rush through the rest of the tie-dyeing, worrying that something's wrong or maybe he's not into me, or maybe something happened or who knows what.

Shula gives us plastic bags to put the shirts in and then she says, "I'm going to let these sit for twenty-four hours and then I'll rinse and wash them for you. So give it a few days, girls."

"Thanks, Shula."

I feel a tap on my shoulder so I spin around on my art shack stool and there's Golfy, sitting right behind me, deep in a lanyard bracelet.

"How long have you been here?" I ask, my heart pounding.

"The whole time," he says. "You guys were totally

bonding and I didn't want to disturb, plus I'm making you some jewelry."

He's making me some jewelry.

I don't think it's possible to love this boy more. Literally not possible. I get up from the stool and sit down on his lap for literally four seconds before I start to feel super awkward.

I want to smooch him right now but I'd never do that because I hate public displays of affection. Plus Gaux is right here and that would be weird.

"These shirts are going to be the best ever!" Gaux high-fives me in the middle of the art shack. "We are official tie-dye masters."

"Well, let's see how they come out first." I pause. "But yeah. Definitely."

We crack up and then Gaux tells us she's going to try and squeeze in a quick swim before shower time.

Golfy and I walk up the hill to hang for a bit.

"Ready for tonight?" he asks.

"Um. Sort of. Maybe. I think so. Yeah?"

He laughs. "Good answer."

We sit side by side against a tree at the top of the hill, listening to the sounds of camp and talking on and off. Not really about anything specific, just random things like the bunk of boys a year younger than us that all got lice and how we haven't had breakfast for dinner once this session.

When we're quiet, I think about the list and all the stuff I want to accomplish today.

Two things down, lots more to go. But for now, I can feel good about Gaux starting her own list and about my tie-dye attempts and hopefully success.

Crushing it, Ari. Crushing it.

17

KAYLAN

WE GET TWENTY MINUTES OF hammock time after dinner but then we have to go back to our focuses for a surprise night session. I try to learn at least one Hebrew word per hammock session. Tonight's is "girl." *Yalda.*

I flip through a few of the other pages I printed out and get to one that lists animals and how to say them in Hebrew.

Kelev—dog

Khatul—cat

Sus—horse

Ari—lion

"OMG!" I yell. "Lion in Hebrew is Ari!"

"Um," Indigo says. "Explain?"

"Ari. My BFF. Her bubbie loves lions. And Ari—her name—means lion. Well, it's not her real name, it's her nickname, but whoa." I pause, letting this sink in. "Also her dog is named Lion! OMG. I'm bugging out."

"I can see that," Indigo says, her eyebrows curvy.

I study a little more Hebrew, all pumped to write Ari about my discovery, but then I realize I can't. Or I'll give away the Hebrew language surprise. It'll have to wait.

A few minutes later, Indigo whispers, "I can't believe you're really doing this."

We're sharing a hammock and a wiggly feeling comes over me. It's kind of that I wish I was over there with Cleo and them but I'm also sort of okay being here, and also feel too nervous about tonight to worry about it that much.

"You're the one who first told me about the girl who snuck out," I remind her.

"True."

We're quiet then for a few moments and then she says, "This list thing. I think I wanna try it, too. Would that be okay? I know we discussed it a little but I just want to make sure."

I sit up, feeling like I've just achieved a major break-through, like Indigo is almost putty in my hands and I'm molding her. "Um, yeah, that would be more than okay. I'd be thrilled for you to start it. Ari and I were hoping it would become a movement kind of thing, and we could inspire girls from all over the country to do it. We kind of wanted to become famous for that, and get on TV, but then we ended up getting on TV for other stuff." I pause. "We'll save that story for another time."

"Wow. Okay. But I definitely want to hear it."

"Indi, I'd love for you to start your own list and I'd love to help you. Do you have a friend you'd want to do it with or . . ." My voice trails off when I see her sad green eyes. I wonder if Indigo has friends at home. It's suddenly hitting me that she might not.

"On my own, I think. I want to change some things about myself and this may be the best way to do it." She sits up and rubs her eyes. "I feel like I come on too strong for people. I have a hard time connecting. Kaylan, you're the first person, since like second grade, who I feel actually likes me for who I am."

My throat tightens. I don't want this to be true.

"Indigo," I start. I don't know what else to say.

"Don't feel bad for me. I'm fine. I just want to improve myself."

A moment later, we're told it's time to go to our focuses and I tell Indigo I'll see her later.

"Okay, but I'll see you in the room to wish you good luck before you sneak out, right?"

"Definitely."

All throughout evening session, my heart is pounding. I can't focus on anything here—not on our improv routine or the stand-up or even the sketch we're trying to write.

"I just need to get to lights-out," I tell Otis. "I'm feeling so antsy."

"I know. Soon enough." He puts a hand on my shoulder. "Soon enough."

Back at the room, I write Ari a quick letter even though by the time she gets it, everything will be done already. I might have gotten caught by then and sent home and this whole experience ruined. At least this includes my being daring and my sneaking out and my tie-dye. I deserve a triple JHH for something so scary. I love that we have a list item completion ritual like the JHH but it's always a little sad to jump in the air, high five, and hug by yourself.

Dear Ari,

Tonight is the night. I'm sneaking out and stealing stuff from the infirmary and doing this unconventional tie-dye approach. I don't know why I'm putting this in writing. I probably shouldn't since they could use this against me in a court case. I wouldn't have to go to court, right? I mean, the worst thing that happens is that I'm never allowed back at Laurel Lake. I guess that's pretty terrible. I really love it here and I want to be here. I'm sorry I suggested this for the list. It was a bad idea. But we can't change it now. The good news is that my roommate, Indigo, is starting her own list. She's younger than we are, don't worry! More on that later.

Pray for me, okay? I am so nervous.

I love you. Xoxoxox Kaylan

PS If I get caught and you never hear from me again because I'm grounded for life and sent to military school just know the most important thing: I'm grateful for you!

PPS Yes, let's wait to decide on the language until we get home! We'll still have plenty of time.

The counselors come around to all the rooms and tell us that it's time for lights-out. I'm under my covers in my clothes but they can't see that. I've put new batteries in my flashlight and I'm ready.

"How long are you going to wait?" Indigo whispers.

The truth is we're allowed to talk during this time but people always whisper when they're nervous. Or scream. I guess one or the other. Nervousness and anxiety brings everything to an extreme.

"I'm meeting Otis outside in fifteen minutes," I say flatly, without emotion.

"Is he scared about sneaking out?"

"I'm not sure."

It's always so hard to talk when you're nervous. I think it's because your body is using so much energy feeling agita that you don't have any extra resources to talk and move your mouth or have your brain think about making conversation.

"It's gonna be fine, Kaylan. The counselors are never

outside," Indigo tells me. "They all hang in the lounges on the first floors of the buildings, so just make sure you walk around the back and not the side and they won't see you through the windows."

"Okay, good tip." I breathe in and breathe out and breathe in and breathe out. "I appreciate your help, Indigo. I think I'm just scared and kind of regretting this."

"Do you ever regret stuff you put on the list?"

"Sometimes," I say. "Although I can't think of any now. I'm the kind of person who always remembers a situation positively. I guess people call that a revisionist historian?"

She laughs. "You always remember really bad things positively? Like times you were sick or had a fight with a friend or whatever?"

I pause to think about it for a minute. I wonder if I remember the thing with Ari positively, when we had a big fight about Marie doing the list with us and didn't talk for a bit. Or do I remember the thing about when everyone went out for ice cream without me positively? Or when Tyler was mean to Ryan at that party? Or when my dad left?

Not that. No. That I remember as horrible. One hundred percent horrible.

"Not everything, I guess. My dad left a few years ago. It still feels as horrible now as it did then." My throat is a lump of mashed potatoes. I wish this wasn't coming up right now. I wish my brain didn't settle on this string of memories.

"That does sound horrible," Indigo replies. "But we can't think about that now. For you to embark on this journey, you need to think positive. Happy thoughts only."

I smile even though Indigo can't see me in the dark. I don't know why she has so much trouble making friends. There's something so beautifully refreshing about her.

"Only puppies and rainbows for you and those tortilla chips from the dining hall that you love." She giggles. "Oh, and the strawberry lemonade. You love that, too."

"Thanks, Indigo. I appreciate your support."

"I set a timer. I'll tell you when it's time to go. Just close your eyes and breathe for now. Calm. Only calm." She pauses. "Oh, and I'll play a song for you. My favorite Indigo Girls song."

I listen to the lyrics and try to do what she says. *If we ever leave a legacy, it's that we loved each other well. So we're okay, we're fine, baby, I'm here to stop your crying . . .*

When the timer goes off, Indigo says in a soft voice, "It's time. Go forth, my child. You will succeed."

I burst into laughter and pop out of bed.

When I get outside, Otis is right there on the bench where he said he'd be. He's in all black with a black cap on. I don't even own that much black but I'm wearing jeans and a black tank top. I explain to him what Indigo said about walking out the back of the building and avoiding the sides but I'm not totally sure I understand it all.

"It's gonna be fine," he whispers. "Ya know why? If anyone catches us, we'll say we're going to the infirmary!"

I stop in my tracks. He's right. We can say we couldn't find one of the on-duty counselors and we have headaches or something and we'll be set. Then I wonder if this even counts as something daring since we have a perfectly good excuse. I put that out of my mind. Yes, it still counts. I'm freaking out right now with agita! Of course it counts!

We walk silently. Not fast. Not slow. We don't see anyone outside, which makes sense because all of the on-duty counselors are in the lounges in their buildings.

Finally we get to the infirmary. We stop a second outside and Otis puts his hands on my shoulders and then pulls me in for a hug. It's totally unexpected but amazing. "This is funny. This is actually really funny. This is a perfect bit," he whispers, pulling back from the hug. "So who is diverting the nurses' attention and who is taking the stuff?"

"You talk. I'll take," I whisper back. "Let's do this."

"Can I help you?" one of the nurses says when we walk in. "Why are you both here?"

She looks at us out of the corner of one eye.

Oh, right. We are both here at night. That means we

166

both have to talk and have an ailment. I'm not sure why I keep forgetting the plan.

"We just passed each other along the way," Otis says. "I have a stomachache. Those tacos for dinner didn't sit right with me."

She does a slow, doubtful kind of nod. "Let me get you some seltzer. Sit down here a minute." The nurse guides Otis to one of the chairs. "I'll be right back to help you, dear."

"Now!" Otis loud-whispers. "Go!"

I go back to the closet. Middle shelf. Bottom shelf. I grab a bottle of rubbing alcohol and shove it in my sweatshirt pocket and grab two eyedropper bottles and put them in the back pocket of my jeans.

My heart is pounding so loud I'm sure the nurse can hear it when she gets back with Otis's seltzer and says, "What can I do for you, honey?"

"Um, I just have a sore throat. Too much talking in comedy." I giggle. "Ouch! It even hurts to laugh. Ironic, right?"

I hope this doesn't say much for my future career but the nurse isn't finding me very funny.

"I'll give you a lozenge. I'd recommend getting some rest." She hands me a few. "Now go back to your buildings, you two. Do you need an escort? I don't want any funny business."

"Irony again!" I laugh. "We're in the comedy focus."

"I got that." She forces a fake smile.

Otis and I leave the infirmary and I make sure to keep my arm on the side of my sweatshirt so the bottle of rubbing alcohol doesn't fall out.

When we make it a little bit away from there, Otis stops and falls down on the ground, laughing. He puts his arm up to grab my hand. "Come hang for a minute," he says softly.

My insides turn to Jell-O.

This might happen. My first camp kiss on the same night as my first theft.

"I can't believe we just did that." I lie down next to him, and even though we're on the grass it still feels kind of intimate and close. I like that it's dark so hopefully people won't see us and we won't get caught. I mean, this is on the list. So. It's gotta be done. The sneaking out part, I mean. We didn't put *have an amazing camp kiss* on the list. We probably should've, though.

"I know. It was awesome." His eyes are closed but his head is back like he's looking up the sky. We lie there next to each other and hold hands and neither of us says anything for what feels like many minutes.

"I wish we could camp out," he says. "I wish we could sleep here on the grass and look up at the stars all night."

When he says that, it does seem kind of nice, even though I'm not really a camping kind of gal.

He sits up then and turns to me. "I'm so glad we got

paired up, Kaylan. You're literally the funniest person I've ever met."

"I am?" I think about Chad and how he never seems to stop with the *girls aren't funny* bit. How I've just tuned him out by now but how it really does bug me when I think about it.

"Yeah. You are."

We're quiet again then, and my stomach is doing somersaults. I don't know if he's going to kiss me. Maybe he won't. Maybe he doesn't like me like that. Maybe he just thinks I'm fun and funny and that's it.

Also who made the rule that boys have to make the first move? That seems to fall into the *girls aren't funny* category. All these rules for girls that are just sort of there but we don't know when they started or where they came from or anything like that.

I can kiss him if I want to.

I mean, what's the worst thing that could happen? He pulls away and says awkwardly that he's not feeling the situation the same way I am and it's weird for the last week of camp. Okay, I guess that would be pretty bad. But ya know, *do something daring* is on the list. This is it. This may be my daring thing. Even though it shouldn't be. It still is.

"You're funny, too, Otis." I smile and inch closer to him. "I'm just gonna do this because, um, I want to, and if it's not cool, you'll say something, right?"

Before he has a chance to answer, my lips are on his lips. He's not pulling away.

My first camp kiss. And I was the one to make it happen.

"Wow. I did not expect that," he says.

"No?" I ask softly.

"Um, no. I've thought about it for sure but I didn't think you liked me like that and I didn't want to just, ya know, kiss you. I thought about asking you first but then that seemed awkward, so yeah." He laughs and lies back down again.

"Does this sound like a bit?" I ask him. "A sketch about the most awkward kiss ever. Maybe some kind of *Guinness World Records* thing."

"But that wasn't awkward," he tells me.

"True. I know. But the bit could work. . . ."

"I just want to live in real life right now." He smiles and grabs my hand again. "The fact that I came here and I met you and you're so awesome. And you kissed me!"

"Shh," I say, not because I want him to stop talking but because I'm worried someone will hear us.

"Oh, right. Duh. We need to be quiet." He shrugs. "I'm just saying. You're so awesome. And I'm so glad you kissed me."

"I'm glad too."

"We should probably get back now, though, um,

because isn't the list thing that you sneak out without getting caught?"

"Yeah. It is."

"Let's go." He gets up off the grass and grabs my hand and pulls me up and we walk quietly and slowly back to our buildings. "We'll do the tie-dye tomorrow during hammock time. It'd be hard to see in the dark anyway."

"That makes sense."

We get to my building first, and we stop at a place between windows so no one will be able to see us from inside.

"Can I kiss you now?" Otis asks me. "One more quick kiss."

"Yes, of course." I smile. "Thank you for asking."

So he leans over and he kisses me and then I say, "Bye, Otis. See you tomorrow." I walk back inside and I touch my lips with my thumb.

Back in my room, Indigo is already asleep and I don't want to turn on my flashlight and wake her up.

I'll write Ari first thing in the morning. In the meantime, I start a draft letter to her in my head.

I don't want to forget any of the details.

18

ARI

"ARE YOU SURE YOU WANT to do this?" Hana asks me. We're whispering in the bathroom in the middle of the night, after all the counselors are in bed asleep; the whole camp is silent and still.

Hana is by far the most cautious of the group but I can't let that get in the way of the plan.

"I have to," I remind her. "The list."

"You don't *haaave* to."

"Hannie, it's okay." I pull my hair into a low ponytail. "I mean, what's the worst thing that can happen?"

"Um, you get kicked out of camp," she loudly whisper-yells.

"Not gonna happen." I reach out and pull her in for a tight, reassuring hug. "All good."

I can't hear the negativity. It's not helpful. I'm doing this and that's it.

Zoe and Alice are up on Zoe's bed looking at magazines under the glimmer of an almost dying flashlight.

"Good luck, Ar," Alice loud-whispers.

Zoe adds, "Crush this. But also don't die and don't get caught. K? Love you!"

"Love you guyssssss!" I loud-whisper back, quickly glancing for the hundredth time to make sure the counselors are sound asleep. Thankfully, they are.

Golfy is outside the bunk waiting for me. I guess he made it to my side of camp with no trouble. That's a good sign.

"You just strolled over here? No big deal?"

"Kinda sorta not really."

"Um, explain, please." I smile at him, and he puts his hands on my cheeks and kisses me. Quick and spontaneous but very magical.

"A few of the guy counselors were on one of the nearby bunk porches. Not on duty or anything, just hanging out." He shrugs. "No clue what's up with that, but anyway, I had to run around the other side of the bunk, but I made it. The thing is, I think there are counselors out and about. I'm not sure we should do the golf cart thing right now."

"Really?" My heart pounds. I'm not sure I can count

this as sneaking out since I haven't gotten very far. I mean, I guess I can. But it's sort of too easy. But another part of me is relieved that we're not doing the golf cart thing tonight. Really relieved.

"Yeah. Also, the golf cart thing could really get us kicked out," he says. "Like using camp equipment. I have another idea, though," he says. "Ready to hear it? First of all, let's sit."

We lean back against a tree, so close the sides of our arms are touching. I rest my head on his shoulder. I wish we hadn't chosen this middle-of-the-night sneak-out. I'm kind of tired.

"Let's get one of the boats from the lake, and paddle a little. That doesn't seem as dangerous, plus there aren't any bunks near the lake. I doubt anyone would see us."

I think about this. It seems oddly familiar to the kayaking Kaylan and I did on our first list and I don't want to repeat.

"I'm not sure about that one," I whisper. "Maybe we save the something daring for another night. I'm kinda tired."

"Okay, we can save it," Golfy whispers. I keep my head on his shoulder and we stay there like that for a while, not even talking. Just listening to the breeze through the trees and the crickets and a train far, far, far off in the distance.

"I have a plan for Charlie and Pres," Golfy says. "Tomorrow, Shabbat dinner, let's get them to sit with us, and I think we can make this happen."

"You do?"

"Yeah."

I want to ask more questions but truthfully, I'm kind of sleepy. I close my eyes and snuggle in closer to him. My head is in the perfect crook of his neck. Like we're two pieces of one of those gigantic toddler puzzles. He smells like anti-itch bug bite lotion and the chicken fajitas we had for dinner, but I don't mind it.

In fact, I love it. It's a delicious combination.

"Ari! Golfy!"

We're jolted out of a deep, heavy, forget-where-we-are-when-we-wake-up sleep.

"Huh? What?" I ask groggily.

"You slept outside!" Alice kicks my foot gently. "Come on. Seriously! We just got up and when I saw you weren't in your bed, I ran out here. Luckily you didn't get very far! Come on! The counselors are gonna notice you're gone really, really soon."

"Oh, Snickers!" Golfy yells, and gets up in a huff. He brushes off the butt of his sweatpants. "I slept on the wrong side of camp!"

"You gotta go, Golfy!" Alice whisper-yells again. "You

guys! This is soooo nutty! You slept outside!"

"See you at breakfast!" Golfy yells back to us as he sprints away.

"Oh my goodness, Al. What if he gets caught? What if people were looking for him? What if he gets kicked out?"

"Shh. Calm down." She puts an arm around me and we walk back to the bunk. "He can just say he went for a morning walk."

"He can?"

"Yeah."

"But he's in his clothes from last night!" I yell.

"Right. He didn't change this morning. Whatever. Just relax. Golfy knows how to talk to people. He'll make it work."

I hope she's right.

Alice instructs me. "Go in through the bathroom door and pray that the counselors don't see you, and if they do, say you were getting a towel off the clothesline."

"I don't have a towel, though."

"Okay, so say you were putting one out on the clothesline. Or get one! Whatever." Alice shakes her head. "Why am I doing all the work here?"

I laugh a little, but the truth is I still feel kind of out of it and groggy and confused. But also rebellious and excited that Golfy and I literally slept outside all night. Side by side. Under one of Camp Silver's most beautiful trees.

This is big. A moment I'll remember forever. Something I'll tell my grandchildren.

I go inside the bunk and find Zoe in the bathroom. "Where were you?" she sings. "You little rebel girl."

My cheeks turn to fire. "Shh. I'll tell you later."

I grab my shower caddy off the bathroom cubby and brush my teeth and wash my face, still feeling the exhilaration of last night. Nothing even happened but so much happened. I wonder if I can count it as the *doing something daring* thing even though I didn't plan to do it. The sleeping outside part, I mean. I wonder if something can be considered daring if you didn't know it was going to happen ahead of time.

"Were you just outside?" Charlie asks me from the sink next to mine, where she's dotting her face with moisturizer.

"Yeah. Had to hang a wet face towel." I shrug.

"Is the grass really wet?" she asks.

"Um, no." I touch the butt of my pajama pants and look down to make sure I'm not covered in mist or sap or some mystery outdoor substance.

"You feel okay, Ari? You seem off or something."

I giggle. "Oh, I'm fine! Tired. Gonna nap during nikayon. I know it's clean-up time, but it's also unofficial nap time. Right?"

"Not really, but okay." She smiles, a little confused.

"Hey, Charlie." I catch her before she walks back to her

area. "Want to sit with us for Shabbat dinner tomorrow? Golfy and me. Probably Alice, Hana, Zoe, too. And I think Golfy asked Pres."

She looks at me a little sideways, suspicious. "Sure, Ari. Sounds nice."

We have a few minutes before breakfast so I write Kaylan a quick letter.

Kay—I gotta make this quick because breakfast is really soon. But guess what? I did the sneak-out and then—you're never gonna believe this—Golfy and I fell asleep by a tree and we slept there ALL night. We didn't get caught but it was kind of shocking when we woke up. Crazy, right? Does this count as my something daring? Even though it was unintentional. Let me know. Good luck with visiting day. You'll probably get this letter after visiting day, though.

Anyway, I love you! What's new with Otis? And Indigo? When is your talent show? I hope you have one!!! Fill me in.

Xooxoxxoxoxoxoxoo FOREVER

Ari

When we get to the dining hall for breakfast, Golfy's sitting on one of the benches out front.

"Hey." He gets up when he sees me. "Did you get in trouble?"

"Not a bit." I smile, proud. "You?"

"No. Kind of frightening they didn't know I was gone, or . . ."

"Nah." I shrug. "Don't question it."

Gemma and her friends run past us and say, "Oooohh. Lovebirds!" and then cackle to each other.

"We are lovebirds," Golfy says. "I like that. Can we make a plaque that says lovebirds?"

I scrunch up my face. "I think we can do better. Let's hang during breira?"

"Yeah. Cool. See ya."

Golfy walks on ahead of me into the dining hall and finds his table. I sit at mine and pour some milk into my disposable bowl of Cheerios and think about all that's happened in the past twelve hours.

Turns out sitting-up-against-a-tree sleep isn't the most restorative, though. I'm pretty tired.

I think I could fall asleep right here at this table.

I look over at Golfy at his table throwing Kix in the air and trying to catch them in his mouth. And then all the kids at the table take turns throwing them and he tries to catch them.

He is the best.

We *are* lovebirds.

No doubt about it.

19

KAYLAN

"I LOVE THE DETERMINATION," INDIGO says as we walk over to the lake area for hammock time. Otis and I are doing our eyedropper tie-dye today and I'm so excited. I just want to start already.

"The list brings it out of me. You'll see it does the same for you."

"Are you sure?" she asks.

"Yes. One hundred percent."

As we walk I keep my mind on the tie-dye and on Indi's list, but there are teeny-tiny agita bubbles in my stomach that I can't seem to pop. Visiting day is tomorrow, and my dad and his person are coming and I just can't picture that in my head. At all.

My dad. His person. My mom. Ryan.

It's not how I ever imagined it would be. It's not how I wanted it to be.

"Hey, Kaylan," Chad yells from down the path, a guitar strapped to his back.

"Hey," I grumble.

This kid will not leave me alone. We don't even have that much time left here and he is still annoying.

"Still trying to be funny?" he yells.

I cannot take this anymore.

"What is his deal? For real?" I say under my breath, not really asking Indigo.

She shakes her head. "No idea."

"Chad! Come over here!" I yell back.

This is happening. I am shutting this down. Enough is enough.

He does this sheepish little smile and traipses over to us like he's all sophisticated and cool and everyone thinks he's awesome. None of that is true.

When he's finally in front of us, I put my hands on my hips and glare at him.

"Chad, you have been doing this *girls aren't funny* thing all summer. You know that, right?"

He laughs and nods.

"It's not cool. Do you know that?"

"Um."

"First of all, it's not true. Second of all, it's sexist. Third of all, it's borderline harassment at this point."

He's silent. So is Indigo. Although I can feel her cheering me on in her head. She stands up straighter and I feel her solidarity.

"You need to stop. There will be people out there in life who will not be as patient as I am. I could have reported you to Rob or Paul or anyone. I could have gotten you kicked out."

"Um, let's not go—"

I interrupt him. "No, I will go where I want to go because society has changed. You need to change with it. Women aren't putting up with this nonsense anymore. I was kind to you because I felt bad for you. But enough is enough."

He adjusts his guitar strap; he doesn't meet my gaze.

"You hear me?"

He nods again, still looking down at the pavement.

"I asked if you hear me, Chad."

"Yes. I hear you. I'm sorry," he mumbles.

I grab Indigo's hand and we keep walking to the lake.

"Wow, Kaylan," she says after a few quiet moments. "That was something."

"It was. I had to do it. I know he's weak and insecure and he doesn't know what to do, but that's not an excuse."

"No, it's not. You're right."

We're almost at the hammocks when Indi says, "So

was that your something daring? I thought the infirmary was. Can you have two? Explain, please."

"I guess I have two." I shrug. "Not sure. I'll have to consult with Ari. Or maybe that was my *make a difference*. . . . I need to think about it."

"Proud of you, Kaylan."

"Thanks." I smile. "I'm proud of me, too."

Otis is already by the lake on one of the hammocks. His hands are tucked behind his head like a pillow and his eyes are closed. I can see little strands of his hair through the hammock holes and from this angle it looks long enough to braid. I wonder if he'd let me braid his hair. I wonder if this is a weird thought to have.

"Do you want to make a shirt? Did you bring a shirt?" I ask Indigo.

"Nah and nah. I just want to watch."

We walk over to Otis's hammock and I watch his chest bobbing up and down. He's really asleep.

"I think I have to wake him up." I turn to Indigo, feeling a little overwhelmed by this. It's kind of intimate to wake someone up. Awkward. You don't know how they'll respond.

"Yeah, we only have about a half hour." She looks at her watch. "We don't have enough free time here. Gonna write that on the end of summer questionnaire."

"Same," I say.

We stand there watching Otis sleep for a few moments, talking about nothing really, but trying to be loud so that he wakes up.

"What's going on?" he asks after a few minutes, sounding groggy.

"Time for tie-dye!" I sing, cheerful. "Time for tie-dye! Time for tie-dye." I laugh, pleased with my new song. "Hey, that's a good bit! It could be a daytime talk show called *Time for Tie-Dye* and there are guests and they talk and stuff, all while tie-dyeing!"

"Love." He rubs his eyes and then takes a slip of paper and a pen out of his cargo shorts pocket. "Writing it down."

We're quiet for a minute and then Otis inches forward on the hammock. He says, "So, Kaylan, I spent a lot of time thinking about which shirt I wanted to give you. And I settled on this one. A favorite."

He spreads it out to show me.

Owl Creek Elementary School

A plain white shirt with simple black letters.

"I loved my elementary school and I want you to have this shirt." He smiles. "Tie-dyed, of course."

"Awwwwwwwww," Indigo makes a sad-touched-verklempt kind of face. "Wait, you guys planned to switch shirts to tie-dye?"

"Yeah," I say.

"So which one did you bring, then?" Indigo asks me.

"My favorite shirt from my favorite place." I hand it over.

Otis reads, "*The Brookside Pool. The place to be.*"

He looks up at me.

"It's my community pool," I explain.

"Is it really the place to be?" Otis cracks up.

"Of course it is!" I smile. "It's my favorite place in the world."

"I love it."

He leans over and hugs me in a far-away kind of way, like our arms are close but our legs are far from one another.

"Okay, you two, um, can we get to tie-dyeing?" Indigo asks. "We don't have much time!"

Otis gets out the Sharpies, and I set up the eye drop squirters. I took little cups from the bathroom and pour rubbing alcohol into all of them.

"So basically I think we just draw a design and then squirt on the rubbing alcohol through these little droppers and then we're set. It spreads the dye around. Then we let it dry, find somewhere to wash it, or maybe hand wash it, I don't know." Otis hands me a red cup. "Oh, and you can use this to trace for the design. Like if you want circles and stuff."

I look around for Indigo and find her on the hammock behind us, jotting stuff down in a notebook.

"What's she doing?" Otis mouths.

"Not sure. I think starting her own list."

He considers this for a minute. "Oh. Cool."

We continue designing our shirts and talking about comedy bits and then he says, "Can I introduce you to my fam on visiting day?"

"Um." I hesitate. "Sure."

I want to ask if I can introduce him to mine but I'm not sure that's such a good idea. My dad coming. With his person. I barely know how the interaction with my parents will go, and then I'm bringing someone new into it.

"You look nervous." Otis makes an over the top curvy-eyebrow kind of face.

"Yeah, visiting day feels like a big ball of molten lava agita this year," I tell him.

"So tell me how you really feel about it?" He bursts out laughing.

"Bit alert!" I yell, falling backward on the grass. I pop back up. "Best sketch idea I've ever had! People say really outlandish, extreme things and then another person, completely seriously, deadpan, says *so tell me how you really feel about it.*"

"Love!" He high-fives me.

We finish our shirts and Otis takes them back to his room since he says he has a great place to let them dry.

I spend all of afternoon comedy session thinking about visiting day and how it's gonna be.

Finally I realize what I probably should have realized

years and years ago: there's no way to prepare for most things in life. None. I just need to go with it. See what happens.

"Otis," I whisper during a quiet writing burst.

"Yeah?"

"Improv. Visiting day. That's what it's gonna be."

"Explain more."

"I have no idea how it'll go. I need to think of it as an improv exercise."

"That works," he whispers.

"You know, the *yes and* thing?" I ask him. "How you just basically say *yes and* to whatever the person before you said and then you add to it, and that's how you keep the sketch going?"

"Of course, yeah." He smiles.

"I think I gotta *yes and* visiting day." I pause. "Just go with it."

I lean back on my elbows on the floor and stare at the ceiling and take deep breaths.

"I like it," Otis says. "It's gonna be great."

It's gonna be great.

I just need to believe him.

20

ARI

"REMIND ME OF THE PLAN," Alice says after she puts the hair dryer down. She blows the hair away from her face with her tongue.

"Okay. We're sitting with Charlie and Pres at Shabbat dinner tonight. Golfy too. And some of his boys, I think. And Gaux and her friends are gonna sit with us. Do you want Oren to sit with us too?"

Shabbat is the Jewish Sabbath and pretty much the most important Jewish holiday even though it happens every week from Friday night to Saturday night. There's always a special dinner on Friday—with delicious braided bread called challah and grape juice, and we light candles, too.

"Maybe." She thinks about it for a second. "I'm not sure."

I nod. "So, to be honest, I'm getting a little nervous about Charlie and Pres. What if it's not right? What if it doesn't work out? What if I can't make it happen?"

"Make what happen exactly during a forty-five-minute dinner?"

I roll my eyes. I've explained this so many times already but every time I do, the less confident I feel. My throat stings a little. "Loyal to the List, Al. But do you think this one has gone too far?"

"Loyal to the List," she groans. "I think?"

A little bit later, we're all dressed in white and we leave the bunk. It's a camp ritual that everyone wears all white on Shabbat. All over the hill people are playing guitars and singing and groups of friends are holding hands. We walk down to the outdoor sanctuary and we sit through the service—the interpretive dance and the readings and the prayers and the songs—and all I can think about is Charlie. I look over at her, down the bench, and her curls are pulled into a low ponytail. Her legs are golden tan; one silver flip-flop hangs off her foot. She's so beautiful. I can't imagine Pres loving anyone else.

I look around for him. He's three rows behind us, sitting next to a guy counselor on one side and a girl counselor on the other. My stomach somersaults. What if he is already with someone else? What if I'm too late?

I tap my foot on the rocky gravel and scratch my head and chew my pinkie nail and pray that this service ends soon. I know that's the exact opposite of what I should be doing since we're literally in a service praying and all I want is for it to be over. I silently apologize to God in my head and move forward.

I just need this to happen. I need this to work. For the list, of course. But also for Charlie. And also for the love of camp relationships. I don't want them to end. I mean, I know I broke up with Golfy. But that was different. And I'll never to do it again.

"Are you freaking out right now?" Alice whispers to me.

"Yes!"

"It's gonna be okay, Ar. You're not, like, responsible for Charlie's love life? I get the list and everything. But it is what it is."

I shrug. I agree with her in some sense but not completely.

When the service ends, we leave the outdoor sanctuary and walk to the dining hall for dinner. We usually have to sit with our bunk but on Friday nights, people can sit wherever they want for dinner. That's why this is such a perfect opportunity to start the rekindling.

Golfy and I make eyes at each other across the path, on the way to dinner. He's my partner in this. He gets it.

After a little bit of shuffling and table scrambling, we're seated and all together.

Golfy, me, Alice, Hana, Zoe, Gaux, Charlie, Pres, a few of Golfy's friends, one of Pres's friends, and Gemma, too.

"Shabbat Shalom!" Gemma yells to the table. It's amazing that this is the same girl who sobbed her way through the first half of camp.

I really did make a difference. In this small but very important way.

After the blessings for the candles and the wine and the challah bread, we start eating.

Well, everyone else does. Not me.

I'm too focused on Charlie and Pres to eat much of anything.

Charlie doesn't eat much either. She picks at her chicken and potatoes and sips her iced tea.

"It's amazing we both have nicknames," Gaux says to Pres. "I mean, I basically came to camp with a nickname and really hoped it would stick and it did and now I'm set for life."

Charlie cracks up from across the table. "You are definitely set for life."

"Are you all staying all summer?" Pres asks us.

We all nod and then Gemma says, "I'm not. I kinda wish I was. But I'm also excited to have a few weeks at home without my darling sister Arianna." She rolls her eyes.

"Ah, feel the sisterly love." Pres laughs.

So far I am not seeing much of a rekindling. I mean, it's fine between Pres and Charlie, but nothing amazing. He's pretty much talking to his friends and she's talking to hers, and that's it.

We finish dinner and walk to the quad for Israeli Dancing.

I follow behind Charlie and her friends, not too close so they can see me, but close enough that I can eavesdrop.

"He's anti me for sure," she says. "Whatever. I need to move on. This isn't happening."

They all mumble something, and it's obvious they're sick of hearing about this.

Maybe Charlie does want to move on and maybe that's a good idea. I wish we hadn't added this one. I regret everything about it.

We can't control other people, and we most certainly cannot control two other people. I want to write to Kaylan and take this item off. I don't know if we have time to add something new. We may have to settle on one fewer list item.

And then it hits me. Something major. Something important.

Maybe we can start to accept that it's okay to fail sometimes. Maybe this is a lesson we need to learn. Maybe *learning to accept failure* should be a thing on our list, an alternate for the two counselors falling in love.

"So that went well?" Golfy throws an arm over my shoulder and walks with me to Israeli Dancing.

"You think?"

"I mean, they seemed chill together?" he says like a question. I think he's just saying it went well to make me happy.

"It didn't go well, Golfy. I don't think he's into her," I admit, defeated. "He's just not."

Golfy stops walking. He looks at the grass.

"What is it?" I ask.

He stares at the ground. "I need to tell you something."

My heart pounds and I expect the worst. He wants to break up; he loves someone else. Of course. He's getting me back for what I did to him during the year. I deserve this.

We lean against a tree, and I wait for him to say whatever it is that he has to tell me. But then he kisses me. Pretty out of the blue, pretty romantic.

"Golfy! You made me so nervous!"

"What? Why?"

"Because you said you had to tell me something and I figured it was bad news."

"Arianna Simone Nodberg! Stop that negative thinking this instant."

He links arms with me and we walk back to Israeli Dancing. He asks, "What happens if you fail at something on the list?"

I look up at him. "I've been wondering about that, but I don't know; it hasn't happened yet."

"I see," he replies. "Well, first time for everything, right?"

I shrug. "I guess. Yeah."

All night, I dance with my friends but my heart's not in it. My heart is splintered when I see Charlie off to the side, her head on a friend's shoulder. And my heart splinters even more when I see Pres walk off with Amanda from the art shack.

What is he thinking? Doesn't he know he's making a terrible mistake? Also, I'm not sure they're supposed to leave Israeli Dancing. Maybe I should report them and get them in trouble. Payback for what he's done to Charlie.

When we're back at the bunk after lights-out, Alice says, "Yeah, I think you're gonna need a new plan." We're all sitting in a circle, cross-legged on the floor in our pajamas, eating Pringles. "He's not into her."

"Definitely not," Hana adds. "He's way into Art Shack Amanda. She has a belly button ring."

"She does?" I squawk.

"Yeah, she wore a bikini to free swim the other day," Zoe shares. "The day you were tie-dyeing."

I lean back against one of the poles of my bunk bed.

"Are you gonna be okay, Ar?" Alice asks. "If this doesn't work out, I mean."

"Well, I still have over three weeks, so maybe some other couple can work? Do we have time to get Charlie to fall in love with someone else?"

"Honestly, this is weird," Hana says. "I support you and your missions but I'm not into participating in this one."

"Thanks, Hannie." I roll my eyes, but I get how she feels. This one is tough. I truly don't know what to do about it. "I'm gonna get into bed and write Kaylan and tell her about my struggles. Visiting day tomorrow. How are we feeling about it?"

"Fine," Alice says. "Excited for some real food."

"Same." Zoe comes over to sit next to me. "Don't stress about this, honestly. Maybe we could help someone else find true love."

"I guess. Maybe. I'm writing to Kaylan to see about an amendment. We've never done it before. But that doesn't mean we can't do it now."

Cozy under my covers, with just the right amount of light from my flashlight, I start writing.

Dear Kaylan,
First of all, good luck with visiting day tomorrow. Second of all, I'm wondering what you think about an amendment to our list. This get two counselors to fall in love thing isn't working out for me. My counselor Charlie (Charlotte really) is in love with her boyfriend from last summer, Pres (Barack really, get it?), and I thought I could get them back together but it's not looking good. I think Pres is with this girl Amanda from the art shack (she has a

belly button ring!) and who knows. Charlie is still in love with Pres and she cries about it all the time. With three weeks left of camp, how am I going to get her to fall in love with someone else? Feels unlikely. I tried, though. I've never failed at a list item before.

I stop writing, feeling beyond defeated. I look over the list.

Ari and Kaylan's 13¾ Things to Build and Improve on Our Complete and Total Amazingness

1. Perform in a camp talent show. (so glad you said it counted even though Alice did it with me) ✓

2. Write at least one letter to each other a week. ✓

3. Sneak out of the bunk at night without getting caught. ✓

4. Keep a gratitude journal. ✓

5. Get two counselors to fall in love. (going to cancel and admit defeat)

6. Be able to have a full conversation in another language. (to come when we're home)

7. Draw a portrait of each other from memory. (to come)

8. Do something daring. (sort of, maybe, I don't know)

9. Get a younger kid at camp and/or at home to start their own list. ✓

10. Master the art of tie-dye. ✓

11. Make a difference. (also unclear. We need to discuss)

12. Tell our dads one thing we'd like to improve about our relationship with them. (TOMORROW! ACK!)

13. Make a time capsule to capture our lives at exactly 13 ¾ years old and bury it somewhere in Brookside. (to come)

13 ¾. Keep our friendship strong. (always and forever) ✓

What should I do? Add in something else? Postpone until next summer? Maybe we should always allow one carry-over item if we can't finish it? Ugh, Kay! I feel terrible. I really want to make it happen but it's not looking good. I might try to have the chat with my dad tomorrow on visiting day. Or is that a huge bummer?

WAHHHHHH!!! I miss you so much. I feel so miserable about this. But here are a few good things. I'll share my last gratitude journal entry with you so I don't end this letter on a sad note.

Gemma finally being happy at camp.

Golfy kissing me out of the blue during Israeli Dancing.

Alice showing me how to make a pinwheel in a mosquito bite to stop the itch.

Grilled cheese & tomato soup day.

Another postcard from Bubbie! Favorite line: When you get home, would you like to work on Yiddish together? It could be our secret language! ☺

As for the language, yeah, I'm okay with waiting until we get home. But since Bubbie mentioned it, maybe Yiddish? Maybe she can help us? I don't know! ☺

I love you, Kay! Hope visiting day goes well. Good luck with your dad and his person.

Xoxoxoxoxoxoxoxo Ari

21

KAYLAN

I WAKE UP AT FIVE thirty in the morning as if it's a nor-mal time when someone should be starting the day. I'm not even sure if I can call it waking up, though, because I don't sleep at all the night before visiting day because I'm too worried. I don't even think I can call it agita anymore. It's more serious than that. It's a full-body stress where I literally have no idea what will happen.

My mom; my dad; his person; and my brother, Ryan. This dynamic feels insane. Too much. Too close. And at camp visiting day. It's not right. I should have said no. Put my foot down about this. But there wasn't a chance to do that. No one even asked me.

I stare at my tie-dye shirt drying on the top of my dresser; I wonder when it will be ready to wear.

I look at Indigo and wait for her to wake up because

I need someone to talk to right now. Anyone. I can't be alone with my thoughts anymore. But she doesn't budge. She's sound asleep, under her covers, breathing with her mouth open.

I get out of bed and move around, hoping that will cause her to stir and she'll wake up. I grab my shower caddy and go to the bathroom to wash up. I come back and dig through my drawers to find an outfit. Nothing. This girl has the ability to sleep.

Finally, her alarm goes off at seven thirty. I sit on my bed staring at her.

"Um, Kaylan." She grumbles, rubbing her eyes. "What are you doing?"

"Ind, I'm freaking out. My dad. His person. My mom. Freaking. Out."

"Can I just say I love that you call her his person? Like you know her name and her role in his life. But his person. I like it."

I sigh. "Well, that's all I can say about her. She's a person and she's his and that's it. Anything more feels icky."

Every time I go down this path with Indigo I feel bad about it. She's a product of a second marriage so I feel like I shouldn't say anything. But right now I can't hold my tongue. I need to just be open and honest.

"I know what you mean," Indigo says softly. "Well, I don't really because I've never been in this situation but I can imagine it. It feels icky." She puts her feet on the floor and goes over to her dresser to grab her shower caddy.

I ask, "How did your stepsiblings feel when your parents got together and got married and stuff?"

She stops right before she leaves the room to head to the bathroom.

"Um, I don't really know because I wasn't alive and I never asked them and they're not really so into me, so I guess not great?" She shrugs. "I'm gonna go with not great."

She leaves then and goes down the hall and I'm left alone on my bed with my thoughts. Maybe I dig too deep with people and ask them things they don't really want to discuss. But not all the time. I also avoid hard conversations. I push away things I don't want to think about. Like with my mom. And Robert Irwin Krieger. Avoid, avoid, avoid. Even with Ari. She has no idea about any of it, really.

My heart pounds and I don't know why I didn't realize this until now.

Zoe! What if she knows more than I realize? What if she's told Ari things I don't even know?

"You're gonna be okay, Kaylan," Indigo says when she gets back to the room, zapping me back into the visiting day stress. "Honestly. I think it'll be a minute or two of awkwardness and then it'll be fine."

"You think?"

She nods.

"Do your stepsiblings come on visiting day?"

"Never. They're in their twenties and have way more exciting things to do." She turns away from me and grabs something to wear out of her top drawer. "I'm okay with it, though."

Sometimes I wonder if Indigo is really okay with the things she says she is. Maybe that should be on her list. *Figure out what I'm okay with and what I'm not okay with.* She says it all the time, *I'm okay with it,* but there's sadness under the surface, lurking. I can feel it. I wonder if she is really okay.

I guess that's for her to unpack, though. Maybe I'll suggest it. Or maybe not. It has to be at the right time.

We get to breakfast and Otis is waiting for me outside, and my more-than-agita subsides a little. Not completely.

"You okay?" he asks.

I do a slow nod but it's not true. I'm not okay.

I stumble my way through breakfast and eat a few bites here and there, feeling the agita, and then pushing it away, and then feeling it again. I try to breathe and meditate like Ari taught me, but it's only half working.

After breakfast we go to the lake area and hang on the hammocks and wait for our parents to arrive.

Otis's parents arrive first. They're pretty much how I pictured them. Earthy. His dad wears hiking sandals with socks. His mom has a fanny pack and not a trendy one.

"I'll introduce you later," Otis says.

Soon after, a lot more people arrive, including Indigo's parents and Cleo's dad.

Finally, my mom and Ryan traipse in. Ryan drags his feet behind her, looking at the ground, hair in his eyes, clearly annoyed that he has to be here.

"My girl!" My mom wraps me in a hug. "I have missed you so much."

I don't know why but I feel guilty when she says things like that, even though I've missed her, too, of course.

"You look so wonderful," she goes on. "So tan, though I hope you're wearing sunscreen!"

"I am, Mom." I roll my eyes, still in the mom hug, and I try to meet Ryan's gaze since he's standing behind me. But he's still staring at the ground.

She pulls back. "Let me look at you again. Kaylan! You've gotten even taller!"

"I have?"

I wonder how long this can go on and if we'll ever talk about more meaningful things or if my mom will spend all day observing me like I'm some exotic animal in a zoo. I look around for Otis to tell him that would be a great bit, but I don't see him.

"How's it going, Ry?" I ask, because so far he hasn't even acknowledged my presence.

"It's chill," he mumbles. No further questions from him. Or I should say no questions at all. He doesn't ask any. "Going to lie down on this hammock. I'm exhausted."

"K, cool. Good talk." I laugh to myself and stand there watching Ryan get onto the hammock, holding tight to the sides so he doesn't fall over.

A few minutes later, I feel a pat on my back and turn around and I pray that it's Otis even though I know it's not.

My body freezes. I look at my mom, who appears to be scrolling through her phone, trying to keep calm and keep it together. Ryan's now fully settled on the hammock with his eyes closed and his earbuds in.

"Hi, Dad," I say, trying to sound cheerful.

"Kaylan! Hi!" he says.

"Hi!" His person (Amy) is over-the-top cheerful. So cheery it seems like she could cause something to explode.

We keep just going around saying hi to each other and finally my mom greets them with a clenched-teeth smile and forced politeness.

"So? Can we get a tour?" my dad says, all breathy. "We'd love to see the place. I'd love to see what my hard-earned dollars are being spent on!" He laughs but no one else does. Of course he'd bring up the money. It's not like he's the only one paying. I contributed and so did my mom.

Way to get visiting day off on a happy note, Dad!

Thankfully my mom ignores it and his person keeps smiling like it's a tattoo and permanent and there's no way for her face to be any other way.

"Hey! Kaylan!" I hear someone yell.

I whip around and see Otis with his parents, all smiley and casual, just strolling across the lawn like everything is wonderful and peaceful and calm and they love life.

"Hey!" I yell back.

They make their way to us and I introduce everyone.

"Nice to meet you, Otis." My dad shakes his hand. This is my dad's favorite thing: being charming and smiley and friendly to strangers. He turns it on like it's an oven light. And then turns it off the same exact way.

We stand there and chat for a second, and Otis's mom and my mom talk about camp and labeling clothing and how they expect that everything will get lost.

"Have a lovely day!" Otis's mom says. "We're off to figure out lunch."

"We should do the same," my mom replies. "What would you like, Kaylan?"

I think for a second. This choice is all up to me. "Well, there's this deli in town that the counselors really like. It seems kind of like Harvey Deli, which I miss soooooo much. So maybe we can go there?"

"I was actually thinking sushi," my dad chimes in. "I read about this place online and it seems great."

"No sushi," Ryan says, not even looking up from the game he's playing on his phone. "I had this bad experience a few weeks ago, and I puked for three days straight."

"Thanks for sharing, Ryan." I roll my eyes at this whole scene, wishing that visiting day wasn't even a thing. I don't want these people here.

"I'm good for whatever," my dad's person says, smiling.

No one asked you, lady.

We debate it for a little while more and then decide on the deli. My dad and his person will do sushi for dinner.

The rest of the day feels like sitting on thumbtacks. If I adjust myself just so, we're fine. But if I move ever so slightly, I feel a pinch in my skin.

We set up a picnic near the lake, and we're mostly quiet as we eat. I don't mind it, though. Talking to each other would be way worse.

"So, Kaylan, how is everything going?" my mom asks after a bite of her chicken salad sandwich. "Is this a one-summer thing or would you want to come back again?"

"Um, yeah, I'd love to. The comedy program is really awesome. And the friends I've made are great," I say, brushing some sesame seeds off my shorts.

"We'll see about the cost, though, right, Kay?" My dad side-nods.

"You're not the only one making the decision," my mom says. "The truth is, I—"

I jump in, "Okay, guys, next summer is next summer. Let's just pause for now."

My dad's person is on her phone, playing a word puzzle

game. I think she's only a few years younger than my dad but she seems way, way younger. Ryan's on his phone playing some kind of violent thing and they're both only half here.

I feel like I'm a crossing guard but for my parents' comments and exchanges. Or maybe it's a chair umpire at a tennis match. I don't know. What I do know is that it doesn't feel right. This back and forth monitoring.

This isn't my role. I shouldn't have to do it.

I expected this in some ways, but not completely. And even if I expected it, there was no way to prep for it.

I want to have the chat with my dad. I want to have it now.

"Hey, Dad, can I talk to you for a minute?" I muster up the courage to ask him this and then brace myself for an awkward response.

"Uh, um, sure." He's tentative and nervous.

I feel bad leaving my mom with my dad's person but she's so busy with her game, it probably doesn't even register. "Hey, Mom, you should go around the corner and check out the art studios. They're really impressive."

"Oh!" Her voices rises, overflowing with relief. "A great idea! I'll do that."

My dad and I walk off a little bit from our picnic spot near the lake. We sit straight up on hammocks across from each other.

Loyal to the List. Let's do this.

But also, loyal to myself, to making improvements, to healing. Loyal to all of that, too.

"So what's up, Kay?" my dad asks.

"I wanted to talk to you."

"Right. That's why we're here." He laughs but I don't find him funny. Not at all.

"I want to talk about our relationship." I clear my throat. "I want to see if we can improve things between us."

He nods.

"First of all, I don't like how you're always so cryptic. Every time you write me it seems like a big bucket of knives is going to fall on my head."

He laughs but I'm not trying to be funny.

I continue, "You never really say what's happening or going to happen or whatever. Maybe you think you're protecting me or something but you're not. It just makes me worry more. And you know me, I already worry a ton. More than a ton." I pause, waiting for him to say something, but he doesn't. "So that's one thing."

He nods again. I can't tell if he's speechless or bored or what. Maybe he's worried about his person.

"Anyway, and also, I feel like I'm always a referee between you and Mom. I know you left and I know you don't love her and I know you have a new wife." My voice catches in my throat. The tears will flow soon but I don't want them to. I push them back, far away, as far as they can go. "But you still share kids. You still share memories. Isn't there any little corner of your heart where you can find kindness and sweetness and happiness with her? The tiniest corner."

"Kaylan, I—" He stammers. "Your mother and me. It's complicated."

"People say that as a way to get out of difficult things," I reply. "Lots of things are complicated. It doesn't mean we don't try. This conversation is complicated."

"It is. That is true."

"And?" I ask.

He tries to meet my gaze, but I turn away. "And. Well. I. I'm glad you said something."

"That's it?" I stammer.

He scratches his forehead and it seems like he's trying to say something poignant while not feeling anything at all.

I blurt out, "Do you want to be close to Ryan and me? Do you care about our relationship?"

"I do. And actually I wanted to talk to you about something." He pauses.

"See? Cryptic again. Bucket of knives again. All the time. Just say it. Just say it, every time. No warning. Just say it."

I feel myself getting hot and sweaty and angry all over again. He doesn't hear me. He doesn't get me. I don't even feel like he knows me.

"Amy and I are planning to move to Brookside some-time this fall. Before Christmas." He pauses, maybe waiting for a reaction from me. Hard to say. "We love Scottsdale, but we want to be closer to you. I sort of mentioned it to Ryan but it wasn't set in stone at the time."

I'm speechless. Really and truly. Ryan *was* right when he casually mentioned it. This is actually happening.

"We're looking at the apartments downtown by the train. There are great amenities and even a rooftop pool and I know how much you love the Brookside pool, so."

I interrupt. "I'm loyal to the Brookside Pool. Very loyal. I can't be visiting other pools."

He laughs. "Anyway, so I think it'll be nice to be closer to you and Ryan and we'll work out some kind of visit schedule."

My throat tightens. Is this going to be some kind of every-week deal that kids of divorce have? One day during the week and every other weekend or something. Because no. I don't want to do that.

"Thoughts? You haven't said anything."

"I don't know what to say. It'll be an adjustment. Another adjustment. I'm always having to adjust to new things, changes, and I hate it. I hate change, Dad! Don't you see that? And you're always forcing changes on me."

"Kaylan," he says softly.

"Don't Kaylan me!" I yell. "I wanted this talk to be about me, and it's about you. And Amy. And your move back to Brookside. Enough. I'm not going to spend my last week at camp thinking about this."

I get up from the hammock and walk back to the pic-nic area, hoping my mom had a nice visit to the art center and didn't suffer too much with Amy and Ryan.

"Kaylan, come on. Don't do this," I hear my dad say from back at the hammocks. He doesn't try to follow me.

I did what I needed to do for the list, of course. But also for myself. I was open and honest.

And I feel lighter.

One brick off the very large tall tower of bricks resting on my shoulders.

22

ARI

I WISH I COULD SPEAK to Kaylan and discuss visiting day with her, and ask if she had the talk with her dad, and find out how it went. I can't, though, and it's frustrating. We're not allowed to have phones at camp, even on visiting day, and I feel weird using my mom's phone to call Kaylan's mom's. We wouldn't have privacy to talk anyway.

I wake up before everyone else in the bunk on visiting day morning and I look over the list, trying to pretend that Kaylan is here with me, by my side, glancing over my shoulder.

I wonder if Kaylan performed in the talent show yet. I don't think she's mentioned it or maybe it's the last night of camp for her. I also need to hear back on the *something daring* thing, if sleeping outside at night counts. And the *make a difference?* I don't know if I've done that. I guess I have with Gemma, but is it big enough? And maybe I've made a difference in Gaux's life, too.

Do we ever really know if we've made a difference? It seems kind of like a life-long goal that's never really complete. But what about the whole *save a life, save the whole world* thing in Judaism? Even making a difference in a small way has the potential to change things in a really big way.

I rest my head back on my pillow and close my eyes. It's hard to do this list so far away from one another. It was supposed to keep us close, but it's making me feel so far away from my best friend. Not distant in love, but distant in distance. I guess that's just a fact of the situation. And the thing with Zoe's dad—this secret I've been keeping—it's starting to get to me. In a real, deep, powerful way. It's not my news to share, but the guilt is still tugging at me.

My mind swirls around and around. I look across the bunk, and when I see that Alice is up, too, I hop down from my bed, scurry over to hers, climb up, and get in next to her.

"Hi, Al." I rest my head on her shoulder.

"Hi, Ar."

"Can I talk to you about something?" I whisper.

"Of course, my doll. What it's about?"

"It's actually about Zoe."

"Zoe?" she asks. "Is this about how she's obviously the prettiest girl at camp but has no idea? I wonder about that, too. She honestly doesn't know she's literally supermodel beautiful."

"Um, no." I giggle. "She is super pretty, but I'm talking about the thing with her dad and Kaylan's mom being serious and, ya know, making future plans. I've sort of known about it all summer, but I haven't told Kaylan and now it's really starting to stress me out."

"Oh yeah. That is stressful." Alice crinkles her eyebrows. "I don't have any advice. But I don't think you can say anything to Kaylan. I think her mom needs to tell her."

"Yeah, that's what I keep reminding myself." I pause, shifting on the bed. "But do you think she already knows and hasn't told me?"

Alice shrugs. "I don't know. Honestly. But also, your boarding school thing? You didn't tell her about that either, did you?"

I shake my head. My stomach turns gurgley.

"For BFFs, you keep a lot of secrets." Alice scrunches up her face like she's regretting that she said that.

"Well, sometimes we protect each other's feelings, and that's the priority," I whisper, sitting up in the bed. "We had a whole thing about it—about what we prefer—being totally honest or protecting each other's feelings. But this feels different, kind of like a new variety of secret. We shouldn't be keeping them; I shouldn't be keeping them."

We stay there in Alice's bed for a little while longer, talking and then not talking and then talking again. I wonder how I'll feel when I see Zoe's dad today. I wonder if my parents know, if Kaylan's mom has said anything to my mom when they run into each other at the grocery store or if my mom ever shows up at book club.

"Pres and Charlie aren't gonna rekindle," I admit. "I think it was a failure to put that on the list. I'm admitting defeat."

"For real? Official defeat?" Alice sits up and leans against the wall behind her bed. "You never do that."

I exhale. "I have to in this case, but I think that's important, too. A necessary thing this list is teaching us."

Alice thinks about it and listens as I talk on and on about this.

"AlKal," I whisper. "Do you think I've made a difference this summer? So far."

"Made a difference how?"

"Well, it's on the list, and we just wrote *make a difference*, but we didn't know what that really meant or how we'd do it, and now I wonder if I have. I mean, there's still time, but just a check-in." I pause. "What do you think?"

"You make a difference in my life every day just by being your amazing Arianna Simone Nodberg self. Just saying your name out loud makes me smile."

"That's kind, Al. But for real."

"I feel like yes, but maybe I'll make a list later of all the ways you've made a difference." Her face perks up. "See, I can make lists, too!"

I want to talk to Alice about the looming dad talk but I don't. I avoid it. Push it away. Pretend it's not gonna happen even though it's definitely happening and definitely needs to happen.

After breakfast, we all go back to the bunks to wait for our parents. We hang on the porch and when the cars start pulling up, we get excited but nervous at the same time. There's something about not seeing people for a few weeks that makes seeing them again feel strange, even when they're your parents. I think it pretty much proves that you can get used to anything. We're used to not seeing them; we're okay with it now.

Gemma's with me on my bunk porch; she's making a string bracelet that's tied to her water bottle. Most of the other parents are here already, but ours aren't. They're pretty much always late to everything. Drives me nuts.

"Do you wish you were staying second session?" I ask her.

"Kinda sorta not really," she replies. "I'm happy here now. But I also wanna go home. My comfy bed. Snuggles with Lion. Also I want some time there without you."

"Gem!" I kick my foot against hers. "That's kind of rude."

"Sorry." She looks away. "Camp is great, though. You were right."

"You're admitting that I was right, right now? Wow."

She's quiet then.

"Are you saying camp has made a difference in your life?" I ask. "That I've made a difference?"

She focuses on the bracelet string stitches but then she looks up at me and she says, "Definitely. I never realized Jewish stuff could be so much fun."

I crack up. "Yeah, that's one way to say it."

I decide I'll write Kaylan a letter and tell her I'm going to JHH the *make a difference* thing. I know I only made a difference in a small way, but sometimes small ways become big ways, and I think this counts. And who knows what will happen from here, other small ways I can make a difference.

"Hi, girls!" My mom jumps out of the car and runs over to us.

"Hiii!" Gemma runs over to meet her, but I stay on the porch, taking in the scene. I need to prepare. I need to get ready for this talk with my dad. I want it to happen today. I want it to be meaningful and good and important.

We hug and talk and then hug and talk and on and on. And then we settle on Koi for lunch, a Chinese place a mile away where each table has one of those circle spinny things in the middle that makes it really easy to share food.

We eat lo mein and General Tso's chicken and scallion pancakes and dumplings. It's a feast. A real feast. And then after that we go back to camp to hang out on the Adirondack chairs and maybe swim or maybe go boating. We don't know yet.

"How's Golfy?" my mom whispers as we walk up the hill back to my bunk.

"Great." I smile, sort of forgetting that I'm talking to my mom. For a second it seemed like she was a friend and that mildly freaks me out. Do I want my mom to be a friend? Maybe one day when I'm, like, thirty. Not now. I don't think so.

"Details you want to share?" My mom does that casual mom-ish smile that I hate where she thinks I can't tell she's prying for info but it's so obvious and I can totally tell.

"Not really. Sorry." I'm quiet then, feeling a little guilty that I was rude.

"Ari! You can talk to me. I'm your mother."

If I had a dollar for every time she said that, I'd be able to cure homelessness in this country. "I know, Mom."

She goes on, "Plus I love to hear this stuff. It makes me happy. I get pleasure from my children. You know that, right?"

Ew. Why is she such an over-the-top mom right now? I can't take it. Maybe it seems even more jarring since I've been away from it for four weeks or maybe she's had four weeks to not talk like this and now it's bubbling over like a pot of water on the stove. No matter. It needs to stop.

"I know that, Mom. I'll tell you when I'm ready."

"Tell me what?" She squeaks like I'm hiding something major, something like Golfy and I are engaged or who knows what.

"Nothing! There's nothing to tell. Mom. Stop. For real." I brush some hair away from my face and walk on ahead of her. Today was the day I was supposed to have an open dialogue with my dad, not her. And here I am feeling the need to have an open dialogue with both of them. She may need a refresher on the talk I had with her two years ago—about understanding that I'm growing up, that I'm not a baby anymore.

"Hello, Nodbergs!" we hear someone say, and I zip around to find Zoe and her dad on the hill a little bit behind us. My mom struts over to them like she's best friends with Robert Irwin Krieger, and I jog a little to catch up with them. Gemma and my dad are having a catch in front of her bunk, and I'm not sure they heard.

"Hello, Robert," my mom says, all formal-sounding and weird. I don't understand how she doesn't know how to talk to people or be normal. I don't get how she's gotten through life this weird and awkward. "How's summer treating you?"

Everything she says annoys me. Literal nails on a chalkboard.

"It's been wonderful. I've been in Brookside a bunch, and Colleen and I have been in the city a bunch, too. We're going out to the Hamptons next weekend."

I look at Zoe as he talks and I wonder how she feels. It's different than with Kaylan's dad and his new wife because her mom died and her dad is alone and I know she wants him to be happy. It's not like he had a choice. But I wonder if it also feels icky and weird and uncomfortable. I don't know. She shuffles her feet on the grass and looks at me, doing her signature Zoe eye-bulge, lips-curved-down thing, and I crack up.

"Zo, come talk to me. I need to ask you something." I pull her off to the side and we sit down against a tree. "I can't deal with visiting day." I almost said I can't deal with my mom but I always feel weird saying that to her. It seems cruel.

"Same, it's the most awkward day. I'm always relieved when it's over." She makes a braid out of strands of grass and then tucks it in my hair in an artful kind of way. "Is it total wackiness that I could be stepsisters with your BFF one day? I mean, take a step back. This is super wacky."

"It is wacky. When Kaylan and I put *find the perfect man for Kaylan's mom* on our list last summer, I'm not sure we thought we were going to actually accomplish it."

"You're super weird to even put that on a list. You know this, right?"

I laugh and lie back on the grass. "Yeah, we are weird.

That's why we love each other. We're both super, super weird."

A few moments later, Robert Irwin Krieger and my mom walk over and then Gemma and my dad, too, and I'm still lying on the grass trying to relax and not get bogged down with visiting day.

"I'm gonna take Gemma boating," my mom says. "Anyone want to join?"

When my dad doesn't jump in and answer, I say, "Actually, Dad, want to spend some Dad-Ari time?"

He hesitates. "Um, yeah, um sure."

He's probably so caught off guard since we literally never spend time just the two of us, and when we do it's sort of this awkward silence where he looks at me like I'm an alien and not the daughter he's known for thirteen and three-quarter years.

"I thought maybe we could walk over to the pottery studio," I say. "I wanted to show it to you."

Truthfully he doesn't care about pottery, but I couldn't think of anything else and I needed to say something.

Gemma and my mom get ready for the lake and my dad and I wait for them on Adirondack chairs on Gemma's porch.

"How's it going, Dad?" I ask. "Bubbie writes me every week and it's amazing. She may teach me Yiddish when I get home! It's kind of incredible she's made such an awesome recovery."

"Yeah," he replies. "Very good."

He's quiet in a way that seems off, even for him. Like there's something he's not telling me.

"She's okay, right?"

"She is okay," he answers. "But, Ari, she does struggle. We can't deny the fact that she can't do all the things she used to do. There are good days and bad days."

"I know that. I mean, yeah. Of course. But even still."

We're quiet then, and when Gemma and my mom come out ready for boating, we walk down the hill with them.

"Have fun," I say when we get to the lake.

My dad and I walk around camp and the awkward silence is so awkward that I regret putting this on the list. I start to wonder if I'll regret everything that I put on the list and maybe that means all the things are on it for a reason. Or maybe on one list I should put *something you won't regret later on*, but how can I really know that at the time I make the list? I can't.

"So, Dad," I start. "I just wanted to have a little chat with you about our relationship." I debate telling him it's for the list since he knows about the lists because he's always our laminator. Maybe I'll get to that later.

"Okay . . ."

I wait for him to ask a question or two, but nothing. He's just quiet.

"For example, this moment, right now." I pause. "I don't

feel like we're connecting. I don't feel like you get me."

"I get you, Ari. I love you. You know that, right?"

"Yeah, I know that. But I wish we could be closer. I feel like things are awkward between us sometimes."

"Oh, um. I didn't realize you felt that way." He stops walking and rubs his head.

"Come, let's go sit over here." I guide him to Green House Lawn, and we sit on benches across from one another. "I'm not bringing this up to be mean or anything, and I know it may seem like it's coming from out of the blue. I just want to have a closer relationship with you. That's all."

"Go on."

I sit back on the bench. "It seems like it's always Mom running the show and you just go along with it. But then other times it just seems like you're kind of absent. I don't know."

"I have a lot on my mind, Ar." He looks up at me with his sad eyes, like he carries a small house on each of his shoulders. "I'm not absent. I'm here. Usually struggling to try to figure out how we can make everything wonderful for you and Gemma."

I'm quiet; my throat is lumpy.

"So it's not that I'm not aware of everything or thinking about it. I'm actually thinking about everything all the time, but trying not to make that your problem."

"Okay, well, I'm glad you told me now. For so long it

seemed like you don't know how to talk to me, like it's always strained between us. I don't want that."

"I don't want that either." He sniffles. For a second I think he might cry but then I realize that it's actually only allergies. "I'm glad we had this talk. And I'm really going to make more of an effort. Maybe we can do once-a-month dinners, just the two of us, or once a week, even. We'll see." He pauses and his eyes look brighter. "You're growing up so fast. I want to savor the time we have while you're at home."

He sniffles a little and when I look up at him, I see that he really is crying a bit. He wipes a few tears away with his knuckle. Seeing my dad cry makes me cry and soon we're both sobbing, side by side. He puts an arm over my shoulder and we stay like that for a few minutes.

"I hope you know you can always come to me," he says. "To talk about important stuff or silly stuff or any stuff." He pauses. "Hopefully it snows a lot this winter so we can take out the food coloring and dye the snow again like we did when you were little."

"I hope so. That would be fun."

"Ari!" I hear someone yell, and without even seeing him I know that it's Golfy. He's walking by with his parents and his sisters and I'm having a flashback to visiting day last year when I was so nervous.

"Hello, Mr. Nodberg." My dad gets up and he shakes Golfy's hand like they're friendly but not best friends.

Like maybe they're passing each other at temple after Friday night services.

"Hello, Golfy," my dad replies like it's painful for him to call him that and he wishes he could just call him Jonah but he knows he can't.

They chat for a second and then my dad starts talking to Golfy's parents. Golfy's sisters run off to hug people and Golfy and I share a bench. He puts his arm around me and then pulls it away and then puts it around me again.

"Is this weird? To sit here like this in front of our parents?" he whispers.

"Not really. I don't think so." I laugh for a second. "How's visiting day so far?"

"Pretty chill. We had a pizza picnic from Four Brothers and then went out for ice cream—espresso cookie, of course—and now we're back. We may go boating or swim or who knows."

"Nice." I look up at him. I want to count his freckles. Or maybe take a pen and connect them. They're the perfect golden brown, not too dark but not too light.

"Listen." Golfy leans in closer to me and whispers, "Noah was telling me that they definitely don't lock the golf carts at night. Get this." He taps my knee, all excited. "They leave the keys right in them. We can totally do this. Seems way easier than I thought at first."

"Really?" My stomach flips over a few times.

"Yeah, let's wait until, like, the second-to-last night of camp, and then just take a golf cart, drive a little together, and then return it. It'll be so fun."

"What if we get caught?" I ask, and look up at our parents chatting, hoping they can't hear our discussion. They seem to be talking about mortgage rates and if it's feasible to buy a second home in the Berkshires near camp and rent it out for ski season.

"We'll be okay," he assures me, and I mostly believe him, but not one hundred percent.

"Let's think on it a little more." I rest my head on his shoulder and then pick it up when I see my dad glancing at us in a lovey but too dad-ish kind of way.

My parents, Gemma, and I spend the rest of visiting day walking around and swimming and touring the pottery studio. Then they head to Gemma's bunk to finish packing and load all of her stuff into the car.

"Sure you don't want to stay, Gem?" my dad asks for the hundredth time.

"Sure. But I had fun," Gemma reassures them. "Thanks for your help with that, Ari."

"Anytime," I reply. "Actually, not anytime because I don't think I'll need to do it again. But you know what I mean. Anyway, make sure you take care of Lion until I get home, Gem!"

Later that night, I'm in my bed ruminating about the day and the talk with my dad. I JHH the talk by myself in an understated kind of way so my bunkmates don't think I've lost my mind.

I think about Golfy and the golf cart and if we should do it or not, and what would happen if we got caught and kicked out of camp. Would we be kicked out for life or just this summer? I don't know.

I take out my clipboard with my stationery and write to Kaylan.

Dear Kay,

How are you? I can't wait to hear all about visiting day. I just JHH'd the talk with my dad thing. It went pretty well. I'm not sure we really uncovered anything too amazing but we did have a talk and I do see his point of view and that he has a lot on his mind and all of that. I hope he sees mine. I think we're gonna try and make more of an effort with our relationship.

How are things with Otis? Are you a couple? Will you stay together when you get home? What about Indigo? How far does she live from us? She sounds cool. I want to meet her.

I can't believe I only have three more weeks here. Why does time at camp go by so much faster than time at home? I bet you're so sad to leave Laurel Lake and I am so sorry. That is the worst feeling. Leaving camp is a deep-pit-in-your-stomach kind of sadness. It takes so long for it to go away. The only thing that'll cheer you up is counting down to next summer. Trust me on that one.

I'm just realizing I need to send this letter to your home

address. If I send it to camp you'll be gone before it arrives. Oh, that just made me so sad. I didn't even realize the last letter I wrote you at Laurel Lake was the last camp letter. Isn't that strange? How we rarely know the last time we do something is actually the last? I guess in this case I could've realized but in life we can't. Like when we turned my basement into Barbie World and would spend hours playing, we didn't know the last time we played Barbies was the last time, but we haven't done it in over two years. Do you know what I mean? Sorry this letter is so rambly. I feel so emotional. I just love camp so much. And I miss you. And I want to savor all the moments here but I am so excited to see you at home, too.

And I love Golfy. I know that now. One hundred percent. Please remind me of this in February when I forget because it's freezing and dreary and blah.

I love him. He's just so magical.

Ew, how cheesy am I right now?

Okay, I need to stop this letter because I'm freaking myself out.

I LOVE YOU, KAYLAN MARIE TERREL!!!!!!!!!!

xoxoxoxo Arianna Simone Nodberg, the magnificent

23

KAYLAN

"WHAT'S YOUR UN-TALENT GONNA BE?" Indigo asks me after we've showered. We're in towels, with little water-absorbing wraps on our heads, and we're lotioning up, soaking in that amazing shower-after-a-hot-day feeling.

The talent show at Laurel Lake is actually called an un-talent show. Since we're all here for talents basically, the talent show is not a time to showcase them. That happens every day in each of our focuses.

The un-talent show is what happens the last night of camp. It's basically an open mic kind of thing and everyone can just go up and do whatever they want. It's a Laurel Lake tradition and sometimes it goes until midnight. They only stop it when there's no one else who wants to perform.

"I don't know. Something funny, obviously," I explain.

"But not too over-the-top funny."

"Yeah."

"What about you?" I ask her, digging through my drawers for my black tank top.

"I wanna sing random songs," she tells me. "All on a theme . . ."

I think she's waiting for me to say I want to do that with her, and I kind of do. "Ooh! What about if all the songs had the same word in the title?"

She grabs a white sundress off a hanger. "Yes! We have time to practice. But it'll be even funnier if we don't practice."

I smile. She's right. Maybe she should've been in the comedy concentration. "Sounds good, Indi."

I pause a minute and look at her and get this throat burn all-over-sad feeling. I'm going to miss sharing a room with her, miss our talks, miss her perspective on life. On the bus I thought Cleo would be my instant BFF, and she's fine and cool and whatever, but Indi is something special. I wish Cleo could see that; I wish everyone could see that.

"I'm gonna miss you, Indi," I say softly because I'm not sure how sappy I should really get. For all of her deep thinking, she's not super cheesy or sappy or emotional. She just is. Matter-of-fact. Honest. Aware. "Promise we can keep in touch?"

"Of course, Kay. Literally, how is that even a question?"

She faces the closet and slips the sundress over her head. "I can take the train anywhere, so does your town have a train station?"

"It does." I smile.

"Then I'm there. I'll show up at your doorstep when you least expect it." She widens her eyes, all spooky. "I'll just hang until you get home. I won't break in or anything."

I laugh a little and say, "How come your parents let you do whatever you want? Do you love it so much?"

"Sometimes yes. Sometimes no." She sits back on her bed and puts her feet up on the footboard. "I wish they cared more, but they're so into being busy with their own stuff and they know I can handle it, so that's just how it is."

I feel sad for her right then, picturing her lonely at home, roaming around. She reminds me of Harriet the Spy in a way, without the spying, I guess, and without the nanny or the cook. I don't actually know what it is. But they seem similar.

She goes on, "I'm not gonna be like that. I'm not like that now. I think there's an art in stillness, an art in just gazing out a window or relaxing on a porch or being alone with your thoughts."

I listen to her talk and kind of wish I could take notes and write down what she says. She's so wise but I'm not sure she realizes it, which makes her even wiser.

"Anyway, so, yeah, I can basically do whatever I want."

She giggles. "I'll come over all the time if you want me to. And I can't wait to meet Ari."

"She's gonna love you, Indi. For real. I see you guys totally bonding."

We talk for a little while longer and we discuss the ideas she's written down for her list.

"Here's what I have so far," she says.

Indigo's 13 Things to Become MORE AWESOME AS I EMBARK ON TEENAGERHOOD List

1. *Eat as many different cuisines as I can.*
2. *Find all the bridges that have walking paths and walk across them.*
3. *Babysit for some of the kids in my building.*
4. *Call my grandma once a week.*

"I love it," I tell her. "But you may need a few silly ones sprinkled in."

"I'm not so good at silly," she admits. "People tell me all the time I'm an old soul, and I think that's why I have trouble making friends. I can't be goofy enough."

"There you go!" I exclaim. "Be more silly! Or do something silly once a week! Anything like that. Could be so great! And it's an area you want to work on." I get so excited about this because she's already awesome but she's going to become even more awesome. "Add that to the list!"

This is totally making a difference. No one can deny it.

One hundred percent I am making a difference in Indigo's life.

I lie back on my bed for a few moments before we need to go to dinner and I put my arms behind my head and I think about the summer here. I feel good. It's truly been everything I hoped for and more.

Sometimes, though, in moments of gratitude, I'm instantly plagued by little agita bubbles. I don't know why it happens or how it happens and it almost seems like my brain is trying to play tricks on me. I have agita about my dad and his person moving to Brookside and what it'll do to my mom and to Ryan and to me.

Not now, agita bubble. Go away. I'll deal with you later.

Indigo and I walk over to dinner together and we keep talking about her list and what she'll do at home the rest of the summer. It cheers me up a little, and pulls me out of the agita funk.

"Read a lot, I guess," she says. "And then my parents always plan a trip for the whole family at the end of August. We all go to Maine and drive through the whole state and try to eat a lobster roll in each town. We go in separate cars but it's like a caravan. It's kind of fun. Actually it is fun. It's probably my favorite family tradition."

"That sounds awesome, Indi." I link arms with her. "Wait, I just realized something. We never discussed when you're starting the list or your timeline or deadline or anything."

"Maybe I should do the whole school year," she muses. "Start on the first day of school and end on the last?"

"Yeah, that's great. Ari and I have never done one like that but there's so much growth in a school year. It could be really interesting."

"I think so, too," she says. "And the title of the list is pretty open ended, so that's good."

We get closer to the dining hall and Otis is waiting outside for us (I guess me, but he's kind to Indigo and includes her in stuff) on the usual bench.

"Hey," he says, his eyes bright. "Can't wait for all the un-talents."

"Me too!" Indi says. "One of the best nights of the summer."

"I'm so excited to see this," I add. "I hope it's laughs all night. Just an endless variety of people's un-talents."

We giggle about it for a few minutes and walk into the dining hall, and Indigo says, "Is it so shallow to put on the list something like *get a boyfriend*? I'm so not like that but just seeing how much Otis likes you, ya know. I'm jealous. I want that, too."

"Not shallow." I put an arm around her. "Let's discuss later."

After dinner, we all walk to the main theater, bubbly with excitement for the un-talent show.

Cleo and her friends go first, and if this had happened

at the beginning of the summer and I wasn't included, I'd have probably been upset, but the thing is, I'm actually okay with it now. Actually okay for once with not being part of one friend group and being with another (in this case Indigo).

This is a big thing for me, and a huge sign of growth. I feel like my whole life since the Brooke and Lily debacle and their breakup with me has been a stressful sense of needing to be part of a crew, needing to be surrounded by people, included in whatever *the group* was doing.

Their un-talent is a group staring contest and it's actually pretty funny because they sit up there staring at each other until one falls over laughing.

Chad and his friends try to read Shakespeare together and they're dumb about it and I'm not impressed. At least he doesn't bother me anymore, though. I consider that a success. I can count that as *making a difference*, I think. Getting him to realize that his words and behaviors were sexist.

Otis and some of his friends do three versions of this thing called *The Bean Skit* where they basically do the same thing every time but at the end the person playing the director tells them to do it differently: slower, faster, while hopping up and down. Everyone cracks up harder and louder with each time.

Finally, Indigo and I go up onstage. Before the show, Indigo gave the counselor in charge of music a list of our songs, they all have the word *girl* in them.

We sing parts of all of them—"Brown Eyed Girl," "Girls Just Want to Have Fun," "Uptown Girl," "My Girl"—as loud as possible, using the hairbrushes we brought with us as microphones. Everyone claps along and laughs, and at the end Indigo and I grab hands and bow. The whole world feels euphoric and fizzy.

When we're back sitting down, I lean over and whisper in her ear. "Indi, forgot to tell you something."

Her eyebrows curve inward. "What?"

"I'm not doing the thing with Rob and Paul anymore." I pause and realize I should stop talking because people are performing. "It doesn't feel right. For the first time in list-making history, something just didn't feel right."

She nods and thinks for a moment. "Let's dig deep on this later, okay? When no one else is around."

"K." I smile.

At the end of the un-talent show everyone goes to the lake for extended hammock time and it's pretty much just mass chaos of kids running around and people hanging out and finally the lifeguards go up in the high chairs because so many people are jumping in the lake with their clothes on.

"Does this happen every summer?" I ask Indi as we're side by side on a hammock.

"Pretty much, yeah."

We swing back and forth together, and I try to soak in

all of this moment, every drop.

A little bit later, Otis runs up to me, all out of breath.

"Kaylan! I need to talk to you!"

He grabs my hand and I hop off the hammock, feeling a little guilty about leaving Indi there by herself.

"What's up?" I ask when we're off to the side a little bit.

"I'm staying for second session," he says. "I called home, I got permission, and my parents said I could stay. I know it's not a huge thing here, but I want to keep working on my comedy and hopefully do some of the kid open mics this year in the city and places, I don't know, and I just love it here, and I want to stay." He stops talking and grabs my hands. "Can you stay, too? Pretty please. It would be so amazing. More time with you. More hammock time, specifically." He laughs. He knows that's my favorite.

"Otis, that's so awesome." My skin prickles with jealousy. "I can't stay, though. Money is super tight for my family and it was a huge deal for me to even come for four weeks, and I need to get home, and I miss my mom and . . ."

I stop talking because I'd love to stay. For comedy, of course, and for Otis and for the hammock time and the lake and all of it, really.

"Are you sure you can't stay?" Otis looks at me through his gigantic green eyes.

"I can't. But I will keep in touch and I'll write you

letters." I pause. "And you will write to me and we will look up at the sky at the same exact minute every night and we'll feel together." I sniffle because I do wish I could stay.

He stands there and stares at me like maybe I'll change my mind. But I won't. I can't.

Softly, I say, "Please come knock on my window tonight, after lights-out. So we can have a few quiet minutes to say goodbye."

"Don't say this, Kaylan!" he yell-cries, all over the top like he's a character in an old movie who is going off to war. "Don't say it!"

"Shh." I laugh and give him a quick kiss on the cheek.

As I walk back over to Indi on the hammock, I notice Rob and Paul talking to each other, and even though they might like each other, there's also a chance they don't see each other that way at all. And that's okay. That's for them to figure out, not me.

I think it's good that the list led me to realize this.

Led Ari to realize it, too. I'm so glad we could discuss this in our letters, even though we're far away from each other. The list works wonders in so many ways, especially now, keeping us close when we're apart.

Sometimes failure can also be disguised as success.

24

ARI

ONCE GEMMA GOES HOME AND second session starts, it feels like there's a countdown clock to the last day at Camp Silver and not in a good way. It's true that there are some campers who only come for second session and I get their excitement, but for the rest of us, it feels like the end is near. Too near.

We seem to move slower, and maybe it's because we want time to go backward and this is our way of maybe making that happen.

A few days into second session, I wake up way before everyone else and I look over the list for the zillionth time. It calms me, and also helps to remind me of all the things I'm going to do when I get home, so maybe leaving camp won't be as hard.

I haven't worked on the language thing at all, but it's

okay; we agreed to wait until we got home for that.

Deep in my heart, I hope I can convince Kaylan that the language should be Hebrew. And if that's the case, I'll be medium prepared. If not, we might have to really take Bubbie up on the Yiddish thing and study every day with her. Or I guess we could sign up for a crash course online.

Ari and Kaylan's 13¾ Things to Build and Improve on Our Complete and Total Amazingness

1. Perform in a camp talent show. ✓

2. Write at least one letter to each other a week. ✓

3. Sneak out of the bunk at night without getting caught. ✓

4. Keep a gratitude journal. ✓

5. ~~Get two counselors to fall in love~~ Learn to accept failure.

6. Be able to have a full conversation in another language. (TO COME)

7. Draw a portrait of each other from memory. (TO COME)

8. Do something daring. (still TBD)

9. Get a younger kid at camp and/or at home to start their own list. ✓

10. Master the art of tie-dye. ✓

11. Make a difference. ✓

12. Tell our dads one thing we'd like to improve about our

relationship with them. ✓

13. Make a time capsule to capture our lives at exactly 13¾ years old and bury it somewhere in Brookside. (TO COME)

13 ¾. Keep our friendship strong. (always, ongoing, forever and ever and ever so ✓)

I think more about the *make a difference* thing and I decide that I have made a difference—in the lives of my friends, in Gemma's life, in Gaux's life—who knows what else. Is it enough? I don't know. Is it ever enough? I also don't know.

Once you start making a difference, you want to keep doing it.

I guess that's the point.

After a little while of being the only one up in the bunk, and stressing in my bed, I go outside to the porch. I look around at camp first thing in the morning—the mist on the grass glistening in the early sunlight. The sense of sleepiness, quiet, stillness. I love it here. I love being away from everything at home, on my own, in this space that feels mine.

I wonder if the best version of myself is someone who is off on her own, exploring and figuring things out. Independent.

Pretty soon the rest of the girls in the bunk wake up and we're all getting ready for breakfast and my thoughts wind down for a bit.

"Would your parents ever let you go to boarding school?" I ask Alice as we walk down the hill for breakfast.

"Um, doubt it?" She seems far away, like she's not paying attention. "You're obsessed with this, Ari."

I giggle. "Would you ever want to go?"

"Not really. I like home and my home friends. I mean, I like it here and you guys more but I like them, too." She's quiet then and I wait for her to talk so I'm not bombarding her with questions, but she stays silent.

"You okay, AlKal?"

Alice looks at me and then pulls me off to the side, behind a tree. She puts her hands on my shoulders. "I need to tell you something."

"What?"

She looks down at the ground and then back up at me and our eyes meet.

"I snuck out of the bunk last night, and Oren and I kissed."

"AlKal! That's amazing! Your first camp kiss. I didn't even know you were planning this!"

"My first ever kiss." She pauses. "I'd always been lying during Truth or Dare. Don't hate. Okay?"

"I don't hate. I get it." I pause. "But why do you look so distraught? Was it a bad kiss?"

"We got caught." She looks down at the ground. "Rachel

caught us and she said we'd deal with it in the morning and now it's the morning and what if we get kicked out of camp?"

I'm speechless then, really and truly. No clue what to say. What if she does get kicked out of camp? What would I do without her? I want to tell her that everything will be okay but I don't know that for sure. I don't want to be that person who just spews out stuff and then can't follow through or back it up.

She says it again. "What if we get kicked out of camp? I mean, I thought we were okay since you and Golfy literally slept outside that whole night and no one caught you." She pauses and wipes her eyes. She's crying.

"Oh, Al." I wrap her in a hug. "This is terrible. And we can't even focus on the magic of a first kiss and the extra magic of a first camp kiss! And with Oren! He is so cute. And Israeli! AlKal, I am so sorry."

She starts sobbing onto my shoulder. Thick, splotchy, watery tears that land right on my T-shirt. And she stays there sobbing and sobbing and sobbing. I don't know what to say.

"I hate to get in trouble," she adds finally. "Hate it hate it hate it. I hate to disappoint and have people be upset with me. And Oren's in trouble, too. And what if they call our parents?"

We keep walking, smooshed together. "I don't know. Maybe we can talk to Rachel. Or maybe I can say something. Or maybe we can convince her this was a one-time thing and of course it won't happen again."

I stop talking, and we inch away from each other a little bit. I'm fired up that we can change this or talk our way out of it. I know I didn't do it, but somehow I feel involved. I want to help. Maybe this is another little category of my *make a difference* thing.

She perks up a little. "Do you really think so? Do you think there's a way out of this and I'll get to stay at camp?"

"I don't know." I hug her again. "But I want to try. Come, let's walk to the dining hall and we'll find Rachel before she finds you and you'll say how sorry you are, and maybe that you and Oren had to discuss something private and maybe it wasn't the right time and you know you did the wrong thing . . ."

"Okay." She nods superfast like she's taking it all in, and is the tiniest bit hopeful that this can work and she'll find a way out of this. "Thank you so much, Ari. Thank you for trying. I can't believe I was so stupid."

We get to the dining hall and take our usual seat at our bunk table in the back by the salad bar.

"Should we go talk to her now?" Alice whispers.

It seems Hana, Zoe, and the other girls in the bunk don't know what happened. I feel awkward about it but there's nothing I can do.

"After the blessings," I say.

Once the blessings are finished and everyone is

milling about, pouring orange juice and going up to the cereal and oatmeal bar, I tap Alice's knee, signaling that it's time to go. We make our way through the dining hall and find Rachel at the unit head table at the front near the stage.

"Hi, Rachel," I say, confident yet polite. "Can we talk to you for a second?"

She hesitates a little but then gets up and we walk outside the dining hall together.

I nudge Alice to talk first.

"Um, I just wanted to say I'm really sorry about leaving the bunk after hours." She sniffles and it's hard for her to get the words out. "I am so, so sorry. I had to talk to Oren about something private and we shouldn't have been out of the bunk at night but we were and I am just so sorry." After that she starts full-on bawling—deep, heavy sobs. "I am so sorry. Please don't make me leave camp. It's my favorite place in the entire world."

I look at Rachel, trying to figure out how she's going to respond.

She's quiet as she shuffles her feet, her arms folded across her chest. She looks down at the pavement. "Alice, this is serious. You know that, right?"

Alice sniffles and nods, not making eye contact.

"So I'm not sure what's going to happen exactly. I'm discussing with the directors." She looks off into the distance. "I wish I could give you a definitive answer but being caught out of your bunk at night is very dangerous. We can't allow it to happen."

"I understand," Alice says through her tears.

"We totally get this," I chime in. "And Alice is so, so sorry and she understands how dangerous it is and she's even willing to lead a program for the younger kids about it. . . ."

Alice looks at me, head crooked, confused. I am not sure where I just pulled this from, but it seems like the right kind of solution, or, um, punishment I guess.

"Interesting idea, Ari. I'll consider it. Now please go finish breakfast."

We walk on in front of Rachel but we don't go back to the table. Instead we go into one of the bathroom stalls together, and make sure it's locked, and Alice sobs onto my shoulder again. My T-shirt hadn't even dried completely from the last cry-fest.

"What am I gonna do, Ar?" She sniffles. "My parents are gonna kill me, and how embarrassing that I have to tell them I was with a boy. Oh my goodness, things were way easier when I just stuck with you guys and didn't care about boys and why did I do this to myself?"

She goes on and on forever and people come in and out of the bathroom and breakfast is probably ending soon and I have no idea what to do and I sort of feel like this was my fault because Golfy and I didn't get caught.

"It's gonna be okay, Al. For real. You said you were

sorry. I'm sure people have done much worse stuff. I mean, what's the story about that group of kids who painted peace signs all over Pink House in the middle of the night? They didn't get kicked out. I think they just had to do a major camp cleanup and repaint the building. I mean, people do crazy pranks and, like, actual bad stuff. I don't think this is a get-kicked-out kind of thing. I think Rachel just wants you to feel bad; she wants you to be scared."

Alice looks up at me then through swollen eyes, her cheeks all red and splotchy. "You think?"

"I do. But we need to go. It sounds really quiet. I think breakfast is over and we have to get back to the bunk for nikayon. We don't want to get in trouble." We giggle and leave the stall, and I wash my hands because truthfully I feel kind of dirty after being in here for so long.

The rest of the day goes in slow motion because I'm so nervous about Alice and her punishment and it's too hard to think about anything else. Finally when it's lights-out and I'm under the covers, I decide to write to Kaylan. Maybe I'll just casually mention the boarding school thing.

Dear Kay,

I can't believe you're home! How is it? Are you settling in okay? I miss you! Things are so amazing here and I am so sad that time is winding down. I never want to leave camp! I'm sure you understand that now. I had this idea—what if I went to boarding school? What if we went together? Would that be so crazy? I mean, I know we love our families but they hold us back sometimes. I want to be free. I want to be on my own. I want things to feel like camp year-round. I just get so antsy and tied down feeling at home. What do you think? Here I feel like the best version of myself.

Write back soon.

xoxoxoxoxoo Ari

The next morning at breakfast, Rachel taps Alice on the shoulder, and they walk outside the dining hall together. Oren is with them as well as Seth, one of the assistant directors.

Last night, Alice filled Hana and Zoe in on the whole situation, so I whisper, "Zo, let's go eavesdrop. Come on."

"Huh? I'm still asleep." She spoons some cereal into her mouth like a zombie.

"Just come," I hiss.

Hana joins, too, and the three of us get up from the table, staggered so it's not too obvious, and walk over to one of the open windows at the front of the dining hall.

"This is serious," Rachel says. "Do you understand?"

We can't hear any responses. I assume they're nodding.

"We've spent a good deal of time thinking about your punishment," Seth says. "And I know you two are good campers, and this was a mistake and it won't happen again. Correct?"

Again, silence. Again, I assume nodding. We are standing on the other side of the window so they can't see us.

"We're not going to kick you out of camp," Rachel says. I breathe the deepest sigh of relief. So deep someone could swim in it. "But here's the thing." She pauses and my deep sigh of relief turns shallow, hesitant, pretty unreliable. "You'll be doing early morning *toranut* for the next week. You'll assist the bunk that is on duty and do whatever you can to help."

I look at Zoe and Hana and we cover our mouths to prevent laughter from leaking out.

"That's the punishment?" I mouth. I mean, sure, it's less than ideal to wake up early and help set up the whole dining hall for breakfast since Alice isn't really a morning person. But, hello! More one-on-one time with Oren, and it's not like it's that labor intensive to put out plates and cups and bowls and pitchers of orange juice.

"Thank you sooooooooo much," Alice says. "For real, thank you. I am so, so, so, so, so sorry and it won't happen again."

Zoe rolls her eyes. "Yeah right," she whispers.

I put a finger to my lips, shhing her. "Let's go back to the table so AlKal doesn't know we were eavesdropping. Come on."

We run back and our counselors look half confused

about where we've been, but they're so sleepy they don't seem to have the energy to find out.

"Guys," Alice says, sitting down and hugging me at the same time. "I'm good. I'm not kicked out. Most relieved I've ever been in my whole life."

Zoe, Hana, and I pretend to be surprised.

"Best news ever," I say.

I rip open a carton of chocolate milk and lift it up to cheers with Alice's carton.

"*L'chaim.*" I clink the carton against Alice's even though there's no clink because it's paper. "To life. Our best life ever at Camp Silver."

The whole table starts laughing and maybe I had something to do with Alice being able to stay or maybe I didn't.

Hard to say.

25

KAYLAN

"I NEED TO TALK TO you," my mom says a few nights after I've been back. We're cuddly on the couch, watching a cooking show and eating mini peanut butter crackers. She sounds like my dad with her ominous, cryptic vibe, and it scares me.

"Okay . . ." I stay focused on the cooking show. They're working on an easy lemon ricotta pasta and it truly looks and sounds delicious.

She taps my knee. "Sit up, Kay. Let me see your face."

Uh-oh. This can't be good.

"I hope you will see this as lovely, positive news but I understand that you may not, and I want you to know I will love you forever no matter what. I am not expecting you to be happy for me, but I am expecting you to respect my choices. If possible."

She stops talking and I feel like I'm about to pass out. This is not how one should talk to an agita-inflicted person. Not at all. I'm surprised she doesn't know this.

"So please listen to me. And please hear me out," she continues, almost waiting for me to jump in. But I'm too scared to speak.

"Mom, please just say it. Whatever it is doesn't need this kind of buildup. Truthfully nothing needs this kind of buildup. It's always best just to jump right in and say whatever it is." I can't look at her. I stare at the TV, waiting for her to speak, wishing I had a plate of this lemon ricotta pasta.

"Robert and I are engaged." She says it all matter-of-fact, no emotion in her tone or her words. "We don't know when we'll get married. It's most likely years away. We're figuring out the logistics, but we love each other and we want to be together."

Ew. Hearing a grown-up, especially your mom, say *we love each other* just sounds gross. I don't know why. I guess Ari and I played a pretty big role in this so maybe part of me should feel proud? Excited, even. But no. I just feel grossed out and blindsided and one hundred percent weirded out.

"Any thoughts?" my mom asks.

I can feel that my mouth is hanging open. It feels dry, like I need a gigantic glass of ice water. It feels like even if words did try to come out, they'd be pushed back like balls against the bumpers at a bowling alley.

"Um," I finally manage to say. "Congratulations."

"Thank you." She rolls her lips together like even the two sort-of words I said have gotten her choked up. "I've been trying to talk to you about this. And I know it's hard and I know you don't want to hear it. So I wasn't sure how much of it you were really digesting. And I didn't want to talk too much about it before camp because I didn't want you to worry while you were away." She pauses. "I love you, Kaylan. I hope you can see that he makes me happy."

"I am happy for you, Mom. I want you to be happy. I just don't know what to make of this. Will he come live with us, and what about Zoe? I mean, she loves her school. And I love Brookside so we're not moving." I pause. "We're not moving, right? I don't see us as city people."

"It's not happening right away. This could be years off," my mom says. "It's complicated."

"Mom." The word comes out forceful and I turn myself so I'm facing her more directly. "What does that mean?"

She sighs. "It means I don't know what we're doing. We really don't know."

I start to think about the fact that it seems there's more she doesn't know than she actually does, and also wonder why I needed to know this now if there's so much they still need to figure out.

"So what are the next steps or what?" I don't even know what to ask her, or how to feel, or where to go from here.

"We're figuring things out. I just wanted to make sure I didn't keep anything from you. I wanted to be upfront." She readjusts herself on the couch and sips her seltzer. "I wanted to make sure you were clear on what was going on."

"Um, okay. Well, congrats, and thanks, I guess." I get up and grab my water glass. "I need to head to bed. Love you, Mom."

"Love you!" she yells back when I'm halfway out of the room.

After I'm upstairs and cozy in my bed, I start to realize how miserable I feel: I miss Laurel Lake. I miss Otis and Indigo. Ari's not home. Most of the lunch table girls are away, too, but even still I don't feel like making plans with them. The reentry to life at home is too exhausting. And now this with my mom.

I take out the list and look it over, hoping that it calms me. I'll keep working on my Hebrew but maybe there's something else I can do before Ari gets here. Something to help me keep busy.

Ari and Kaylan's 13 ¾ Things to Build and Improve on Our Complete and Total Amazingness

1. Perform in a camp talent show. ✓
2. Write at least one letter to each other a week. ✓

3. Sneak out of the bunk at night without getting caught. ✓

4. Keep a gratitude journal. ✓

5. Get two counselors to fall in love. (ADMIT FAILURE HERE BUT LEARNING TOOK PLACE TOO)

6. Be able to have a full conversation in another language. (SOON)

7. Draw a portrait of each other from memory. (SOON)

8. Do something daring. ✓

9. Get a younger kid at camp and/or at home to start their own list. ✓

10. Master the art of tie-dye. ✓

11. Make a difference. (always ongoing but JHH'd)

12. Tell our dads one thing we'd like to improve about our relationship with them. ✓

13. Make a time capsule to capture our lives at exactly 13¾ years old and bury it somewhere in Brookside. (SOON)

13 ¾. Keep our friendship strong. (ALWAYS & FOREVER)

Reading an almost-complete list is pure awesomeness. And all of the beautiful check marks of things I've finished—amazing. It takes the sting away. All of the other things that are bugging me are there, too, but they don't totally take over my mind.

Tomorrow morning I'll go say hi to my neighbor Mrs. Etisof and tell her I'm home and maybe I can draw Ari's portrait on her beautiful front porch while she paints. She likes to call it her painting porch.

Just the thought of Mrs. Etisof is calming. She's basically human ocean sounds, also a soft blanket against your face.

I take out my gratitude journal and think back to the quote I found years ago: *Interrupt anxiety with gratitude.* At the time, it spoke to me, but it speaks to me even more now that I'm actually practicing gratitude on a daily basis. When you take the time to think about being appreciative and thankful, your mind takes a step away from agita. Gratitude is a literal stop sign on the road of anxiety.

Surviving salmon patties.
My room still being all neat and clean.
New magazines waiting to be read.
Looking forward to back-to-school shopping.
The new strawberries and cream lotion I got from the
    drugstore.

After that, I quickly write to Otis.

Dear Otis,
How's Laurel Lake? I miss it so, so much. I still can't believe you stayed. Who is your new comedy partner? I hope he or she is not as amazing as I am. There's no way that's

even possible so I won't worry. ☺

Today at dinner I thought of a new bit. My mom made these disgusting salmon patties. They were made from real salmon and not a can, but still. Anyway, my brother kept groaning "Salmon patties!" and it made me think how funny that would be if we morphed it into a sketch where people blurted out weird foods at inappropriate times like during a major exam or at church or an assembly in school. This kind of sounded funnier in my head, but let me know what you think.

Please write back soon. Get some extra hammock time for me.

Sniff. Sniff. Wish I was there with you.

Bye! Kaylan

I sleep soundly that night in the shirt from Otis that I tie-dyed and the next morning I wake up early—before Ryan or my mom. I'm used to early camp wake-ups and I wonder if I'll ever be able to sleep in again.

Maybe my mom took the day off or maybe she's going in late today. I pull on some shorts and brush my teeth and go outside to see if Mrs. Etisof is on her porch. She's not out yet but I sit on one of our rocking chairs and look out across the street. I take in the sounds of a sleepy, quiet neighborhood. The birds chirping, maybe an automatic sprinkler off in the distance. It feels peaceful. It feels like the world hasn't woken up yet and I've gotten a head start on the day.

I start sketching Ari in my notebook from memory. I picture the curves of her face and her brown hair and her soft but intense smile. I think about her eyes and the way they always focus in on the person she's talking to.

So far what I've drawn is okay, nothing great. More like a slightly-better-than-stick-figure kind of thing. I'll wait until Mrs. Etisof wakes up. She'll be able to give me pointers for sure.

I start thinking about how much of a difference Mrs. Etisof has made in my life, just by being there, by literally living next door to me. It's not like she set out to make a difference, but she did. Maybe I'm overthinking it. Maybe I've made a difference in someone's life without even knowing it. Maybe I'll continue to do that. I hope so, anyway.

After a half hour of me pondering this, I hear the slam of Mrs. Etisof's screen door and the screech of her rocking chair.

"Helllooo," I sing from my porch to hers. "Good morning, sunshine!"

"Kaylan! Is that you?"

I pop up. "It is!"

"Well, come over here and tell me about camp. What are you waiting for, my dear?"

I run down the steps and across the grass and a minute later I'm hugging Mrs. Etisof, breathing in her comforting sort-of old-lady-soap smell.

"You look absolutely breathtaking, Kaylan!" she says. "You've gotten so tall! And so tan!"

"I have?" I screech. "A lot of the camp program I was at was indoors."

She laughs. "Well, you look great. So talk to me. Tell me all. And don't leave out any of the details."

I tell her all about Otis, of course. And Indigo and how she's starting her own list. And I tell her about the Cleo thing and about how for once I didn't care about being part of a crew, how I was happy with Indigo and my gut said that was the right place to be.

"That's growth," she says. "True growth."

"So now I need to draw a portrait of Ari from memory and I was going to wait until she got home, but I kind of need something to keep me occupied," I say. "Until she gets here, I mean. Is it bad that I don't feel like seeing any of my other friends?"

"Nah. You need to take time for that stuff. You'll see them eventually. Wait until you're ready." She tousles my hair and gets up from the chair. "I'll be right back."

I sit on her porch while she's inside and watch the across-the-street neighbors—the Brownsteins—as they get up to start the day. They have girl triplets—maybe kindergarten age or maybe first grade—and it always feels like craziness around their house. They moved here at the beginning of the school year and the girls are adorable but for some reason they're always running out of the house with only half their clothes on.

Ooh! Mother's helper! I can volunteer to help with the kids, play with them, assist in getting them ready for camp. Or basically whatever the mom needs!

I can keep making a difference!

Mrs. Etisof comes back outside with her giant easel and a fresh sketching pad and these thick wonderful pencils that are so perfectly sharpened they could be an art piece in and of themselves.

"This is for you," she tells me. "I'll leave it out all the time, except if it rains. Feel free to use the whole book. Sketch and sketch and sketch. This is a trial and error thing. Lean into your mistakes." She sounds like she's giving some kind of TED Talk and it's all I can do not to laugh. I love what she's saying but her delivery is hilarious.

Bit alert: Woman who always speaks like she's giving a TED Talk. I'll write Otis about it later.

She goes on. "It's okay to fail. It's okay to hate your work. It's okay to hate the process, but you must carry on. You must have faith in your goals and trust yourself that you will see your way through it." She stops finally and sips her coffee. "Now get to work."

I picture Ari again in my mind. At the Brookside Pool, at the lunch table, in my basement playing Barbies. I picture her during a sleepover, cozy in my bed, sitting next to me on the bus, walking around the neighborhood. I picture her at Martin's, eating an egg and cheese sandwich. I picture her at her happy place, Camp Silver.

I get choked up thinking about her. What a gift she is.

My unicorn. I realized it when we were doing the last list. But it's also something I realize again and again all the time.

I'm so glad we put this portrait from memory thing on the list so I could remember this again and again.

My friendship with Ari is the most powerful, important relationship in my life.

My total honesty friend.

My soul sister in every sense of the word.

26

ARI

THE END OF CAMP MOVES at a different pace than the beginning. Second session is a week shorter than first so it already feels abbreviated. And everyone knows the last week of camp is Color War, or as they call it at Camp Silver, Maccabiah. It means *games* in Hebrew and it refers to the "Jewish Olympics," an international Jewish and Israeli multisport event that first took place in the 1930s.

We know Maccabiah happens during the last week; we just don't know *when* exactly. The break—the official over-the-top kickoff—is always a surprise.

So when you think about it, there are only two weeks of regular camp second session. It's not very much. Plus the fact that it's August is on everyone's mind; it changes things. Everyone feels like summer is gonna be over soon.

There's a sadness in the air but also the sense that we

need to savor it all, stretch it, like my bubbie says.

It hits me that stretching things is another way to think about gratitude. Because you're really taking the time to appreciate every part of an experience.

"Imagine if you were really kicked out," I say to Alice. We're hanging on the hill staring at the sky. "I don't know what I would've done."

"It would have been the worst. For real. The absolute worst." She leans back against a tree. "To be honest, early morning toranut was fine today and it was kind of nice to just wake up early and walk down to the hill to the dining hall alone while most of the camp is asleep."

"It's kind of comforting that it's an easy punishment," I admit.

"Agree." She looks at me. "You think they're all talk with the consequences thing?"

"I don't know." I push my sunglasses to the top of my head since it's gotten cloudy all of a sudden. "But Golfy is still all about this golf cart thing and maybe we should just do it? I mean, there's a week and a half of camp left, and—" I stop mid-sentence. It still scares me. I still don't feel great about it. "I mean, we're good kids generally, so they'd probably be forgiving. . . ."

"Do it the last night of camp," Alice says. "That way if you get caught you can't be kicked out."

"But then what if they don't let us come back next summer?"

"I doubt they'd do that," she says.

The thing is, Alice doesn't sound one hundred percent confident. It's still a shaky kind of endeavor. I'm not sure it's worth the risk. But I also don't know if I can count the sleeping outside thing as the *do something daring* since we didn't plan on doing it. Plus daring can mean different things to different people. I sort of wish I'd come up with what daring means to me before we put this on the list.

"Hey, Ari," Gaux says, out of breath from running up the hill. "What's up?"

"Just hanging out. You?"

"Same." She plops herself down and takes a sweaty piece of paper out of her pocket. "Check this out. I think I'm really on a roll!"

Gaux's LIST OF 8 COMPLETE AND TOTALLY
AWESOME THINGS TO DO With Astrid Before We
Turn 9 and While We Live on Opposite Coasts

"The title is very long," she admits. "But I'll work on it."

Alice and I crack up.

"I can't believe you've recruited little Gauxy into your list." Alice shakes her head. "Only Ari would do something like this."

1. Swim in the ocean at the exact same time—
Astrid in the Pacific and Gaux in the Atlantic

since we're on opposite coasts now, booo-hoooooo.

2. Convince our parents that we need to visit each other three times a year.

3. Come up with a catchphrase that only the two of us understand.

4. Have a minute of the day where we are always thinking about each other.

5. Make each other a friendship bracelet.

6. Send each other a pair of our pajamas so we can always feel close.

"You are def on a roll, Gauxy!" I high-five her. "This is awesome. And I barely gave you any guidance."

"I'm awesome. I mean, obviously."

"Obviously," Alice and I say at the same time, and then fall back laughing. We laugh at ourselves all the time but I think it's because we stay up too late every night and we're so tired that the next day everything and anything feels hilarious to us.

"I need more ideas, though," Gaux says. "It's hard because I want it to be stuff we can do apart but also together."

I reassure her. "You'll get there. For real. Has Astrid weighed in? Or does she even know that she's going to be doing this?"

"She doesn't know yet. I figured I'd call her when I got home from camp and tell her." Gaux makes another braided bracelet out of strands of grass. "By the way, when do you think Maccabiah is going to break?"

"Monday." Alice talks with her eyes closed, lying back on the grass. "Night. After dinner. That's my guess."

I sit up. "I don't think so. I think Monday after breakfast. Then three full days—Monday, Tuesday, Wednesday. Thursday and Friday are chill days. Saturday is packing and banquet. Sunday home."

"Can we not discuss home?" Alice asks. "Please. Too sad. Way too sad."

"Agree," Gaux says, folding the list again and putting it in her pocket. "Wait, I forgot to tell you the most important part."

Our eyes perk up.

"My whole bunk is making a list! Stuff we can do during the year until we're back at camp again!" She stands up and runs in place for a second, all hyped. "How fab is that?"

"Ultra fab," Alice answers. "Ari, can you please JHH the *make a difference* thing because you totally have made a difference and also because I can't hear you obsess about it anymore."

I crack up. "Love that you remember the term JHH. Yay, AlKal. And I kind of already have, but the *make a difference* thing may be ongoing, like *keep our friendship strong*."

Gaux bursts into laughter and falls back on the grass

but then hits her head on a tree root. She's not really hurt, though, so we all laugh uncontrollably for a few minutes. "I love how they have their own language," she says finally, when she's able to talk again.

"Oh! Gaux!" I say. "You need to learn the JHH!"

She giggles. "I do?"

"Yes!" I stand up and tap her foot with mine to get her to pay attention. "So you jump in the air. Well, you and the friend you're doing the list with. You do it together. Then you high-five. And then you hug! This is the ritual for when you finish something on the list." I pause. "Come, let's try together."

We practice the JHH a few times, and we stay on the hill for the rest of breira talking and laughing. Golfy comes and finds me at the end.

He puts his head on my shoulder and scoops me into a side hug. "What am I gonna do without you?" he asks. "For real, though."

"For real, though. I know."

"Okay, I can't handle all this lovey-dovey stuff." Gaux gets up and brushes off the butt of her shorts. "See ya, peeps."

Alice jolts up. "Oh! My job is mail collector today and I forgot to get it. Be right back!"

She runs down the hill like a little kid, and Golfy and I laugh as we watch her skip from the bottom of the hill all the way to the main office.

"So golf carts. Do something daring?" he asks, his eyes wide.

"I don't know, Golfy. I want to." I shift on the grass and move away from him a little bit. "But I don't want to get caught. I don't want to get in trouble." I pause.

"This could become a story we'll tell our grandchildren? JK. JK."

"Golfy! Wow!" I slap his arm.

"I was kidding." He shakes his head. "Sheesh."

"Me too. Sorry."

I mean, I obviously know he was kidding but sometimes Golfy can be so weird when it comes to stuff like that.

"But the golf cart? Yes? Please say yes?"

I shake my head. "Why are you so obsessed with this? I don't get it. It was an idea we had for my list and now you're soooo into it."

"I like making memories with you."

His eyes turn sad and thoughtful and I just can't take the cuteness. I look around to make sure there aren't people standing right near us, and I pull him in for a quick kiss.

"You're cute." I smile. "I'll think about it. I wanna do it but I'm scared. Maybe if it was the last night of camp? That's what AlKal suggested."

"Okay." He sighs. "That could work."

We're quiet then, thinking about the dilemma, when Alice runs up the hill with the mail.

"Wow, almost forgot this," she says. "Can't believe I'm such a slacker. Here. You got a letter." She drops it on my lap.

It's from Kaylan. I rip open the envelope and read.

Dear Ari,

Home is fine, nothing crazy, haven't seen the lunch table girls yet but I have been working on the portrait of you from memory with Mrs. Etisof.

I have a question: Did you know about this Robert Irwin Krieger and my mom getting engaged thing from Zoe? Please say no. I really hope it's no otherwise I feel like you've kept something from me and that is not who we are. We are TH friends, remember? We tell each other everything; no secrets. Not PF. I don't want my feelings protected; I just want real truth. We had that whole debate. I think I said TH, but now maybe I didn't but anyway, this is a big thing and I was totally caught off guard and now I'm kind of freaking out and you're not here and I can't call you and this is the longest run-on sentence in the history of letter writing probably.

I really miss Laurel Lake and Otis and I can't believe I'm home without you AGAIN. Also my dad is moving here, and I wonder if there is ever a time of calm or if life is always just mini volcanoes erupting every few minutes? Is that life from here on out? Ice buckets on our heads, ready to drop. That's how it feels to me.

It's two in the morning and I'm super emotional right now. Please write back right away. I miss you so much.

Love and stuff, Kaylan

PS Boarding school? How long have you been thinking about this?! Not something we can discuss in letters. Def an in-person, sleepover, soul-searchy, heart-to-heart kind of conversation.

My throat is clenched tight and I shove the letter in the front pocket of my jean shorts. I did keep it from her. I know I did. Just like I've kept the boarding school thing secret. And we are TH friends. But that can't be one hundred percent of the time. It just can't. Some things need to simmer. To resolve. To become clearer in my mind before I talk about them.

I feel like the worst friend ever. But the thing is, I still don't regret my decision.

Golfy looks at me like he's waiting for me to talk. But I can't. My thoughts are a jumbled word search in my brain.

I get up from the grass and brush off the butt of my shorts. "I gotta go, Golf. I'll see you at dinner." I sniffle and walk away, back to my bunk.

"Ari, you okay?" he yells.

I give him a thumbs-up behind my back because I don't want him to follow me.

I'm not sure if I'm okay.

27

KAYLAN

"HELLO, KAYLAN." MRS. BROWNSTEIN MEETS me at the door. One triplet is hanging on one leg and another is hanging on the other. Unclear where the third one is. "What can I do for you?"

I giggle. "Oh, it's what I can do for you! I'm home from camp and not doing much and I figured I could lend a hand over here. Not that you need it. You seem to have things totally under control but if you wanted, um, some extra help."

My mom told me once to never make it seem like mothers are doing a bad job or failing or disorganized or literally anything. She always reminds me to ignore tantrumming toddlers in the grocery store. *Just look away,* she hisses. *All they want is for people to ignore it.* Apparently Ryan was a terrible baby and a terrible toddler and people were always weighing in and offering my mom advice and it drove her crazy. Too bad he's a terrible teenager now, too. I guess he had a few good years between like six and ten. Who knows for sure, though.

"I could be a mother's helper to you!" I say after Mrs. Brownstein just sort of looks at me dumbfounded. "Whatever you need. Play with the girls or help them get ready for day camp or whatever."

"Kaylan, are you sure? You really want to do this?" She steps back and opens the door wider. "I mean, look at this place. It's like three tornados hit all at the same time."

Her house does seem to be mass chaos. Somehow there's a sock hanging on the ceiling fan. An entire container of yogurt has been dumped in the middle of the living room floor.

"I really do." I smile. "I love kids, always wished for a younger sibling, and I'm home and my best friend is still at camp."

Mrs. Brownstein looks at me a little iffy. "Um, well, that's a lovely offer. And I definitely do need help." She looks around again. "So I guess, come on in! First thing is to try and locate Maya and see if you can help her get on her bathing suit for camp. They swim first thing so it's easier to get them ready here but she never wants to. Devra and Eden are fine with it but it's a huge nightmare for Maya."

"I'm on it!" I take off my flip-flops and leave them

by the door and go on a search for Maya. "Maya! Where are you?" I sing. "Are we playing hide-and-go-seek? Oh, Maya . . ."

Mrs. Brownstein smiles at me as she gathers some materials to clean up the spilled yogurt. "I'm glad you're here, Kaylan. Really."

I run up the stairs feeling this new sense of positivity and purpose.

Making a difference. Maybe it's more for me than the Brownsteins. Or maybe it's for both of us. Whatever it is. As I'm doing it, I'm not thinking about the my-mom-and-Robert-Irwin-Krieger thing and if Ari knew or not. So that's good.

It kept me up most of the night, tugging at me like a leg cramp.

"Maya? Maya, where are you?" I sing as I search the upstairs. A few minutes later I find her hiding under her bed, peeking out at me from under the pink eyelet dust ruffle.

"Hi! Kaylan! You found me!" She pops out. "Wanna play again?"

I laugh. "Well, Maya, it's time for camp. Can you show me all of your bathing suits and we'll pick one out for you to wear today?"

She makes a less-than-excited face.

"Please, pretty please with sugar on top," I say. She leads me over to her dresser and opens the top drawer full of bathing suits. "Ooh, how about this hot-pink one? I love the ruffly sleeves."

She nods. "It's my favorite."

"So wear it, and hurry, hurry." An idea pops into my head. "Ooh, I'll set a stopwatch on my phone and let's see how fast you can get ready for camp. K?"

"K!" She wriggles herself into the hot-pink one-piece and quickly pulls on a pair of tie-dye shorts with a purple T-shirt. "Ready!"

"Oooh, one minute and three seconds! Wow!" I grab her hand. "Come, let's run downstairs and find your sisters. I bet it's time to go."

We get to the front door and Devra and Eden are all ready with their backpacks on, shoelaces tied tightly, skin glistening from lots and lots of sunblock.

"You ready, My?" Mrs. Brownstein asks, all cheerful.

"Ready!"

Mrs. Brownstein smiles at me and hugs Maya tight. I high-five the other two triplets and follow them out onto the front porch.

"Thanks for all of your help, Kaylan." She taps me on the shoulder in an awkward mom-ish kind of way, after we've gotten the triplets into the car. "Tomorrow same time?"

"I'll be here!" I walk across the street, back to my house, feeling pretty good. That was only like a half hour of work and yet I feel like I really helped out, eased the morning chaos in the Brownstein home.

My phone buzzes and when I look down to see who is contacting me, I realize I can't ignore her anymore.

Since I've been home, Cami has sent twenty-three texts and called five times and I've let them all go to voicemail.

I'm home. It's time for me to act like it. Ease back in. Really reenter life in Brookside.

I text her: **Sorry! My phone wasn't working! Pool this afternoon? 3pm? Xox!**

I think it's okay to white-lie every now and again. I needed time and space to process Laurel Lake and I wasn't ready to see any friends from home. I think back to last summer and how Ari felt this way but I didn't understand it. I couldn't have understood it, though. But now I do.

Telling my friends I wasn't ready to see them would've hurt their feelings. So a white lie to protect feelings is okay.

I think back to the TH or PF friends thing, and maybe we're not always one way. Maybe it switches back and forth. It's a gut feeling kind of thing, to know if you need to protect someone else's feelings or if you can be totally honest. And in this case, I know with one hundred percent certainty that I need to protect Cami's feelings.

OMG! I was so worried! Yes! See you there my looooveeeeee. I'll tell the others, too.

I was kinda hoping it could be just us, so I could really ease my way in, but I guess not. Oh well. This will be more like a deep dive than a toe dip, but maybe that's better. Maybe you do need to just take the plunge in these times.

I go back to Mrs. Etisof's even though I know she's not home. She's out for her morning kayak paddle. But she said I could come anytime to work on the easel, so I take her up on that.

I grab one of the sketching pencils and draw Ari from memory. I picture her in the backyard when we make s'mores, hair still wet from a day at the Brookside Pool. All of her features just come to me. I truly feel like she's here with me right now. Not like in a terrible *she died and I feel her presence* kind of way. More that I just know her so well. I really do know her by heart.

Finally, I finish, and I step back and admire it. I open the photos on my phone and compare the zillion pictures of Ari that I have with the portrait I just sketched.

Pretty close. Pretty crazy, kind-of-hard-to-believe close.

I pat myself on the back.

I snap a picture of it and then email it to myself and go inside and print it out.

"Where have you been?" Ryan asks me, turning off the TV.

"Around. Why?"

"Mom didn't know where you went. Apparently

Robert"—he makes a gagging face—"is coming over tonight and she's making a nice dinner and she wants us to be on our best behavior."

"Oh."

Truthfully, we haven't had much to do with Robert. They see each other on their own and they don't involve us. I know my mom had been trying so hard to tell me that they were getting closer and I avoided it this whole time.

Now the whole thing just feels so all-of-a-sudden.

"How gross is this?" Ryan asks, and I'm totally thrown for a loop. Ryan hasn't talked to me about anything significant in two years, I'd guess. He never opens up about his feelings. Everything is *whatever* to him. "Are you completely and totally grossed out?"

I sit down next to him on the couch. "Were you this grossed out about Dad and Amy?"

"I mean, sort of?" He thinks about it for a moment. "Maybe not as much."

"Why?" I ask, trying not to sound judgmental. "Isn't it the same kind of thing, though?"

He shrugs. "Feels weirder with Mom."

I want to pull apart this moment like string cheese so I can really dig deep and figure out what Ryan's feeling. He's actually talking to me again! This is huge! I want to dissect it and analyze it and make sure it keeps happening.

278

"I think anything with grown-ups is weird," I admit. "Like with love. It's all so ewwww, ya know."

"Grown-ups?" He laughs, mocking me. "You sound like you're in preschool."

He turns away from me and flips on the TV again, some sportscaster show where they just talk on and on about one game like it's the most important thing in the world.

I'm mad at myself for saying that word, like it totally just upended the conversation. But how would I know he'd react like that? Maybe I can start it up again.

"It is gross," I admit. "I agree with you."

"Okay." He doesn't look at me; he focuses on the TV, even turning it louder like he's trying to make it clear he doesn't care to talk to me anymore. Fine. He opened the door to conversation and then he closed it, but that doesn't mean it won't open again.

I sit there with him for a few moments, trying to pay attention to the sports show like maybe we can share an interest, but I'm so bored my mind wanders in every direction imaginable.

"Oh, Kay! You're back!" I turn around and see my mom coming into the den in a flowy, flowery sundress. Her wet hair is tied up on her head in a loose bun. She looks tan and relaxed and just a very cheerful shade of happy. "Did Ryan tell you Robert is coming for dinner? I'm going to grill some steaks and make that quinoa salad you love, the one with the dried cranberries? And asparagus. And that lemon ricotta pasta we saw on that cooking show."

My first instinct is to tell her I'm staying at the pool for dinner with Cami and everyone, make up some embellished lie. But then I catch myself. I don't do it.

"Sounds delicious, Mom. I'm really excited about that lemon pasta."

Ryan groans and looks at me like I'm a traitor. But the thing is, I am excited about it. The whole meal sounds delicious. And when my mom is this kind of cheerful, it's just too pleasant to ignore.

I want to be a part of it. Even if does have to do with icky *grown-up* love stuff.

I run up to my room and write out a quick letter to Ari before I get ready to head to the pool. I know I said three to Cami but I think I'll go early, get some lunch, lounge, maybe read a little. Maybe there are ways I can carve out hammock time at home, even without a hammock. Or maybe I can convince my mom to get one.

Dear Ari,

Check out my portrait of you from memory! JHH worthy, right?

I started being a mother's helper for the Brownstein triplets today. I feel good about it. I think that's one of my make a difference things. Plus how I put an end to Chad's sexism. And Indigo, too. We'll see. I guess it's good to make a difference in as many ways as possible. I can't stop!

Also, since we failed at get two counselors to fall in love, I feel better that I was able to make a difference in more ways than one.

Guess who is coming for dinner tonight?

Robert Irwin Krieger.

Crazy.

You still haven't written back to my letter about that. Please do.

Love you, Kaylan

PS I'm going to the pool to meet Cami and everyone now. Don't be jealous. LOL. ☺ xoxoxoxoxo

PPS I know how reentry from camp felt for you last summer. I get it now.

PPPS I'm starting to get really worried that you're actually gonna go to boarding school.

28

ARI

MACCABIAH BREAKS ON SUNDAY NIGHT. The last full Sunday of camp. We all expected it to happen Monday night so it's really a surprise. Even though I've never experienced a Maccabiah, I kind of feel like I have because I've heard so much about it.

We're all in different areas of camp for evening programs when a message comes over the loudspeaker. "Please go to the quad immediately for a required safety drill."

So we groan and walk sluggishly and annoyed and when we get there, we see a fire truck and all of the Olimers (the oldest campers, going into tenth grade) standing on it wearing different colors—red, blue, green, and gold. They're screaming, of course.

We know this is real. The next three days we'll be

divided up into teams—playing sports, making art, doing dances, singing comedy songs and fight songs and alma maters. Sweating, crying, laughing, knowing the end of camp is so close we can feel it but trying to enjoy these last days at the same time.

My friends and I sit close together, as if that'll help us all be on the same team, even though we know it won't.

Our hearts pound as they read off our names and we go to our different teams for a quick meeting and then there are fireworks over the lake. I'm not on a team with any of my friends but I am with Gaux, and we're on gold, so that's good.

Golfy and Alice are on green together. I wonder if they'll spend the whole time strategizing about the golf cart thing. Oren is on red with Hana and Zoe. I'm jealous they got to be together.

I'm trying to be into this and excited because it's Maccabiah and people wait all summer for it, but the truth is, there's a pit in my stomach. And it's not just about the golf cart agita, but that's part of it.

It's the Kaylan thing. The secret I kept from her that I kept pushing down, further, further down all summer. But now I can't push it down any further because summer is pretty much over, at Silver anyway, and also because Kaylan asked me about it.

"You okay?" Gaux whispers to me. We're sitting next to each other during the fireworks—the true kick-off to

Maccabiah—and I feel a little silly since I'm not with anyone my age.

I'm trying to manage my thoughts and keep myself from freaking out. We're not wearing any of our team colors yet since they were just assigned but we're sitting with our teams, on the path to competition.

"Yeah." I don't want to get into it with her. She's too young and she wouldn't understand.

After the fireworks, we have the first event—tug-of-war. We all get our team color bandanas. I tie mine on like a headband.

I'm toward the back since all the little kids are at the front of the rope, and I pull so hard, as if I really have a role here, a chance for our team to win. I go back and forth between pulling with all my strength and wondering what will happen with the boarding school thing. I know it's too late for this coming year, but for the following year, I think I can make it happen.

I want to make it happen.

I want to be the best version of myself all year long.

After we lose tug-of-war and it's time to go back to the bunks, Golfy finds me on my way up the hill. He drapes an arm over my shoulder. "Going somewhere?" He cracks up, and I do too because his laugh is still so contagious.

"I'm freaking out," I tell him. "I kept something from Kaylan and now she knows and she called me out on it and I feel sick."

"Oh, um, wow." He stops walking and I do, too, and we sit down against one of the trees. We're not really supposed to be doing this because it's almost lights-out and we need to be in our bunks getting ready for bed.

"Yeah. Oh, um, wow."

He repeats it and then we just keep laughing and saying *oh um wow* over and over again.

"That'll be how we respond to any intense news or situation from now on, okay?" I lean my head on his shoulder. "Like our secret not-so-secret language."

"Noted." He kisses the top of my head for a second and it feels like such an adult thing to do, especially since he's never done it before, but it's also pretty comforting. "So, listen, here's the thing. You need to just tell her, whatever it is. One hundred percent honesty. It's weird that people can never see this or understand it, but honesty is truly the best approach. Because people can't really be mad at you for being honest."

"They can't?"

He hesitates a minute. "No. Because you're speaking your truth. You're just saying it, you know what I mean?"

"I guess, but I don't know. It really wasn't my place to tell her this, but I still feel bad about it. And also she was away at camp; I didn't want to upset her. And—"

"I get it," he says. "So say that exact thing. I gotta go and find some green clothing for the next few days. Have anything you can lend me?"

"I'll check. Do you have any gold for me?"

"Yes!" He jumps up. "The Malkin Family 2018 Cruise T-shirt is kind of gold, kind of yellow, but it'll work. It's yours."

"Oh my goodness." I smile. "Really? I feel so honored. Can I keep it for real or just for Maccabiah?"

"Let me give it some thought." He gives me a quick kiss and runs to the other side of the hill to his bunk. I think about what he said the whole way back to mine, but it still seems iffy, and also not something I want to write in a letter. This is going to have to wait until I get home and Kaylan and I can discuss it in person. Maybe it's easier to be honest when you're face-to-face, or maybe it's easier to be honest in writing.

Hard to say for sure.

That night, we all dig through our cubbies and trade clothes in all four colors, and by the end of the night I have a pretty big stack of gold stuff, and I don't even have the shirt from Golfy yet.

Everyone goes to bed early; there really isn't any late-night chatting tonight and I'm left alone with my thoughts. There's only a week left of camp. I don't want to go home. I don't want to face Kaylan after she knows I've kept something from her. I don't want to be away from my Camp Silver friends or be away from Golfy.

It all went too fast.

I figure I should write the lunch table girls before I

come home. At least they're okay with group letters, and of course I send them to Cami's. She wouldn't have it any other way.

Dear Cami, Marie, M.W., June, Amirah, and Kaylan (since you're home now):

Sounds like summer has been awesome for all of you. I can't wait to hear about all the adventures in person. So funny that Saara is back in action and she wants to be friends with us again. I feel like I don't even remember what she's like. Also fun that you have a new pool crew—Jules and my old friend Tamar? Love it. Sorry it's taken me so long to write back.

Camp is awesome and I'm so sad it's ending soon but I won't bother you guys with that. Hmmm, what else can I tell you? It's Color War now, which is really cool. I'm on the gold team. Golfy is great and I still love him and I guess that's it. After this summer, I only have two more summers to be a camper. Isn't that unfair?

I'm excited for some pool days when I get home, and hopefully we can go to that place to get the amazing pies like you did last summer when I was away. I'd say write back but I'll probably be home by the time it arrives here, so don't worry about it.

Have fun!

Love xoxoxoxoxox Ari

29

KAYLAN

Dear Ari,

It's taken me a few days to write this because I am so mad. I'm sorry to send this during your last week of camp and you may not even get it since who knows how slow the mail is. But here it is:

Robert Irwin Krieger came over for dinner the other night. We all had an okay time. Well, not Ryan. He sulked through the whole meal and barely ate. I was having a fun time and of course you came up, and Camp Silver and Zoe. And guess what? Robert Irwin Krieger told us how happy Zoe was to get the news BEFORE SHE LEFT FOR CAMP that they were planning to get married. I mean, I guess it's possible that she didn't mention it to you but I really doubt it. So here's the thing: You knew about this and didn't tell me? That my mom was literally getting married?!

I can't believe it. I am hoping there's an explanation for

this. I am hoping you can help me sort this out because right now I'm madder at you than I've ever been in my whole life. So mad I want to rip up this list and never do one again. I never even want to talk to you again because I can't trust you. We are soul sisters (I thought so anyway) and the bestest of BFFs (also thought so) and people like that don't keep stuff like this from each other. No way. Not at all. Never. Ever. Ever.

I am so mad I can barely write this. See that droplet in the top corner? That's my sweat. My angry sweat droplet.

Write back ASAP and explain yourself.

—Kaylan

I shove the letter in an envelope and even address it. But then when I'm about to put on the stamp, I picture myself putting it in the mail slot. I stop myself.

I shove it in my desk drawer.

I can't send this.

"I'm sure she has a good reason," Cami says from the lounge chair next to me later that afternoon. She's not one to usually defend Ari so I'm tempted to believe her even if I don't want to. "I mean, she's your bestie. She wouldn't just not care to tell you."

I think about it for a few seconds. "It seems off, though. She knew how this would affect me. And she probably just didn't want to deal with it when she was at Camp Silver, the most perfect place in the world and blah blah blah."

Everyone's quiet after that, which basically just means Cami since she was really the only one responding this whole time, anyway. The rest of the girls have been silent on the subject, probably too scared to get in the middle of it.

"Let's change the topic," Cami says. I kind of get it since I've been pretty much obsessing about it for three or four days now. I've lost count. "Tell us more about Otis. And where does he live again? And when can we meet him?"

I adjust the hair under my visor. It's so humid out that it's sticking to my forehead. I don't even feel like being at the pool. That's how annoyed I am. "He lives in Portland, Maine, so I have no idea" is all I can manage to say.

"I love Maine," June adds. "We used to go every summer."

"How come you don't anymore?" Cami asks, sounding bored, but like she's trying to keep the conversation going.

"I dunno. I guess it's too expensive. Everything is too expensive, apparently." June flops over onto her stomach, turns her head away from us, and closes her eyes. Maybe she'll explain more later.

Jason's playing Ping-Pong against a little boy and I watch him from the lounges, feeling annoyed at his steadiness. How nothing seems to really bug him. And he can just do his thing all the time, never flustered, never worried about who is around. I want to tell him how Ari betrayed me but I also don't. I'm so annoyed that I'm even annoyed at myself for being annoyed. If I could run away from myself for a little bit, I would.

"Well, how's mother's-helpering going?" Cami asks, and everyone laughs at her.

"*Mother's-helpering*, Cam?" Marie asks. "That's not a word."

"I know that." Cami rolls her eyes in my direction and gets up in a huff. "I need more water. You guys are dehydrating me with your attitudes."

When she's far enough away that she can't hear, I turn to the others. "Has she been like this all summer?"

"Sort of," Amirah says. "We didn't hang every day. That's only been a thing since you came home. She became super close with Saara, which is just the weirdest. I wonder what'll happen when we're back at school."

"We did hang a lot, though," M.W. contradicts her. "Probably too much. We're all sick of each other."

Amirah scoffs, "Speak for yourself! I'm fine with everyone."

After that everyone is huffy in a silent way where it feels like you could only cut the tension surrounding us with one of those fancy knives they use on cooking shows.

When Jason's Ping-Pong match ends, I get up and walk over to him since none of my friends are talking to each other anyway.

"Hey," I say.

"Hey." He picks up a few stray balls and the paddles and walks over to the office to return them. I'm not sure if I should follow or go back to my lounge, so I wait a few steps and then traipse over to the office.

"How was your summer?" I ask.

"Fine. Yours?" He leans against the wall and pulls one foot up, standing there with a knee bent. "I took a sick trip to Colorado. It's really awesome. I think I'm gonna go there for college and then live there forever."

"Oh, cool. You have it all planned out."

"Yeah, pretty much."

We laugh for a second and he doesn't ask me anything and I wonder if I should just walk away. "I'm so mad at Ari," I blurt out, feeling the need to discuss this with another person. Someone new who isn't sick of it yet and can hopefully help me figure things out.

He sighs. "Kaylan, you always do this. Do you know that? Ari does it, too. When you're mad at each other, you come to me like I'm some kind of mediator or whatever. It's weird."

"I do not always do it," I say defensively.

"You do. Whatever. I can't help you. Sorry you're so mad at her again." He shakes his head and walks away, getting his phone out of his pocket and staring at it as he heads to the snack bar. "You'll work it out like you always do."

I stand there a little dumbfounded and then slump

back to the lounges, trying as hard as I can to not look sad or frustrated by Jason's comment. I wonder if he's right.

"I can't take anyone today," Cami whispers when I make it back there. "Everyone is annoying."

"I agree."

Sometimes you need someone like that, someone who will just agree with you and be grumpy with you and lean into the grumpiness. It's not a good thing most of the time, but sometimes you need it.

And right now I am at an all-time-high grumpiness level.

"Come. Walk with me." Cami taps her foot against mine, which is another thing that annoys me, but I ignore it. I think this is one of those days where it would be best if I spent it all by myself and sorted out my feelings. But that's pretty much all I've been doing since I got home from Laurel Lake. I might as well change it up a little bit.

We walk around the pool and past the snack bar and then over to the basketball court and then down this walking trail that really leads to nowhere special except this little bench next to a babbling brook. I'm not even sure it's really part of the Brookside Pool property but I think it's okay that we're here. We're quiet and it feels peaceful but so strange since I'm walking with Cami. She's never quiet.

"I think I may want to reinvent myself for this year," Cami says finally. "I'm sort of over everyone. Not you. But everyone else. I think that's why it's been so refreshing to have Saara around."

"Oh." I stare at the little ripples and bubbles in the water. "How come you didn't write me at camp about Saara?"

Cami shrugs. "I dunno. Figured I'd see if we were still close by the time you got home. You know how she is."

I nod. "Yeah."

Cami goes on, "I mean, not that I'd do a list, but . . ." Her voice fades away and I know what she's saying. Cami does want to do a list, maybe even with Saara, and she wants me to say it's okay and she wants me to help her. But this is different than with Indigo.

"I don't really think you need a list, Cam." I start talking in that way where I don't know what I'm saying but somehow I'll figure it out on the journey of speech. "You're so self-aware and confident and everything. I don't even feel like a list would work for you."

I'm pretty sure she can tell I am just making this up and spewing words from my mouth, but maybe not. She's quiet, though, and doesn't respond for a little bit.

"Okay. I didn't really even want to do that," she scoffs. "I just couldn't think of anything."

Oh, this is not what I needed. Cami annoyed at me.

"Cam," I start. "I didn't mean to say you couldn't do a list. I was just saying it doesn't seem like the plan for you."

"I get it, Kaylan. Just stop. Whatever. I'll figure it out. Let's talk about something else."

I clear my throat. "Did I tell you Ari wants to go to boarding school? I don't know if she will, but she does."

"No, you didn't tell me." Her voice lifts a little at the end and it bugs me that it does but I don't dwell on it. She'd be happy if Ari went to boarding school; she'd have me all to herself. "You really think she'll go?"

"I have no idea." I pick at a patch of dry skin on my arm. "I feel like probably no, but maybe?"

I don't even want to keep discussing this, but I'm happy to not be discussing Cami's list. I wonder if it's a bad thing that I'm so protective of the lists, but I am. Sometimes you just want something to be yours, and if it's not totally yours, only shared with a select few.

We finish the pool day and I'm not really in much of a better mood than I was when we started.

I see why Ari wants to go to boarding school. Sometimes you really feel like the best thing to do is get away from literally anything and everything.

This is the end of summer and I'm in a terrible mood.

I want to feel light and breezy, the way I did at Laurel Lake. I want to be the human equivalent of one of Indi's flowy, flowery skirts.

If I try hard enough, maybe I can get into that mindset again.

30

ARI

"IF I'M NOT A GENERAL when I'm in Olim, I will literally be the saddest person in the world," Alice tells me as we're walking down the hill for the final night of Maccabiah. Tonight each team will sing a fight song and an alma mater and we'll also do comedy sketches. It's one of the best nights of summer. Also, the saddest. The alma maters are what makes it especially sad, though, because they're basically songs about how awesome camp is, and how much we love it, and how miserable it is to leave at the end of the summer.

I say, "I think you will be," even though I have absolutely no idea. But it's still two years away and we don't really need to worry about it right now.

"Who do you think the boy generals will be?" she continues. "Definitely Golfy. Maybe Oren, if he comes back and learns more English. That kid that everyone calls Duke because he only wears Duke University tees probably will, too. He's an up-and-comer."

"Up-and-comer!" I burst out laughing. "AlKal, who even are you?"

"No idea." She laughs. "I crack myself up, too."

One of the zillion things that amazes me about Camp Silver is that we spend four days broken up into teams in a competition and we literally don't care who wins. I mean, we want our team to win but it's not a big deal. We're more focused on the fact that camp is ending and summer is over and we have to wait an entire year to be here with these people again, our soul-mate friends.

We get to the New Facility, which is really an airplane hangar that's been at camp for at least fifteen years, but we still call it the New Facility, sometimes the Newf for short. I smooch Alice's cheek and we part ways to go to our different teams. "Bye, AlKal."

Gaux pats the floor, letting me know that she's saved me a seat.

"Are you gonna cry tonight?" she asks me.

"Probably." I smile. "You?"

She giggles. "I don't know. Maybe."

"Are you so excited to see your new house?" I ask her.

"Yeah! I have a window seat in my room." She claps. "I'll take pictures and send them to you."

"That would be amazing, Gauxy."

I pull her into a side hug and then we're quiet because it's time to start all of the songs. Alma maters will be last. They want us to save our crying for the end.

The night goes by in a blur because there are so many things I don't want to focus on. Most of all, I don't want to think about camp ending and leaving these people. I don't want to think about going home and reentry and adjusting to the whole back-to-school routine.

When it's time for our alma mater, our whole team gets up and stands in a circle, arms around each other. I have to lean down a little to put my arm around Gaux, but it doesn't bother me. She smells like bug spray and strawberry kiddie shampoo, and I wish someone could make a candle of this fragrance so I can bring it home with me and have her with me. She's such a little ball of comforting sunshine. A ray of positivity and excitement and happiness. A little firecracker of a girl.

She's the embodiment of that Life is Good brand.

I look over at her and I smile and then she makes a silly face at me and we both crack up but then our generals shhh us and we stop talking.

"I come back to see that you remember me," we sing, high-pitched and squeaky, "another year's begun. See our friends return; still our fire burns in the heat of the summer sun. You're the pony on my carousel, you keep my summer spinning, one year older now, still you show me how, through your eyes and grinning . . . this is heaven in my eyes."

We all start crying then and the whole camp is silent because everyone can see and hear that this is the best alma mater in the history of Camp Silver, or maybe even in the history of sleepaway camp, hard to say.

"As the stars climb over the Berkshire mountains, the golden sun sets over the hills. Tie the smiles of your friends to your heart with the ribbon, 'cuz if you come back, I will."

We sing on and on, and I decide that the first thing I'm gonna do when I get home is take this wrinkly, tear-streaked, golden-yellow song sheet and give it to my dad to be laminated. He's the lamination king, and also this will give us a chance to connect over something super important to me. A first test of our new, always-evolving, trying-to-be-close-to-each-other relationship.

I wipe my tears with the shoulder of this gold T-shirt I borrowed from Zoe. It says *Tower Records* in big red letters, and apparently it used to be her dad's. She only brought it because she worried she'd need gold stuff for Maccabiah. Lucky for me, she brought a lot of gold stuff. I wonder if she'll let me keep this T-shirt, though, especially since it's stained with my tears.

I'm so out of it, exhausted, and zoned out from crying that I don't even notice when the winner is announced.

I only realize it when the entire green team is on their feet hugging and crying and cheering.

"Guess green won," Gaux says. "Blargh. Kidding."

"Ha, I don't really care." I wipe my eyes again because my left eye is still tearing. "Golfy will be happy! Alice too!"

After a few minutes of celebrating green's victory, the whole camp mixes together—a rainbow of colors all hugging and loving each other and not caring that three-quarters of the teams lost.

"Oh, sweet victory," Golfy says after pulling back from our hug. "Green! Go green!"

I crack up. "Since when are you so competitive?"

"I'm not. I'm totally messing with you. I don't even care." He hugs me again. "Arrrriiiiiii. Can we please make a plan so I can see you pretty soon after camp ends? My grandparents are taking us on a trip to Acadia National Park straight from camp but then after that?"

I nod. "Yes. Definitely."

My heart dances a little in my chest, like a soft sway someone does when the person is really feeling the music, and is in the moment and not thinking about anything else.

"Speaking of my grandparents, how's Bub? You haven't mentioned her in a while."

I smile. "She seems good? She writes me every week. She wants to teach me Yiddish and she reminds me to stretch the summer and really appreciate everything. All summer I've been feeling so grateful that she's been healthy. I write it down in little print every day, under all the other things I'm grateful for."

He smiles and pulls me into a hug. "I love that." We stand there looking at each other for a few minutes, talking about grandparents, and then he says, "I'll find you on the hill before lights-out. K?"

"K."

I watch him walk away into the sea of color and somehow I've lost Alice somewhere in there, too. I can't find Hana or Zoe or even Gaux, but I don't really mind. It doesn't feel like the times I couldn't find Kaylan in the cafeteria at school. It doesn't feel like I'm alone. It almost seems as if I'm invisible but in a good way—looking out on something magical, sipping it slowly through a straw, taking it all in.

This place.

These people.

I could write Camp Silver in the gratitude journal every day for the rest of my life and it wouldn't be enough appreciation.

This place has changed me in the best possible way.

I stare out into the room of people hugging and crying, balloons of all the colors flying to the ceiling of the New Facility.

I memorize this moment. A snapshot in my mind that

I put in my pocket to save. Like when we picked up Lion and he was in the back seat with Gemma and me. And then we went to Bubbie and Zeyda's for Chinese and he was jumping up trying to get on Bubbie's lap.

I have an imaginary photo album of amazing moments in the back of my brain.

I go back to them again and again and again.

And somehow each time I revisit them, they become stronger, more important, even more wonderful than when I lived them.

I guess that's what gratitude is. It's not really about filling a journal, though that's great. It's remembering to pay attention all the time, to snap those memories and save them and show appreciation again and again and again.

31

KAYLAN

Yo Kaylan,

I'm leaving Laurel Lake tomorrow so this is your last letter from me. It's also your first and I'm so sorry about that. No time to write. Also, I lost my pen for a few days. I know, I know. I could've borrowed.

It's been great here but first session was better. My comedy partner was this kid named Frankie, he was only ten, and he wasn't very funny, but he tried. Hammock time was kind of boring without you. My roommate was this kid Drew, he came all the way from Oklahoma—crazy, right? He was fine. I dunno.

I hope we can find time to hang during the year. Good luck with your parents. When is your dad moving?

Anyway, I wrote my home address as the

return address, so write me, or, uh, I guess we can go to texting when I'm reunited with my phone. I have your number and I'll text soon.

— Otis

"Um, how do you always find the cutest boys in the world?" Cami asks after reading the letter from Otis for the tenth time in a row. She studies it like it's classic literature.

We're out on my back patio, lounging and contemplating what to do for the rest of the day.

"Always? Huh? What other boys?"

She thinks about it for a minute. "I guess only Jason. Well, you did love Tyler but he's a jerk and I never liked him."

"Noted. Thanks, Cam."

"Does Tyler still hang with Ryan? I never see him at the pool, come to think of it. Actually, I never see either of them."

I breathe in and breathe out. Cami's been at my house since ten this morning and she's supposed to sleep over and I'm exhausted from her nonstop chatter. My brain can't process information that fast. Or even respond to what she says.

"I heard Tyler had to do, like, intense summer school because he almost failed all his classes," I mumble, praying we can just sit quietly for a few moments. "And Ryan hates the pool. He likes to be inside."

"I get it. My sister Jane is the same way but that's because she has such fair skin—she cannot tan AT ALL—so she's scared of sunburns."

I nod, not responding. I have no more words to say. My brain is asleep.

I think she gets it because she's quiet then and she closes her eyes and I just stare at her like that, hoping it lasts for a long time.

She does end up falling asleep and I doze off, too, and then my phone buzzes.

I wonder if it's Otis. I wonder if he's home already.

Hey, Kay. Moving date got moved up. Amy & I will be there next week. Looking forward to having you over. Love, Dad

Okay, first of all, eww. Why do parents sign their text messages? And second of all, just eww. I don't want to come over. I don't even want to know where the apartment is.

I ignore it for now and close my eyes and think about happy things.

Ari will be home tomorrow and even though I am so mad at her, I am still excited to see her. I guess that's how you know someone is a true soul sister best friend. I am literally furious but my heart beats with little pats of excitement when I think that she'll be home soon and we'll be back together again.

"Kay, you need anything?" My mom comes out in a sundress, her hair tied up in a loose bun again. She has that relaxed and happy look, the same one she had when Robert Irwin Krieger came over. I guess it's kind of her permanent vibe now.

"No, we're fine," I reply with my eyes closed.

"Okay, well, I'm heading into the city for the evening. I'll be back around midnight, I'd guess, so you know the rules: no firepit, no stove, no letting strangers in, no parties, no—"

"Mom." I sit up and turn to face her. She's only going an hour and a half away and she acts like she's going to be climbing Mount Everest and gone for days. "I get it. Thanks. Have fun."

She says "Kaylan" in her warning voice and I do a deep breathe-in, breathe-out again.

"We're okay, for real. Please. Just have fun."

After my mom leaves, Cami and I go back to our naps.

A little while later, Cami shoots up. "Why are our schedules so late this year? Don't we usually have them by now? Did something happen?"

I groan, a little annoyed by Cami's intensity. "I think there was too much chaos last year when everyone got their schedules so early. People kept wanting to make changes and everything," I explain. "So they're sending them out super late. Like the last week before school starts."

We talk about that for a little while longer and I keep debating if there's a nice way to tell someone that you really want them to go home. Is that a thing that's okay to say sometimes or literally never? I don't know.

It's just that Cami seems so anxious herself and on top of my agita it feels over the top. Plus the text from my dad that he's literally going to be here next week, and the fact that Ari's coming home tomorrow.

It's too much. I need space. Quiet. Alone time.

"Cam, I don't feel well," I say, making an over-the-top sad sort of sick face. "I think it was that BLT we got and then the ice cream. It's all swirling around in my stomach right now."

"Oh no." She inches closer to me and puts a hand to my forehead, checking to see if I have a fever. "You don't feel warm."

"I don't think it's the flu, Cam," I say with more energy than I should if I'm really trying to make this sickness believable. "I just really don't feel great. I think I need to be alone right now. I feel like I might puke."

I stand up, trying to force the point, but she stays seated, so then I just sit back down and rest my head back and close my eyes and pray that this does the trick.

I need her to go. I need to sort out this agita on my own.

No one can help now but me.

32

ARI

IT'S THE LAST NIGHT OF camp and most of our stuff is packed up in our bags on the bunk porch. We've already had dinner and the last Havdalah of the summer. It's a short little service that marks the separation between the Sabbath and the rest of the week, but the last one of the summer feels like it also marks the separation between camp and the rest of the year.

Now we're all allowed to just hang out pretty much until lights-out. Some people try to stay up all night, but I'm not sure how many of them really make it.

"Okay, as soon as everyone is in for lights-out, we'll both leave our bunks calmly," Golfy explains. "Don't make a scene. If anyone asks us where we're going, we'll say the infirmary."

We're sitting smooshed together on the hill near my

bunk, leaning against our favorite tree.

"Are you suggesting that because Kaylan and Otis used the infirmary in their plan?" I ask, laughing.

He looks at me with twisty eyebrows. "Um, I'm not *that* up on what Kaylan does."

We both start laughing for a little while and then he goes on explaining. "Anyway, the golf carts are kept behind Ranch House. I've checked many times, and the keys are always right there, on the seats." He eye-bulges. "How ridiculous is that?"

I lean over and whisper in his ear, "They probably don't expect anyone will steal them."

He nods. "True. So anyway. I'm going to hang with my friends for a little. A half hour after lights-out, I'll meet you on the side of your bunk. Look for me."

My heart twirls around like a ribbon in one of those ribbon-dancer performances.

A little bit later, Alice and I walk back to the bunk, arms over each other's shoulders, and I feel like I'm about to throw up. I can't even speak.

I ask myself what my gut is telling me right now. Yes or no? We've been talking about this pretty much all summer and yet I am still not sure I want to do this, if I want to be *this* daring.

We're in pajamas, and all of us are in our usual spots on the bunk floor, crying and laughing and then sobbing and then laughing again.

When it's time to meet Golfy, I don't want to leave. For a few reasons. One is that I really want to stay with my friends. The other is that I'm scared out of my mind about this.

"I think there's still a group of counselors on the porch," Alice says. "How are you gonna do this?"

I clench my teeth together. "No idea."

My stomach is twisting itself again and again like a washcloth that needs to be wrung out. My throat is tight. My neck feels swollen.

"Guys, I have a bad feeling about this," I mumble, covering my mouth because I think I might throw up. "I just don't feel right. And now I don't know what to do."

Alice stands up and wraps her arms around me. "Arianna Simone Nodberg, my love. Listen, you're stressing because you've never done this before. Golfy comes from a long line of Camp Silver people and he knows what he's doing." She pulls away and then raises her eyebrows. "Loyal to the List. You haven't done anything daring yet, and you know you're not gonna when you get home."

"Sleeping outside all night?"

"Doesn't count." Alice shakes her head. "You didn't plan on it."

"Since when is Alice such an expert on the list?" Hana asks. "I don't get it."

"I may start my own," Alice muses.

"Just go, Ari," Zoe says. "Honestly, the last night of

camp is a free-for-all. It's not gonna be a big deal. This golf cart thing has been talked about all summer and can I just say it'll be a little disappointing if you end up not doing it after all this? Please just go, drive the golf cart a few feet, and come back so we can hang with you?"

When she puts it that way, it feels calmer, easier, not a whole-night experience but a short thing I can do quickly. It'll be memorable but not last forever.

"Ooh, that crew of boy counselors just left the porch," Alice says on her way back from the bathroom. "Go now. I mean, not this second, but I have a feeling our counselors will come in soon and go right to bed. Then you should go."

A few minutes later, they come in and crawl into their beds, and my friends and I look at each other wide-eyed.

"Now. Go!" Alice hisses. "Be careful. Don't stress. Have fun. I'll talk about this in the toast at your wedding!"

I roll my eyes. "AlKal!"

The rest of the girls giggle as I grab my hoodie off my bed. I sneak out of the bunk through the side door from the bathroom and before I even know what's going on, I'm outside with Golfy.

"Just follow my lead," he whispers. "No talking."

For the last night of camp, everything feels very still and quiet. There really isn't anyone around. I guess people are hanging out in their bunks, or maybe they're in far-off secret camp places where we can't see them.

We walk down the hill in silence. It's so quiet, I wonder

if my flip-flops are making too much noise against the grass. Golfy holds my hand the whole time and even though we're quiet, I feel connected to him, like he gets me and he knows me and I can be myself around him.

When we get to Ranch House, we walk behind the building and lean against it with our backs straight like we're already hiding from someone.

No one is here, though. The only things I can see are the little flickers of light on the lake and a few stray fireflies. We hear crickets and some homemade wind chimes off in the distance and that's it.

Maybe this will be easier than I thought.

"There they are," Golfy whispers, and points to a line of three parked golf carts. "We'll get in, the keys are already in the ignition, we'll do one lap around the building and then park it, and that's it."

"That's it?" I ask.

"Is that daring enough for you?"

"I think even the fact that we're out at night, right now, not in the bunk and all the way down the hill is daring enough for me."

"Got it. Let's go."

He grabs my hand again and we tiptoe over to the golf cart. We get in quietly and I squeeze the sides of my seat as tight as possible. My palms are sweating onto the cracked vinyl and little droplets are dripping down from my forehead but I don't want to let go of the seat to wipe them away. I blow the hair out of my face but it doesn't really work.

"Ready?"

I nod but I'm not ready. I just want this to be done already. So I guess in that sense I am ready. Ready for it to be over.

He turns the key and the golf cart revs. The engine isn't as loud as I expected it to be in the deep silence of the night.

I clench my teeth together and close my eyes as he drives. And it's not like he's going very fast or anything. After a few seconds, I realize I can open my eyes and maybe experience this without paralyzing fear. Maybe things are okay. We're in the golf cart, he's driving, there's no one else here.

We're doing this.

My body relaxes. I'm glad Golfy encouraged this. Kaylan will be proud, too, and then maybe she won't be as mad that I kept the Robert Irwin Krieger thing from her.

"Who is that?"

My body freezes. I clench the sides of the seat again.

Golfy brakes rather abruptly and my whole body falls forward.

We're parked in the middle of Green House Lawn, sort of at an angle since I think we're half on a tree root.

Pres is standing in front of us.

"Why are you two in a golf cart?" he asks.

We're silent.

"I said, why are you two in a golf cart?"

"Um, it's kind of a long story, actually." I talk really fast and then nervous-laugh. "You know I am a major rule follower—here and at home—and my best friend and I have this list and one of the things on it was *Do something daring* and so I thought this could be fun and Golfy was just helping me. Don't blame him. And I know this all sounds unusual but please, please, please don't get us in trouble." I start crying.

I start sobbing in the golf cart, holding my head to my knees and dripping tears and snot all down my leg. And I don't even have a tissue.

No one says anything. Not even Golfy. I think he's shocked.

"Get out. Now."

Pres doesn't seem to care that I'm crying.

"This is serious. Not what I expected from either of you. Especially on the last night of camp."

I wonder why he's down here, but I know I can't ask.

"Go back to your bunks immediately."

"I'm really sorry," I say again. "It's just that I—"

"Go back to your bunks, I said," Pres hisses.

I've never heard him this angry. I wish he'd said something about the punishment so we'd know what to expect.

Golfy and I walk back to our bunks in silence, except for my constant crying. He puts an arm around me and then pulls it away and then puts it around me again. I know he feels terrible. I can sense it.

"It's gonna be okay, Ar," he whispers as we part ways to go to our bunks. "I promise."

"You do?" I ask. "How do you know that?"

He shakes his head. "It's gonna be okay," he repeats.

When I get back into the bunk, my friends are all cuddled together on Alice's bed, half-asleep.

"What happened?" Zoe whispers, and pats the tiny bit of space on the bed for me to sit down.

I start bawling. "Pres caught us. We're in huge trouble. I know we are."

They ask me a million questions and I don't have the answers and I don't want to talk anymore. I can't believe this is how I'm spending the last night of camp.

"I need to go to sleep," I whisper. "Or fret on my own under my covers. Either way."

I go back to my bed and cry for the rest of the night. People *usually* cry on the last night of camp, but this is different.

This is not how I expected camp to end. This is not how I wanted it to end.

I knew it was a bad idea, but I went along with it anyway.

And the feeling I have now is worse than any punishment the camp could give me.

33

KAYLAN

ARI COMES HOME TODAY AND even though I am so mad at her, I am still so unbelievably excited to see her. Plus there's the fact that I have been saving a surprise for her all summer.

When I thought about what language to learn so we'd be able to have a conversation, it seemed so obvious.

Hebrew, duh.

She already knows a bunch and she's so passionate about it, and it's a language that my mom and Ryan don't know at all, so we can totally have secret chats. It was kind of a no-brainer. But I didn't want to tell her because I didn't want her to suggest alternatives and I didn't want to have to debate it.

I just wanted to make a decision and stick to it.

I'm not the old Kaylan who second-guesses everything

and overthinks and stresses.

Sometimes I just go with my instincts. And this was one of those cases.

I text Ari: **Call me as soon as you get home. I know reentry and blah blah but this cannot wait. I have to talk to you. Welcome home.** ☺

I know I'm being overly aggressive but it's already three in the afternoon and I don't want one of those experiences where she takes forever to see me, and then all of the feelings fade. I need to be honest with her about what she kept from me, I don't want to push this down and bury it. I want to be upfront and truthful so we can get past it.

No lingering fights. Just honesty.

Ari writes back pretty quickly.

I'm home. I'm coming over.

Okay, that is not what I expected. At all. And now I'm nervous. Pacing around my room, trying to prepare. I don't know why I feel the need to clean up, but I do.

"Ari is coming over," I yell down the stairs. No one responds, so I yell it again.

"Okay! Who cares?" Ryan yells back. My mom still doesn't say anything. To be honest, I'm not even sure she's home.

A few minutes later, the doorbell rings, which is already super odd since Ari always just walks into my house like she lives here. I run downstairs to greet her and when I do, I see her standing there: shoulders slumped, hair a mess, visible bra strap under a tank top, something Ari truly hates.

"Are you okay?" is the first thing that comes out of my mouth because she really looks horrible. "Did something happen?"

My mind flashes to Bubbie, but I'm too scared to say that out loud.

She nods. "Yes. Something happened."

My heart races. I guide her up the stairs like she's suddenly blind and when we get to my room she falls face forward onto the bed.

Does she not realize I'm mad at her? But how can I be mad at her when she looks like she narrowly escaped death?

"Ari," I whisper. "Do you want to talk?"

She sits up finally and starts crying, and then she rubs her eyes. I get up to hand her a tissue and then she says between sobs, "The *do something daring*." She pauses to catch her breath. It's hard for her to get the words out. My heart pounds and a sense of dread creeps over me. "Golfy encouraged me to drive a golf cart together and so we did and now we may not be able to go back to Camp Silver."

"Ever?" I gasp.

"Ever." She buries her head in the pillows again. "We waited until the last night of camp to do it because we

figured we wouldn't get kicked out but then we got caught and now this is our punishment."

"Can they really do that to you?" I say so quiet it's almost a whisper. That sounds like the worst punishment they could ever give to anyone.

"I guess," she whispers back. "We don't know for sure but they said they'll need to really think about if it's safe to have us back at camp."

Hearing her say that out loud really stings. Ari Nodberg, rule follower, honors student, perfect human. Of course it's safe to have her at camp! It's better than safe. She makes the camp even more amazing.

And then I remember again: I'm mad at her!

"Ari, I hate to do this when you're hurting so much but here's the thing, I really need to talk to you about something else pretty serious." I pause and wait for her to respond. "Can you please sit up and can we please talk?"

She doesn't move at all. Maybe she's fallen asleep.

I go downstairs to get us a few cans of seltzer and the freshly washed grapes from the fridge and by the time I get back up to my room, Ari's sitting on my bed with her knees pulled up, writing something, leaning on my lap desk.

I glance over her shoulder but then she pulls away from me and keeps writing.

I look over the list again and try to think of how to start the conversation in Hebrew. It's not like I can really talk about anything important in the language. My words are limited. But based on the words they use at camp, and the words I've learned, I think we'll at least be able to JHH and check it off the list.

Then hopefully we'll talk out about how I'm mad at her and resolve it quickly, and then we can make the time capsule. Oh, and Ari has to draw the portrait, unless she did it already and didn't mention it to me.

Ari and Kaylan's 13 ¾ Things to Build and Improve on Our Complete and Total Amazingness

Ari	Kaylan
1. Perform in a camp talent show. ✓	1. Perform in a camp talent show. ✓
2. Write at least one letter to each other a week. ✓	2. Write at least one letter to each other a week. ✓
3. Sneak out of the bunk at night without getting caught. ✓	3. Sneak out of the bunk at night without getting caught. ✓
4. Keep a gratitude journal. ✓	4. Keep a gratitude journal. ✓
Get two counselors to fall in love. X New item: Accept failure.	Get two counselors to fall in love. X New item: Accept failure.

6. Be able to have a full conversation in another language. (to come)	6. Be able to have a full conversation in another language. (to come)
7. Draw a portrait of each other from memory.	7. Draw a portrait of each other from memory. ✓
8. Do something daring. ✓	8. Do something daring. ✓
9. Get a younger kid at camp and/or at home to start their own list. ✓	9. Get a younger kid at camp and/or at home to start their own list. ✓
10. Master the art of tie-dye. ✓	10. Master the art of tie-dye. ✓
11. Make a difference. ✓	11. Make a difference. ✓
12. Tell our dads one thing we'd like to improve about our relationship with them. ✓	12. Tell our dads one thing we'd like to improve about our relationship with them. ✓
13. Make a time capsule to capture our lives at exactly 13¾ years old and bury it somewhere in Brookside.	13. Make a time capsule to capture our lives at exactly 13¾ years old and bury it somewhere in Brookside.
13 ¾. Keep our friendship strong FOREVER.	13¾. Keep our friendship strong FOREVER.

She looks up at me, and then goes back to writing, and then a few minutes later, she hands me the letter.

Dear Kay,

I know you're mad at me. I know you wish I'd told you about Robert Irwin Krieger and your mom. But hear me out. And this is why I'm writing to you and not saying this out loud because I don't want you to interrupt me. I don't want to be in a fight with you or an almost-fight or a quietly-annoyed-at-each-other-but-not-saying-it fight.

So here's the thing: Zoe kind of mentioned it but she didn't know details. Her dad sort of let it slip out before she left for camp. And when I found out, you were already at Laurel Lake, so what was I supposed to do? Write to you and mention it and then you'd be all miserable and not enjoy your time there? That didn't feel right, especially when I didn't know all the information and Zoe didn't either. And was it really my news to share? Would you really have wanted to hear it from me and not your mom?

We can discuss this but I wanted to at least explain myself first so you can understand where I'm coming from.

Keeping our friendship strong and loyalty to the list are the most important things in the world to me.

Xoxoxo Ari

I stare at her after I read the letter. I don't know if I should respond in writing or speaking.

My anger fades even though I'm not sure it should.

"Were you stressed keeping this from me?" I ask her, sitting up straight, criss-cross-applesauce on the bed.

"Um, yeah. Mega-stressed." She pulls her hair up into a tight ponytail. "Literally thought about it every day. Kay, what you don't realize is that your pain is my pain. I literally feel it. I mean, maybe that means I'm super empathetic but it's not like that with everyone. Just with you."

She starts crying right then, sobbing, tears all down her face, red nose and cheeks. I hand her the tissues and watch her try to calm down and I realize I can't be mad at her. I feel her honesty all the way through.

"I'm sorry you were stressed about it, Ar." I inch closer to her and put an arm over her shoulder.

"I'm sorry, too, and I'm sorry you had to find out and realize that I knew and that you had to feel all this anger." She pauses, sniffling, trying to catch her breath again. "Everything feels lopsided. It was a great summer, don't get me wrong, but it ended on a terrible note, and I knew you were mad, and maybe you still are, and I just feel like running away." She cries again, unable to speak. "I want to go to boarding school and start fresh."

"You mentioned that," I reply. "But really?"

"Yes, really. I don't know if it will happen. But it's what I want. I want to feel the way I feel at camp all year round."

I don't want to get into this right now. I don't want to tell her that's a pipe dream, that it's not reality.

I need to focus on the present moment, and where we are right now.

"Listen, Ari, I'm glad you wrote me that letter." I clear my throat. "Because this whole time I felt like you kept it from me because you just didn't care."

She jolts up. "Really? That's what you thought?"

"I mean, some of the time. Maybe not all the time. But I wondered if you were so consumed with camp stuff that it was like *oh whatever* and then you moved on."

"Kaylan. Stop. Think about what you're saying right now." She looks at me, talking with her eyes, and then gets up to go to the bathroom.

When she gets back, I say, "Listen, I didn't really think that, but it was hard to know what was really going on when we weren't together and I wasn't sure what you knew and didn't." I pause. "Let's table this. We don't need to talk it to death."

"Are you still mad at me, though?" she sniffles.

I hesitate and think for a second. "No. I'm not. I see where you were coming from. I get it now. My perspective isn't always the truth."

Her eyes bulge. "Kay, this is huge growth."

"It is, right?" I smile.

"Yes! You are a new woman." Ari grabs another tissue from the box and blows her nose.

"Ewwww." I laugh. "Don't say woman. You know it creeps me out."

She laughs, too. "I know. Okay, I should probably go home. I literally ran over the second I saw your text. I need to check in on Lion and Bubbie and Zeyda and maybe unpack and then deal with the wrath of my parents, who have probably gotten an email or call from the camp director by now."

"Oh Lord. That is a lot."

She gets up from my bed and slides her feet into her flip-flops. "I'll call you later."

"*L'hitraot*," I say, smiling. "*Kol Tuv*."

Ari turns around, surprised. "Wait, what?"

"Hebrew. Our language. For our conversation."

Ari's eyes bulge. "Kay, really? You learned Hebrew?"

I smile. "*Ken Ken*." I pause, to let her appreciate more of my Hebrew. "You already sorta know it so I figured I'd make it easy on both of us." I pause. "Surprise!"

"I totally back-burnered this list item for when we got home, like we decided," she says, "but I was really hoping it could be Hebrew, too. I figured our backup could be French since we both really want to go to Paris. And then when Bubbie suggested teaching me Yiddish, I considered that, too."

"Yeah, those could've worked," I admit. "But Hebrew is pretty cool."

She runs back to me and hugs me. "*Yalda Tova*." She points to me. "*At*."

"You're a good girl, too." I smile, proud of my Hebrew

skills. It might come as a surprise to people that I could crush it at comedy camp and learn Hebrew at the same time. But I did. I really did.

"Oh, Ari, wait!" I yell when she's almost out of my room. "OMG! I forgot to even mention this, but did you know Ari means *lion* in Hebrew?" I widen my eyes.

"Yeah." She giggles. "I knew that. But that's not why I have my name, because of Bubbie's love of lions, I mean. Arianna actually means *very holy* in Greek or Italian, or both. But also not why I have my name. I don't think there's a reason really. My mom just loved it."

"Crazy coincidence, though!" I pull her in for one more hug. "And you have the same name as your dog!" I giggle. "*Kelev Ari!*"

"*Mishuneh.*" She laughs. "That means *weird*, by the way. In case you didn't get to that yet."

I scribble it down on a piece of paper and wonder if our Hebrew chatter counts as our actual conversation because there's really so much more I can say. That applies to regular life, too, though, and not just this list or another language.

There's always so much more I can say to Ari.

34

ARI

AFTER BREAKFAST THE NEXT MORNING, I walk over to talk to Bubbie. I want to tell her everything about camp, of course, but especially about the last-night debacle. I start with that, and hope she'll have some wisdom. for me.

"You did what?" My bubbie's voice squeaks at the end, the way it always does when she's shocked and surprised. "Tell me the story again. Don't leave out any of the details."

I can tell she's almost proud in a way, but she'd never admit it, especially not to my parents. Zeyda's playing golf with a few of his buddies and it feels nice to have Bubbie all to myself right now.

I start telling her the golf cart story and she interrupts, "Did I tell you about the time we put honey on our counselors' arms and then covered them with feathers from someone's pillow?"

I laugh. "You did, but tell me again."

"That's basically the story." She smiles. "They didn't know what hit 'em!"

My bubbie leans her head back against the recliner, listening to every word of my story, smiling from ear to ear like I'm explaining how I won a Nobel Prize.

"I loved sneaking out at night," she interjects. "Really loved it."

It takes me forever to make it through the story since she keeps chiming in, but I don't mind.

"Maybe you can convey some of this enthusiasm to my parents," I say completely seriously but with a hint of joking. "They don't find it all so entertaining."

"Well, parents don't always see things the way grandparents do. That's why grandparenting is the best role in my life. Too bad we can't skip parenting and go right to grandparenting." She winks at me.

"Bub! I love you!" I slide the walker I'm sitting on closer to her recliner, and pull her in for a hug. Her recovery has been incredible, miraculous, even. I know she still struggles but she's almost back to her usual self.

"Could you talk to them for me?" I ask. "They're really mad and even if camp does let me come back, they're not sure they will."

She shakes her head in an annoyed-but-not-surprised

kind of way. "They'll come around. So will the camp." She pauses. "Trust me."

We talk for a little while longer and then I realize I should probably get home. I still haven't seen any of the lunch table girls and I've been home for two days. I don't even feel like I have the energy to call them. And I've been scared to reach out to Golfy to see what his parents said about the incident. I guess he's been feeling the same way because he hasn't contacted me either.

Even though time with Bubbie always cheers me up and makes me feel like I can conquer the world, an overwhelming sense of ickiness comes over me. I just want to finish the list. We only have a few things left, and I feel like if I can get that off my plate, I can focus on reentry with home friends and getting ready for school. I've loved this list, but I also feel the need to move on from it. To put it aside for a little while.

"Bub, I love you beyond. You know that, right?"

She giggles. "Yes. I love you more."

We go back and forth and back and forth and then finally I let her have it. She loves me more. Okay. I can live with that. Even if it's not true.

I walk home and feel so grateful for Bubbie, that she's still here and able to talk and laugh with me. A few months ago, we weren't sure that was even really possible. But here we are. And I appreciate it more than I could express in any gratitude journal.

I'm almost at my house when my phone vibrates in my pocket. A text from Kaylan.

We're finishing the list tonight. Don't argue with me. I'll explain why tonight. My house or yours?

I hesitate to answer because I think I am sort of grounded even though my parents didn't explicitly say that. It was more of a *you've lost all privileges for the rest of your life* kind of thing. But I did go to Kaylan's right when I got home, and they didn't stop me. Soooo . . . hard to say.

Let me get home first and see how things are. I went over to see Bubbie.

I walk into my house and Lion jumps up so high he licks my elbow. I scoop him into my arms and kiss his head and feel all around gratitude for this little pup. At least he's happy to see me. The unconditional love from a dog (and a Bubbie) can really get a girl through all the hard things. This is necessary, essential stuff.

Gemma's playing with a remote-control car. I almost trip over it. My parents are at the kitchen table, holding their heads the way they always do when they're stressed. Lion runs over to the couch and rests his head on his paw, looking like the happiest creature on the planet.

"Oh, Lion baby." I smoosh into his face. "How did we get so lucky to get you? How? How?" I rub his back. "You're the light of my life."

"Um, Ari." Gemma shoves herself between us on the

couch and Lion pops up onto my lap. "You're weird when you talk to the dog. You know that, right?"

"Yeah. And I don't care. We all know I'm Lion's favorite. So just accept it!" I get up and run away from her as she tries to swat me with a pillow.

"Are not!"

I find it a little strange that my parents haven't really wanted to discuss my transgression at all, but I'll ride it out as long as I can.

I grab a can of seltzer from the fridge and go up to my room. I need to figure out a way to get out of here and over to Kaylan's so we can finish the list tonight. It's usually so helpful to have a list to calm us down and help us prepare for whatever's ahead, and this list has been great, but now I need to be done with it. I need to JHH the whole thing and have some more room in my head.

I do a few quick portraits of Kaylan from memory and I'll admit—none are great, but I'm not an artist. I do an abstract kind of thing, mushing colors together and keeping the shapes of her face vague and broad and undefined.

These are all pretty terrible, but I tried. It has to count for something. I think I really nailed her eyes, and that's her best feature. So that has to count for a lot, actually.

There's a knock on my door and I say, "Come in." My parents stand there looking annoyed and irritated, probably with me but maybe with each other, too.

"Ari, we figured out step one of your punishment." My dad sits down on my desk chair and my mom sits on the edge of my bed. I plop down on my beanbag chair and wish I could make myself invisible.

"Okay," I reply, trying not to sound snarky.

My dad talks first. "You're going to write an apology letter to the camp. Not one letter. A letter to all of the directors, to the counselor who caught you, to everyone you can think of. And they will be heartfelt and we will proofread them and make you redo them as many times as necessary before they are sent out."

I nod. I almost want to do a little salute since he sounds like such a drill sergeant but I know I can't.

"And you will not be able to go for the full summer next year," my mom adds. "Even if they allow you back. It's not happening."

My throat prickles. I'm about to cry but I push it down. If I argue, they'll only enforce this more. If I stay quiet and do my best with everything, there may be a way to negotiate later.

"But if I really apologize and make up for what I've done, please, is there any way I can go back full summer?" I look at my dad, pleading with my eyes. "Dad, try to think about how much you loved camp as a kid, how much this means to me, how sorry I am for what I've done."

He's quiet but his eyes are soulful like he's taking in what I have to say.

This is the first step in our new relationship. Really opening up to him, and not just my mom.

"Get to work on the letters," my dad says, and they get up to leave the room. He doesn't say it but I get an overwhelming sense that he's heard me, that maybe he'll consider my plea.

"I need to do one thing first," I say. "I can't explain what it is but Kaylan is really going through something. You guys have modeled how to be amazing friends. I need to follow your lead. I hope you can understand."

My mom groans. "Ari, enough. You are in serious trouble and you don't even see it."

"I do see it. And I am furious with myself. I'm angrier at myself than you are with me, if that's even possible." I pause and get up and stand there facing them. I almost want to get down on my knees and beg them, but I avoid the temptation. "Please. I won't be gone long."

"I can't discuss anything anymore." My mom sighs. "I'm completely worn out."

My parents leave my room and walk downstairs and I guess I won that battle? Unclear. Either way, it's essential that I leave right now and finish the list.

I need it to be done so I can focus on my past actions and find a way to make amends for all of them.

I look over the list one more time. I grab the portraits so we can JHH that together, and all the stuff I think would be important for a time capsule: photos of us from each year of our friendship, a Brookside Pool Frisbee, my favorite gray tank top—it's getting a little small on me anyway—a Harvey Deli magnet, a shirt I tie-dyed for Kaylan, as many movie stubs as I can find from all the films we've seen together. I find crumpled rough drafts of all of our lists and bring those, too.

I take an empty shoebox from my winter boots off the top shelf of my closet and shove everything in. A snapshot of Ari and Kaylan, BFFs, right as we are now, at thirteen and three-quarters. What a beautiful array of stuff, all of the things that add up to a life of magic and love and the truest sense of soul-sister-ship ever to exist.

I throw everything into my paisley tote and run down the stairs as fast as I can, to try and make sure no one stops me.

I look around and notice that my parents are on the back deck having a heated conversation, talking with their hands. They don't see me getting ready to leave.

Lion jumps for me to pick him up and I do for a second, kiss his head, and then gently put him down.

I walk over to Kaylan's as quickly as I can and when I'm almost there, I feel my phone vibrating in my backpack. I hesitate to look at it, thinking it's my parents, but I do it anyway.

It's Golfy.

Hey, Ari. I'm sorry. I'm thinking of you and missing you beyond belief. I hope we can talk soon. I

shouldn't have pressured you into the golf cart do something daring thing. It was my fault.

I stop, frozen in place on the sidewalk, and think about that for a minute. He did pressure me, but there was also a little corner of my brain that wanted to do it. I can't blame him entirely. But in the future I think I'll listen to the whole brain, not just the tiny corner.

Thank you. I miss you so much, too. It wasn't totally your fault. We'll talk soon. xoxo

When I get to Kaylan's, I burst through the door and run up to her room. "We need to do this quick. I can't sleep over. I'm in so much trouble." I run my words together. "Ready? Ready to finish this and JHH and hug and love each other? And then I go back to being in so much trouble."

Kaylan shakes her head in disbelief. "Yes, ready. Thank you for making this happen. Two back-to-back lists is a lot. I'm glad we agree we need some space. From listing, I mean."

"One hundred percent." I sit down at her desk and unpack all of my time capsule things. "I mean, if we do another one, it can be back-to-school and deadline our birthdays like the original."

"Ari!" She cracks up. "We just said we needed a break."

I laugh. "I know, I know." I take deep breaths, in and out, in and out, trying to relax and recenter myself. "So anyway, here's all the time capsule stuff. What do you have and where should we bury it?"

"I have an idea, but first we need to discuss something." She pulls me up and we go into her walk-in closet, which feels very odd and truthfully I don't know what's happening.

"This is my new thinking spot," she says. "I donated a ton of stuff and I have these two little cube chairs in here. Great, right?"

"Totally." I feel myself starting to sweat since there's no air-conditioning in here, but I try to ignore it. "So what do we need to discuss?"

Kaylan hesitates before she speaks. "The *make a difference* list item. Did we do it enough? I mean, was it big enough?"

I sniffle and try to think. "Um, yeah, because here's the thing. We made a difference in small ways—me with Gemma at camp, and you with Indigo. She never had friends there before, she never even felt noticed or part of anything, you said. Right?"

"Yeah."

"And also you helping with the triplets and Chad. You made a difference in so many ways," I say, feeling choked up. "But if we simply focus on Gemma and Indigo, we took two girls struggling with different things and gave them confidence to overcome their obstacles." I pause. "And then that has a ripple effect. Who knows what they will do with that confidence?"

Kaylan nods. "I get what you're saying."

I talk fast because I'm suddenly so fired up about this. "And also, that *making a difference* thing is never done. In some ways that should have been the three-quarter. It'll go on forever. We'll always wanna make a difference."

"First thing on the next list?" Kaylan hides her face because she knows I'm gonna hit her with something. "Kidding!"

"Okay," I giggle. "So back to my original question, where are we burying this?"

"Follow me." She gets up and grabs a small tote bag of items. Then she gets on the floor and pulls for something under her bed. "I decorated a shoebox for us."

She shows it to me and it looks so beautiful: multicolored stripes wrapping around the whole thing with one little sliver of lacy fabric perpendicular to the stripes. Our names are written in thick purple bubble letters.

Arianna Simone Nodberg & Kaylan Marie
    Terrell—best friends forever
"If we ever leave a legacy, it's that we loved each other well."
Time capsule created and buried: summer 2020
To be dug up and discovered: TBD

"By the way, that's from an Indigo Girls song, 'Power of Two.' The quote, I mean," she says. "I'll play it for you when we have more time."

"Love that you discovered new music this summer, by the way. Such a camp thing."

"Here's what I'm putting in." She dumps the contents of the tote on her bed. "Pictures of us, obvs, a few notes we wrote back and forth in school, a few camp letters, this menu from Hibino with our favorite rolls circled that I always keep tacked to my bulletin board, an empty pint (I washed it) from the Ice Cream Shop, a program from our fifth-grade play, the receipt from when we got our hair highlighted, a piece of that foil thing they wrapped us in after the 5K. Oh! And my portrait of you!" She pauses. "I think that's good, right?"

"It's better than good, Kay. Also your portrait is oddly amazing." I feel myself start to cry and I walk over to her and pull her into an unexpected hug. "I love you so much."

I follow Kaylan down the stairs and outside. As we're walking down the block, I realize where we're going to bury this. Truthfully the only place that would make sense.

We walk really fast, as if we're in a major hurry, and we sign our names in the guest book. We grab an abandoned shovel from the fake sandy beach area in the kiddie section of the pool complex.

"Will this be able to dig real dirt?" I ask.

"I guess we'll see. If not we'll ask Joey to get one of the maintenance staff to help us."

338

"Is this even legal?" I ask, a little out of breath from walking so fast.

"Um, I think so?" Kaylan shrugs.

We walk as far back as we can go until we're in this wooded area where no one usually goes, not that I know of anyway.

Kaylan puts her hands on her hips and says, "Aren't time capsules weird because you kind of never want someone to find it but at the same time you really want someone to find it?"

"You just don't want someone to find it, like, soon. Or for it to be anyone we know. That's the thing. You want someone to find this in forty years. And learn all about us and how magical our friendship is and what life was like for us in Brookside in middle school." I pause. "So bury it. Really deep."

"I'm the one doing the burying? On my own?"

"Kay, you only have one shovel, and it has Minnie Mouse on it, so . . ."

"Be right back." She runs off to get another one and I stand there, in the woods, alone for a few minutes with this beautiful time capsule shoebox, and all of a sudden, the emotions take over. Like a flood of tears pouring out of my eyes. Everything hits me all at once.

"Are you okay, Ar?" Kaylan asks when she gets back. She looks at me, confused and concerned.

"It's all too much," I whimper. "Life is too much. It's

going too fast. And I love you too much. I feel everything so deeply that I can't even understand my own feelings half the time."

"I know, Ar. I know." Kaylan puts an arm around me, and I shift to get even closer to her, resting my head in the crook of her neck. "It's gonna be okay. We have each other. That's all we really need."

I sniffle again and cry onto her shoulder.

"Let's start digging."

So we do. We dig as hard and as deep as we can until finally there's a pretty big hole in the earth. Luckily it rained yesterday so the mud is soft.

"We need to JHH right now, before we put it in," I tell her. "The slowest, most meaningful JHH ever. And then we need to kiss the time capsule box. New ritual."

Kaylan nods like she agrees and there's no debating it.

We jump in the air and then high-five and then hug as tight as we possibly can. And we don't let go for many, many, many minutes.

Finally, we pull apart, and we each give the box a quick kiss.

"Oh! And we need to say three things each that we're grateful for. About each other or life or whatever . . . ," Kaylan adds. "You go first."

I fold my arms across my chest and think for a moment. "Well, I'm grateful that I found my unicorn friend at such a young age so I can go through life with the literal best sidekick in the world. I'm thankful my bubbie is healthy. I'm thankful that we failed at something on the list and survived that failure and that we learned from the experience." I nod, pleased with my answers. "Now you go."

She's quiet, deep in thought for so long that I wonder if I should give her a pass. Finally, she speaks. "I'm grateful that I can be total honesty with you and that I know that now for real. Officially TH friends forever, no debating it. I'm thankful that I finally told my dad I can't handle the cryptic stuff. And I'm thankful that I get to share the camp feelings with you, that I stepped out of my comfort zone and did something hard and came out stronger and better and funnier!"

She bows and does a little jump where she taps the heels of her flip-flops together.

We laugh for a second and then we kneel down and gently lower the time capsule shoebox into the ground as if it's a tiny bird. And then we cover it with dirt and twigs and more dirt until it's really hard to believe there's anything under there.

"Well, I guess that's it," I say. "We did it."

"We did it," Kaylan agrees. "So what should we do now? I mean, I know you're in serious trouble and not really allowed to leave the house or do anything, so . . . not like in the immediate sense of the word. But in general."

"We should be us," I tell her. "Do our thing. Take it one

day at a time. Be grateful, make a difference, all the stuff, basically. Everything. All day every day. But most of all: be us."

"Be us," she repeats. "I like it."

We walk out of the woods, holding hands, and we leave the pool and we continue that way all the way home.

Be us.

In a mixed-up world, where so many things are confusing and so few things make sense, we are who we are and we accept ourselves and we accept each other.

More than that, we love each other.

That in and of itself is pure magic.

The power of two.

It's the only thing that matters.

ACKNOWLEDGMENTS

THANK YOU SO MUCH TO all of my people, especially the lights of my life: Dave, Aleah, and Hazel. Thank you to my extraordinary agent, Alyssa Eisner Henkin, my incredible editor, Maria Barbo, and all of the Katherine Tegen crew: Katherine Tegen, Laura Mock, Amy Ryan, Liz Byer, Jon Howard, Mark Rifkin, Camille Kellogg, Vaishali Nayak, Sam Benson, Rachel Horowitz, and Almeda Beynon. Thank you to Emily Robbins McGinnis for letting me use the words to your gold team alma mater from 1999. From then until forever, I will be singing it and loving it. Thanks to the BWL Library & Tech bunch and last but never least, thank you to the readers. I appreciate all of you; I am so grateful that I get to write books and that you choose to read them. Bridget Hickey, I'm looking at you specifically. Thanks for being such an amazing reader, fan, and friend.

Great books by LISA GREENWALD!

The Friendship List

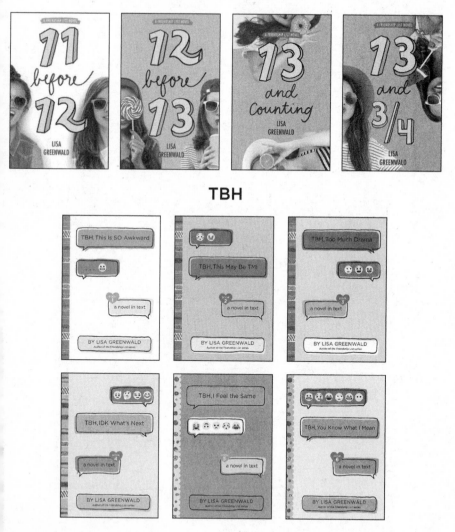

TBH